P9-DVK-401

FELONY
FILE

FELONY FILE

DELL SHANNON

WILLIAM MORROW AND COMPANY, INC.
New York   1980

Library of Congress Cataloging in Publication Data

Linington, Elizabeth.
  Felony file.

  I. Title.
PZ4.L756Fg   [PS3562.I515]   813'.5'4   79-22033
ISBN 0-688-03593-0

Printed in the United States of America.

First Edition

1 2 3 4 5 6 7 8 9 10

This one is for
Doreen Tovey
who likes my books
because I like her books
and hope to see many more of them

In each human heart are a tiger, a pig, an ass, and a nightingale; diversity of character is due to their unequal activity.

—AMBROSE BIERCE

FELONY
FILE

ONE ══════════════════════════

THE FIRST RAIN of the season had arrived, unexpected and early, this sixth of November. In the little forest of tall buildings which was the civic center, lights had come on against the gray darkness. Midway up the rectangular loom of Parker Center, LAPD headquarters, the tall windows of the Robbery-Homicide bureau slithered grayly with the steady downpour; the ranks of fluorescent lighting were on in the big communal detective office.

At the moment, the office was unoccupied except for Sergeant Hackett, who was poring over a typed report at his desk. He glanced up as footsteps sounded in the corridor outside; Mendoza's voice was noncommittal on some polite amenity, and a heavier voice rumbled in reply before a door shut. Mendoza wandered into the office looking dissatisfied. He hadn't been out since the rain began, and was neat and dapper as always in exquisitely tailored gray herringbone, immaculate white shirt and dark tie. He hoisted one hip on the edge of Hackett's desk and said, "That was a waste of time."

"On what?" asked Hackett.

Mendoza flicked his lighter. "That chief security guard at Bullock's, Pierson. A big blank."

"Those other two are down in R. and I. looking at mug-shots, but do you want to bet they draw a blank too?"

"No bets. That was a very cute operation, Art. They tell us this and that, we can deduce the M.O., and it takes us nowhere."

"We are also nowhere," said Hackett, "on this new heist job." He laid down the report. Most of the men in the office had been out getting the first statements on the Bullock's job. There was never a time, of course, when Robbery-Homicide didn't have the heist jobs to work, often several at once, and as a rule they were ephemeral, annoyingly leadless little jobs.

"What about it?" asked Mendoza uninterestedly.

Hackett took off his glasses. "A pharmacy over on Second Street, about eleven last night, just as they were closing. Matt went out on it. I had the two clerks in just now, and took 'em down to R. and I. No go—none of the mug-shots rang a bell. What they tell us, it's a female. Very much a female—stacked, golden blonde, about thirty, good-looking. And all business, with a fairly big handgun. She got away with about four hundred bucks."

Mendoza laughed. "Well, the libbers are getting more equal all the time, Art. No reason they shouldn't start pulling heists."

"She wasn't interested in any drugs, just the cash register. In and out, and neither of them could say whether she got away in a car or what."

"Helpful," agreed Mendoza. But he was thinking more about the Bullock's job, which so far hadn't offered any handles either and was a good deal more important.

[14]

"I'll take no bets at all," he repeated, "that the security men make any shots. Empty gesture. I know, I know, those two said they got just a glimpse of two of them on the way out, pulling the masks off, but—"

"Slick operation all right," said Hackett. It had been. And one that, so far as anybody remembered, hadn't been done before.

There were seven floors and a basement of commodities for sale at Bullock's Department Store at Seventh and Hill. The personnel, accounting, bookkeeping and purchasing departments were on the eighth floor. At the end of a business day, the proceeds from the cash registers of all the various departments were totaled, encased in canvas bags, and shepherded by security guards up to the accounting department, whence the bags were eventually conveyed by the guards to a night drop at the bank. Last night, just after the store closed, as the bags were on their way up, four armed men had materialized in the accounting department, immobilized the guards and the staff remaining in the office, and got clean away with all the bags. The accounting staff was still trying to arrive at an estimate of the loss, and nobody could offer any helpful clues at all. Two of the security guards had had a very brief look at two of the heisters, but their descriptions were expectedly vague.

"John was going back to see the chief accountant. There's no way they can get an exact figure, but an average day—how the hell many departments in that store, and it's not the cheapest place in town—might run to three, four hundred thousand. Some of it would be in checks, but—"

"A very nice haul," said Mendoza, stabbing out his cigarette rather violently. "Anything in from the lab?"

"There probably won't be," said Hackett. "Everybody said they didn't touch anything but the bags and were wearing gloves anyway."

"And where is everybody?" asked Mendoza, looking around the empty office.

"Tom and Jase are down at R. and I. with the guards. Henry's out on a new body, and I think Wanda went with him. I couldn't say about anybody else, I just got back myself."

"There was another body turned up," said Sergeant Lake, coming in with a manila envelope. "George and Conway went out on it. In a house down by the railroad yards. This is a *billet-doux* from the D.A."

"Thank you so much." Mendoza slid out the contents —a little sheaf of official court documents—on Hackett's desk and glanced at the accompanying note. "So. The Hoffman hearing is set for the tenth."

Hackett sighed. "At least the court isn't dragging its heels. Let's hope, short and sweet." None of them liked thinking about the Hoffman case much.

They sat in silence for a moment. The rain slithered steadily down the windows. Mendoza lighted another cigarette. Footsteps sounded in the corridor and Higgins and Conway came in. They looked wet and disgruntled. "So who's going to do the report?" asked Higgins. Conway fished out a quarter and tossed it. "Heads."

"Oh, hell," said Conway, uncovering the quarter.

"What was the body?" asked Hackett.

"Nothing much." Higgins sat down at his desk and got out a cigarette. "Probably an O.D., dumped in an empty house. God knows how long it's been there— couple of weeks at least. The owner found it, and the last time he was there was about that long ago. Male Caucasian about twenty-five. See if his prints are on file." Conway had rolled the triplicate forms into his typewriter and was starting the initial report. "Anything show up on the Bullock's job?"

"I can prophesy right now, it's a dead end," said Mendoza. "Damnation, these smart pros—" That particular M.O. didn't show in any of their files; there was no handle on that at all.

"I see you made a start on painting the kitchen," said Hackett to Higgins.

"What? Yeah, I got the first coat on," said Higgins.

"You missed a spot just behind your right ear," said Hackett, and Higgins swore and felt for it.

"The place needs painting outside too but it'll have to wait till spring. Damned if I'll take on that job. It's been enough of an upheaval to move."

Hackett picked up his report again. For a couple of minutes the only sound was the staccato tapping of Conway's typewriter, and then Sergeant Lake looked in again.

"You've got a new one down," he said succinctly. "Robbery and homicide. Portia Street."

"Oh, for God's sake," said Higgins.

"I'm busy," said Hackett hastily, getting up. "I'm going down to ask records if we have any beautiful blonde heisters on file. Besides, you've been sitting in a nice dry office all day, you're due for some legwork."

"Hell," said Mendoza mildly.

"And I don't suppose I can get any wetter," said Higgins gloomily. They went out reluctantly.

The rain had been completely unforeseen by the weather bureau, and as up to yesterday the temperature had hovered around seventy, nobody had worn a coat this morning. At the front entrance of the building, Mendoza and Higgins stood at the top of the steps for a moment; the rain was pouring down monotonously, and the concrete jungle all around Parker Center looked very wet and uninviting. It was a good fifty yards to the parking lot.

"Damn it, this is a new suit," said Mendoza. Resignedly, they turned their collars up and pulled hat-brims down and launched into the rain. By the time they reached Mendoza's Ferrari they were both dripping.

"Portia Street," said Higgins. "That's up toward Silver Lake." Up to a few years ago, one of the quiet backwaters of town; but recently the crime rate was climbing in that area, which was why the Higginses had sold the house on Silver Lake Boulevard. Mendoza started the engine and backed out of the slot.

It wasn't far enough off to justify the freeway; he went up Sunset, where it curved narrowly here at its beginning; Portia Street crossed it a little way up from Elysian Park Avenue. It was a tired old residential street, modest single houses lining it on each side, mostly frame places dating from the twenties. The houses were neatly enough maintained, with strips of lawn in front. The black-and-white squad was in front of a house midway down the block, a square pseudo-Spanish crackerbox house painted dingy yellow. In the deluge of rain, there weren't any neighbors out staring, but there was a woman standing with the uniformed figure of Patrolman Zimmerman on the little square front porch.

When Mendoza and Higgins joined them the porch was crowded, but neither Zimmerman nor the woman made a move toward the open front door past a sagging screen door. "This is Mrs. Meeker," said Zimmerman, "from next door. These are the detectives from head-quarters, ma'am—Lieutenant Mendoza, Sergeant Higgins."

[18]

"It's just terrible," she said. "Just terrible." She was a nice-looking middle-aged woman, a little too plump, with dark hair; she was wearing a cotton housedress with an old gray cardigan over it, and she was hugging herself, shivering, not altogether because of the cold rain. "I've always tried to be neighborly—we've lived here nearly twenty-five years and the Whalens lived here more like thirty-five, this was their folks' house. They always seemed to get along fine, but it must have been hard for Dave, not that he ever complained, he was such a nice man, so good and gentle and patient—and the Lord knows there wouldn't have been much there worth anything, I know he never kept cash around—and it's bad enough they should break in and rob them, but why they had to—oh, Lord, poor Dave dead there on the floor—" She began to cry a little. "Never did any harm to anybody, and what Dan's going to do without him—and broad daylight, too—it's terrible—Harry and I've been talking about getting out of the city, the crime rate up so high, but this happening right next door, it brings it home. Everybody liked Dave so much, you had to admire them, how they got along—"

"They came in the back," said Zimmerman, "by what I got from Mr. Daniel Whalen. I don't suppose there'll be anything for the lab."

"You never know. There'll be a mobile unit out," said Higgins. Mrs. Meeker was still talking as he and Mendoza went in.

The front door led directly into a long narrow living room. It contained a good deal of old-fashioned furniture: a big couch, two matching chairs, and a TV on a wheeled stand at one end where a small false hearth was built in on one wall; at the other end were a round oak dining table and chairs, and a heavy old sideboard. In the middle of the room sat a man in a wheelchair.

He looked to be about sixty; he had thin gray hair and a long thin face, and his body was thin too and frail-looking. He was neatly enough dressed in gray slacks, open-necked shirt and a blue sweater. He looked up at them as they came in, and said in an expressionless tone, "He's in the kitchen. Dave. I don't know why they killed him. They didn't have to kill him, just for twelve dollars."

At the other end of the living room a cross hall led to the kitchen, two bedrooms with a bath between. The kitchen was square, its old soapstone counters polished clean, no dishes visible, the worn linoleum on the floor clean except for the pool of Dave Whalen's blood spread around his body. He lay flat with his arms out in front of him, as if he was still trying to push himself to his feet. He had been another long, thin man, with scanty gray hair; they couldn't see his face. There was a small service porch, and the outside door there was half open.

"He says they both had knives," said Zimmerman behind them. "His brother was just ready to leave for work—he's a clerk at the J and M Liquor Store down on Fourth, three to closing—when they heard a noise at the back door. He went to look, this one here I mean, and these two louts pushed right in. Both young and black. The other one didn't know his brother'd been killed until they took off—they took his brother's wallet, he hadn't one on him, grabbed some loot from the bedrooms and ran out. That's all he can say, they were young and black. After he called us he called the neighbor woman. She didn't see a thing, and says most of the people along here are at work all day, there wouldn't be many home."

"The lab may pick up something," said Higgins sadly, looking at the body.

"By what she told me," said Zimmerman, "the poor

old fellow in the wheelchair's been crippled all his life
—polio or something—and his brother always looked
after him. Never married, just stayed home and took
care of him, after their parents died. Seems to've been
a quiet, hard-working guy—never much money, but they
got along. Like he says, the louts out after a little loot,
why the hell did they have to kill him?"

But it was, of course, the kind of thing the louts
did. Maybe high on something, or just not caring what
they did.

The lab truck would be on the way. Mendoza and
Higgins went back to the living room. Daniel Whalen
was still sitting in his wheelchair staring at the opposite
wall. Mrs. Meeker had come in and was talking to him,
but he didn't seem to be listening.

"We managed," he said suddenly. "We always managed, whatever happened. I always just prayed it would
keep on that way. I can get myself to the bathroom, fix
myself snacks, when Dave was at work. We knew there
might come a time when I couldn't—we just hoped—I'm
fifty-nine and Dave was sixty-one. Only sixty-one. And
now—and now—what I always dreaded. Just—done—in—
half a minute. Dave *dead*. And I'll have to go to one of
those homes—I'd rather be dead myself. I wish I was."

Mrs. Meeker was crying again. Daniel Whalen beat
one hand on the arm of the wheelchair, feebly. "I can't
—even—open a can for Merlin," he said. "The counter's—
too high. I'm no use—"

There was, Mendoza saw, a large wicker basket at
one side of the gas-heater in the imitation hearth, lined
with pieces of old blanket. In the basket was curled a
rather portly black-and-white cat with very long whisk-
ers and green eyes slitted just now at the strange men.

"Oh, Dan, you know I'll do that—"

"Dave always had to have a cat. I can't even take

[21]

care of a cat, let alone myself. Why they had to *kill* him—about twelve dollars, and Father's old railroad watch and Masonic ring and Mother's cameo pin, that's all—not worth anything really, just sentiment—"

The cat Merlin decided that there was too much disturbance in the room for comfort, and rose and stretched. He had four white feet and a white tip to his plumed tail. Slowly he walked to the front door and waited. Mrs. Meeker hastened to open the door for him and he stalked out.

The lab truck was pulling up outside. Scarne got out of it with Johnson, and Mendoza and Higgins went to brief them. There was always a chance that the lab work would turn up something; they had to try. The louts might have left some latent prints, and they might be in L.A.'s records. The autopsy surgeon might tell them something about the knife. They would get a statement from Daniel Whalen; it might be worthwhile to ask him to look at books of mug-shots. The little loot sounded very ordinary, but if it ever turned up in a pawnshop, he could probably identify it.

Both Mendoza and Higgins were aware that there was a very long chance that the louts would ever be dropped on, a good enough legal case made to charge and try them if they ever were. It was just one of those things.

They stood on the little front porch, lighted cigarettes and looked at the gray veil of rain. "Another wet winter, probably," said Higgins. And after a moment, "I wonder what the other new body was."

The call had come in from the squad car at one-twenty, just as Glasser had come back from lunch. He hadn't seen any of the other men since eight o'clock this morning; Landers, Palliser and Grace were out on the Bullock's heist, the others on something else, but somebody had to mind the store.

Their policewoman, Wanda Larsen, who was bucking for detective rank, promptly got up and followed him out. "New call?"

Glasser cocked his head at her trim blonde person. "You so hot for street experience," he said. "You'll catch pneumonia. Haven't you got a coat?"

"It was such a nice morning—I'll be all right." She had a fairly heavy cardigan. Downstairs, they made a dash from the front entrance to Glasser's Gremlin in the lot. "Where are we going on what?" asked Wanda brightly.

"Don't know—squad just said a body. It's Darwin Avenue."

That was one of the oldest streets in the oldest part of Los Angeles, a shabby, dirty, narrow street of ramshackle old houses. The houses had never been owned by anyone with much money, and a good many of the owners and renters had always been people who spent what money they had on less mundane things than plumbing repairs, broken windows and leaking roofs; most of the houses looked ready to fall down, long unpainted and neglected. They sat on meager city lots; and even the city seemed to have forgotten the street, so that the sidewalks were cracked and broken, the blacktop of the street spotted with potholes.

Patrolman Yeager was sitting in the squad in front of one of the houses waiting for them. "I just decided," he told Glasser, "I don't like this damn job. I'm going to quit the force and start selling insurance or something." He looked at Wanda a little uneasily. "You going in there?"

"Certainly," said Wanda. "What have we got?"

"A bloody mess," said Yeager. "You want me to come with you?"

Glasser didn't think Yeager had been riding a squad long: a year or two on the force maybe. Even in that time, a cop ought to be used to some of the bloody messes they saw on the job. He said mildly, "Well, give us a quick rundown, will you?"

Yeager's roundish young face looked pinched. "A Mrs. Rose Engel called in. Says she came home and found her daughter dead. The kid was nine. There are some other kids, younger."

"That's it?" said Glasser. "Where was she?"

"She just said, at a party. She left her boy friend with the kids. He lives with her. I just got his name, Leon Fratelli. Maybe he's awake now. She's got the hell of a hangover and wasn't talking very straight."

Glasser said to Wanda, "Maybe you'd better stay out here."

"Don't be silly," said Wanda impatiently. "I'm a cop as much as you are, Henry."

The house wasn't very big: maybe five rooms. It had originally been clapboard, and a number of the boards had been cracked and broken loose. Both front windows were broken. It had been so long since the house had been painted, it was impossible to tell what color it had been. There were wide cracks in the cement walk up to the door; there was no front porch. There hadn't been any grass or plants around it for a long time, if ever.

The front door was open. Glasser shoved it wider with one foot and they went in. Various smells hit them at once. This room, apparently intended for a living room, contained little furniture besides an old army cot and a couple of straight chairs. There was a TV in one corner. The floor, rugless, was thick with dust. A baby

[24]

about a year old, quite naked, was lying beside one of the chairs; its lower body was caked in filth obviously many days old. It was a boy, and it was crying feebly in a thin whine.

There was a man sitting on the cot, head down, a man about thirty, with several days' growth of beard on a lantern jaw. He was wearing a pair of dirty shorts and nothing else, and he had a fat paunch beneath a mat of dark chest hair. Somewhere children were crying. In addition to the dust, the floor was littered with miscellany: scraps of dry bread, candy wrappers, beer cans, and unmistakable human excrement.

Glasser went into the little hall off that room, Wanda after him. At the front of the house was a tiny kitchen. Counter and stove were littered with piles of dirty dishes and pans, and there was mold in most of them. The floor was dirtier than that in the first room. There was a table about a foot square by the window, and in a chair beside it a woman sat looking dully at a can of beer in one hand. She was a fat, dark young woman in pink pants and a flowered top; both were soiled and spotted. Her back to them, they could see the engrained dirt on her neck.

Two children, three or four, were tugging at her other arm: children in dirty rags of nondescript clothing. They were both crying.

"Mrs. Engel?" said Glasser.

She looked around slowly. Her eyes were bloodshot, her dark-red lipstick smeared. "Who're you?" she asked thickly. Glasser showed her the badge. "Oh. 'Bout Alice." She gave the nearest child a casual slap. "Shut up, you. Poor li'l Alice. Don' know what happened." She waved an arm clumsily. "Inna bedroom."

They went down the hall and came to an open door. The room was about ten feet square. It held a single bed and an unpainted three-drawer chest. The bed was a tangle of gray sheets, an old brown blanket half on the floor. The body was on the bed: the thin, small body of a little girl—an undernourished-looking little girl, the ribs starkly visible. The doctors would say exactly what had been done to her; it was fairly obvious that she'd been beaten and raped. There was dried blood all over her, and on the bedclothes; her face was contorted in one last scream of agony.

Wanda made a strangled sound. Glasser backed out and went on down the hall. Next to the bedroom was a bathroom. The toilet had been cracked and overflowed a long time ago, and the mess never had been cleared up; there were two ancient chamber-pots, both ready to spill over, in the dirt-encrusted bathtub.

Wanda gulped and said faintly, "I'm s-sorry, I'm going to be—"

"If you're sick here the lab will be mad at you for tampering with evidence," said Glasser. "You'd better go get some fresh air." She fled past the man on the cot, and Glasser shook him by one shoulder. "Fratelli! Can you answer some questions?"

The man just mumbled and shook his head. Glasser came out into the rain and took a deep breath of cold wet air. Wanda was sitting in the back of the squad swallowing determinedly. Glasser got in the front and reached for the mike on the radio.

There wasn't anything for detectives to do here, for a while. Take the man and woman in to sober up in jail. Take the kids to Juvenile Hall where at least they'd be washed and fed. Turn the lab loose, and get the body to the morgue. Later on, one of that pair might answer some pertinent questions.

"You O.K.?" said Yeager to Wanda. "I said you'd better not go in—"

[26]

"I'm O.K.," said Wanda faintly.

"She's getting street experience," said Glasser, and flicked on the mike.

At five o'clock Landers and Grace were talking again to the two security guards from Bullock's, Dick Lee and Bob Masters, who had spent the afternoon looking at mug-shots down in records. They had come up blank.

"I guess I shouldn't have said I might make one of them," said Masters ruefully. He was black; Lee was white. "It was just a second, when those last two took their masks off, just as the elevator door was shutting— I couldn't swear to anything, except they were both white and one had dark hair."

"All I could say, about the same," said Lee. "It was so fast—their timing was so good—they sure as hell knew what they were doing."

"It was a damned slick operation all right," said Landers. He and Grace had been over in the Accounting department of Bullock's most of the afternoon, looking at the terrain, talking to the clerks there. "What sticks out at first glance is that they knew your whole routine."

"And we heard something about that this morning," said Jason Grace in his gentle voice, "but I'd like to run through it again, to get it straight." His regular-featured brown face, with its moustache as neat as Mendoza's, wore a deceptively lazy expression. "What struck me about it—thar's a big store, with a lot of different departments on seven floors. It must take some doing to collect the day's take from everywhere in such a short time."

"Not really, sir," said Masters. "It's planning that does it, all right—a set routine. Like we told you, the store closes at six except for Saturdays when it's open till nine. So at around five-fifteen, the different department heads start to close out the cash registers, see? The amount in every register is totaled and entered on a little form. Then they add up the total of all the checks and put that down too. The cash goes in one little bag and the checks in another, and then they both go in a bag together, marked for that department. By this time it'll be getting on to a quarter of six, and there aren't usually many last-minute customers but if so it's easy enough to add in those sales. As soon as the doors close at six—come to think, it is a kind of split-second timed thing—the department heads take their bags to number three freight elevator. There's one of us on every floor right by that elevator—I'm on the seventh floor. Elevator collects the first-floor bags, goes up to the second floor, and so on. After it's gone up, the guards on the first, second, third and fourth floors, they go down to secure all the street entrances, check the rest rooms, be sure all the people are out. The rest of us go up to Accounting with the bags."

"That would be about what time usually?" asked Landers.

"It doesn't take long," said Lee. "About twenty past?" He consulted Masters.

"Twenty past to half past six," said Masters. "Split the difference. It's all kind of down pat, see? In Accounting—I mean the hall by the elevator where the door to Accounting is—we wheel all the bags in on a big dolly, and there'll be five or six men to handle 'em. They take it in turns. They take the paper forms out of each bag, and seal the bags—that takes maybe another twenty minutes. Tell the truth, I don't know where those forms go, files somewhere, I suppose, they just take 'em into the Accounting office and then they leave and we take the bags down by freight elevator five, that's the one closest to the alley between the buildings." Bullock's store had two separate buildings joined by an arcade below, a mezzanine above. "By that time Decker—he's the ground-floor guard—has brought the van around, we load the bags and drive straight to the bank. That'll be about seven-fifteen, it's only a couple of blocks. The guards there are always waiting, and in three minutes we've handed over to them and the bags are on the way to the vault."

"These birds had to know that routine," said Grace, "to catch you all flat-footed the way they did."

"You can sure as hell say that again," said Lee feelingly. "What the men in Accounting say—they come out to the elevator about six-fifteen, to be there when we come up—these jokers must have hid some place, probably on the seventh floor, until about ten past six. And something else, they knew how to get up to the eighth floor, which not everybody would. That elevator's not for general use, and it's way down at the end of a dead-end aisle in Ladies' Lingerie on the seventh floor. It only goes from seven to nine, where Lost and Found is. Anyway, they showed up at the door to Accounting at ten past six on the dot, and of course there was only six guys there, everybody else had left. All four of 'em had guns, and Mr. Anderson said it didn't take three minutes, three of 'em went to work—they had the rope with 'em—and got them all tied up like packages. Just in time to come out to the elevator and meet me and Bob peacefully riding up with all that loot. There wasn't one damned thing we could do. In about another two minutes they had us tied up, and down they go in the elevator."

"Taking off the masks as they went," said Landers, "to, hopefully, slide out without any trouble downstairs. As indeed they did."

"Yeah," said Lee. "See, the men on the first floor then aren't usually very near that alley door. Two men— Decker and Robinson, but usually Robinson'd be on his way up to the second floor around then. Decker'd have got the van from the parking lot and brought it around to the alley, left the keys in it. And we told you these bastards had on uniforms—not really like ours, but blue —and unless Decker was close enough, he couldn't see it wasn't us, if they slid out in pairs."

"A very smart little operation indeed," said Grace. They had put out an A.P.B. for the van, and it had been spotted an hour ago parked over on Carondelet. It was now in the police garage being gone over by the lab men.

"Not to tell you your business," said Masters diffidently, "but we kind of wondered—maybe one of them used to work as a guard at the store. Knew the routine from that, see?"

"It is a thought," said Grace. That, of course, had occurred to them.

Lee was looking around the big office, at the two detectives, with interest. Only Glasser was there, bent over his typewriter. Lee said to Landers, "Excuse me, but you don't look old enough to be a detective, you know?"

Of necessity, after long suffering, Landers had learned to bear his cross philosophically. He just had the kind of face that would look about twenty until he was a grandfather, and he had to live with it.

It was nearly the end of shift. They thanked the two guards and saw them out. Grace left, and Landers was just going out the door when the phone on his desk rang. He went back to pick it up and found his wife at the other end.

Phillippa Rosemary, unfortunately christened by parents who never dreamed she would turn into a policewoman, was annoyed. "These damn Narco men," she said. "I'm going to be here—" *here* was Records and Identification downstairs— "for at least another hour, Tom—they've got three citizens looking for a pusher. So will you please pick up a pound of hamburger and some frozen french fries on the way home?"

"Certainly," said Landers. "Maybe this kind of thing will convince you to start a family and turn into an old-fashioned homemaker."

"I'm thinking about it, I'm thinking about it," said Phil. "What with all the stupid civilians I've had to deal with today, and now Lieutenant Goldberg telling me all about his allergies—"

Landers laughed. "We'll discuss it later at closer quarters. I'll expect you when I see you."

The chief accountant at Bullock's had come up with a rough estimate of the loot: somewhere around three hundred and fifty grand. Sergeant John Palliser drove home through the steady rain thinking about that very smart job. He had never been especially gifted with ESP—Mendoza was the one with the crystal ball—but a dim presentiment moved in his mind, and as he pulled into the drive of the house on Hillcrest Road in Hollywood he thought, that ought to be enough to last them for a while, but—

Roberta had really been working with the big black German shepherd Trina, who hardly jumped on them anymore at all. She brought him a Scotch-and-water, said there were pork chops for dinner and she'd just got the baby to sleep. "Have you been on that Bullock's thing?—it was on the noon news. That bunch really thinks big—are there any leads on it?"

"Not so far. And I do just wonder—" said Palliser.

Hackett went home, having failed to find any beautiful blonde heisters in their records, to an annoyed Angel and two noisy children. "Seven people came to see the house," said Angel, "and I have had it, Art. Let's for heaven's sake go to those Gold Carpet people— they'll buy the house outright, and we can move." She sounded cross and tired. They had put a down payment on the new house she had found, high up in Altadena, a nice house on a dead-end street; but here they still were in Highland Park, with the local crime rate soaring and two house payments to make for the second month. "I know they only offered seventy thousand, but we might not get much more anyway."

"You're probably so right," said Hackett. "We'd better. George and Mary were lucky." In the background, Mark was being an airplane and Sheila imitating him. "The happy home."

Angel hugged him. "I mean, when we know we're moving, I want to get on with it. I'll call them in the morning."

The Higginses had been lucky because the house on Silver Lake Boulevard—the house which Sergeant Bert Dwyer and Mary had bought sixteen years ago when they were expecting their first baby—had been in a location where the soulless new condominiums were going up. The years had passed too quickly, since it had been a quiet family home on a not-too-busy street; and Bert Dwyer had died on the marble floor of the bank with the heister's slugs in him, and that confirmed bachelor George Higgins had finally persuaded Mary to marry him. These days they had their own Margaret Emily who had turned two in September. Steve Dwyer was past fifteen and Laura thirteen, and—a good thing— they both adored George Higgins. But the years went by too fast.

He knew it had been a wrench for Mary, leaving the old house. The realty firm had bought it, and it would be torn down to make room for another tall condominium. But the new house was occupying her attention; a nice four-bedroom house on a quiet street in Eagle Rock, it needed a good deal of paint and tender loving care. Fortunately, Steve and Laura liked the new school.

When Higgins got home that Friday night Mary informed him that she'd given the kitchen the second coat of paint. "I wanted to get it done, George. But it did take longer than I'd thought, I'm afraid dinner isn't—"

Higgins surveyed her fondly, his lovely Mary, and said, "I see you did. You've got paint all over your face."

"I only finished ten minutes ago—Laura did offer to help but she had her music lesson to study, and Steve just got home—"

"Go wash the paint off," said Higgins, "and I'll take us all out to dinner."

He wasn't thinking about the Whalens, or the other body he'd looked at that day; that was just the job, and after the years he'd spent at the job, he'd learned to leave the current work at the office. See what showed tomorrow.

Mendoza, not thinking much about the Whalens, or

[33]

Hackett's female heister, or the Bullock's job, drove home through the rain, which seemed to be coming down harder. The house on Rayo Grande Avenue in Hollywood wasn't going to be home much longer. Alison's estate—the old *estancia* and winery in the hills above Burbank—was ready to be moved into. The new apartment, constructed for their newest retainers Ken and Kate Kearney in part of the old winery building, was finished; the fence around the four and a half acres was up, and the special wrought-iron gate bearing the name of the house, *La Casa de la Gente Feliz*, the house of happy people. These last few days, Alison had been in a frenzy of sorting out possessions and consulting with movers; they would be in the new house by Christmas.

But he came home to a tranquil atmosphere tonight. The twins Johnny and Teresa, just turned five in August, greeted him exuberantly but settled down again to coloring books. Alison had been curled in her armchair with the latest *House Beautiful*, while the new one rolled on a blanket on the floor. The new one, Luisa Mary, was fulfilling the prophecy of that nurse in the obstetric ward: she was a live wire all right, and her hair—coming in more vigorously by the day—as red as Alison's.

"I have no doot," said Mairí MacTaggart in the door to the dining room, "she'll turn out left-handed, the way she has of going backwards at things. You stay where you are, it's only the steak to broil—give the man time for a drink."

Certainly, when Mendoza was settled in his armchair with the drink (having necessarily provided El Señor, the alcoholic half-Siamese, with his own half-ounce of rye) Luisa Mary was energetically making swimming motions backward and complaining vociferously that she was no nearer her objective—the complicated tangle of the other three cats—Sheba, Bast and Nefertite—curled on the big, round, velvet ottoman.

"We're going to be in before Christmas if possible," Alison was exulting. "It's going to be hell, sorting everything out, but Mairí says better to do it at this end— Lord, we've been here five years, not all that long, but the things you accumulate—"

Cedric the Old English sheepdog galloped into the room with Mairí in hot pursuit. "The creature!" she said crossly. "In the wading pool all summer and footprints all over, and now bringing in the mud—"

Mendoza leaned back and shut his eyes. One of these days he might quit the job, and spend more time with the feudal household his Scots-Irish girl had wished on him. Or maybe not. . . . With the rye warm in his stomach, he was thinking again about that very sharp operation at Bullock's. Dimly, the same presentiment Palliser had known moved in his mind.

TWO

On Saturday morning, with Sergeant Lake off and Sergeant Farrell sitting on the switchboard, they got Nick Galeano back; he'd been off yesterday. He'd heard about the Bullock's job on the news, and was interested to hear what had showed. But Piggott and Schenke on night watch had left them a new heist to work, with at least one suggestive lead—the bartender who'd been held up thought he recognized the heister as some dude around the neighborhood. Galeano and Conway went out on that.

Five minutes after Mendoza came in, he hailed Conway, Palliser and Grace into his office, looking pleased. Hackett had a witness coming in, the second pharmacy clerk from Thursday night's heist; he showed up about eight-thirty and told Hackett just what the other one had. His name was Donald Hopper.

"Could've knocked me down with a feather," he said. "A dame! With a real cannon, and who takes chances with a female with a gun?" He gave a faithful description: maybe about five-five, really stacked, shoulder-length blonde hair, a good deal of make-up, "and real loud clothes, a print dress all sorts of colors, and a bright-red coat. That's about it."

"Just think this over," said Hackett. "Could it have been a man dressed up?"

Hopper didn't have to think. He laughed. "No way," he said instantly, "and Bob'd say the same. I was near enough to tell—no way was that padding, see, and it was a dame's voice, a dame's hands—you couldn't mistake it. That idea don't go. It's damn funny all right, a female heister, but that's what it was, Sergeant."

Hackett started to type up a statement for him to sign. He wondered if the female heister was in anybody else's records somewhere around.

Glasser waited until nine o'clock to call the jail. He was assured that both subjects were in a condition to be questioned. "Care to sit in on round two?" he asked Wanda.

"At the jail, yes."

It had stopped raining about ten o'clock last night, but was looking threatening again. Today, everybody had worn raincoats.

At the jail Glasser talked to the booking sergeant first. "Anything show in the medical examination? A doctor did look at both of them?"

"They were both just drunk," said the sergeant, bored. "Doctor saw them about five yesterday. They're both yelling about getting busted for no reason. You can't hold them beyond, lessee," he consulted the record, "three P.M. Twenty-four hours."

"I know, I know," said Glasser. As they went down the antiseptic-smelling corridor he added absently to Wanda, "They're both in records. First place to look. Rose has one count of prostitution about eight years ago, probation, and Fratelli did six months for a felony hit-run and involuntary manslaughter, four years ago."

"Which I suppose they'd tell us might happen to anybody," said Wanda.

"Nobody likes a cynical woman," said Glasser.

They saw Rose Engel first. The matron had commented dryly, "She's as sober as she ever will be," and looking at her in the bare little interrogation room, they could see that she was far down the line, far gone: her hands shaking, her eyes dull. Her pedigree said she was twenty-nine now; she looked forty. It was doubtful that she'd ever been very intelligent, but the alcohol had dimmed whatever sense she'd had.

"You got no right to hold me," she told them. "I didn't do anything."

"We're not holding you," said Glasser. "You can go any time when you've answered some questions. You do realize your daughter Alice has been murdered?"

"Yeah. Poor li'l kid."

"Where's your husband, Mrs. Engel?"

"Joe, you mean? He walked out on me a long time back—six, seven years. I dunno where he is, but he wouldn't hurt Alice."

"What about the other children, are they his too?" They were younger than that.

She was hunched over the bare table, not looking at them. She'd been bathed, and given a beige cotton uniform, but her dark hair was still unkempt, the dark-red polish on her stubby nails half worn off. "I dunno," she muttered. "I just couldn't say who it was, on Dicky or Linda, I guess I was drunk. Except the baby, it's Leon's."

"All right, about Thursday night," said Glasser. "You left the kids at what time, you remember?"

She shrugged. "I went to a party at Cora's. Cora Miller, she lives over the next block, on Mozart. Leon said he was tired, didn't want to go. I told him to get some hamburgers or something for the kids. The kids were O.K."

"What time was it?"

"I dunno, maybe seven-thirty."

"When did you get home?"

"Well, it sort of went on, the party. I stayed over with Cora, I guess we went to bed about four o'clock. I come home about noon, and that's when I found Alice. Like that. I couldn't get no sense out of Leon, so I went back to Cora's and she said I oughta call the fuzz, so I did."

"There wasn't anybody else there with the kids but Leon when you left?"

She shook her head. "They was O.K. Some real fiend musta got in while Leon was asleep. I dunno nothin' about it, you can't say I did."

"Nobody's saying anything," said Glasser. "You can leave any time."

Out in the corridor, Wanda said, "I hope you called the Board of Health."

"I did. Rose may go home, but it won't be home anymore. Depending on their red tape, it'll get declared unfit for habitation today or tomorrow—I mean Monday. I wonder who owns the place. They'll find out. And probably," said Glasser, "the court will take the kids away from her—God knows they'd be better off at Juvenile Hall or nearly any foster home—and she'll stop getting the nice A.D.C money."

Leon Fratelli wasn't as far down the road as she was, but on the way. He was at least cold sober now; he didn't like cops much, and answered them sullenly. "Listen," he said, "I'm sorry, what happened to the kid, but I don't know nothin' about it. All I know, I went out and got some hamburgers for the kids after Rose left, and then I went out for a couple drinks and when I come home I went to bed."

"You usually sleep on the cot in the living room?"

"No. I been thinkin', and it musta been that guy. Come home with me. I don't know who he is," said Fratelli. "I got talkin' to him in that bar."

"Which bar?"

"Uh, Pete's place up on North Main. I was awful tired, I'd hadda work two shifts, see, the night barkeep was off sick. That's at the Eagle Grill on Fourth, where I work. I was tired. I thought a couple drinks sort of relax me, is all. And I got talkin' to this guy, I never seen him before, he said his name was Sam. Maybe the barkeep or somebody there knows him."

"How did he happen to come home with you?" asked Glasser. "You have a car?"

"Yeah, yeah, I got a kind of beat-up old Ford. Well, that was sort of it. I guess I had a couple too many drinks, and—uh—once I got busted for drunk driving and I was nervous about it and—uh—he said he'd drive me home. He seemed like an all-right guy."

"How was he going to get back?"

"It was only up North Main. About six blocks. Listen, I don't know nothin' about all this, and you can't hold me. I sort of passed out and I never saw or heard nothin'."

Glasser sighed. "You remember what Sam looks like?"

"Sort of. Yeah. He was kind of tall, maybe six feet, and thin. About twenty-five. He had black hair, sort of long." Fratelli shrugged. "Listen, you can't hold me—"

Glasser said, "You can leave any time." And halfway down the corridor he stopped and said, "Damnation. The Board of Health—"

[40]

"I was going to say something," said Wanda, "but you're the detective."

"Yes. They'll get evicted, and how are we to know where the hell they've gone? But there's the A.D.C. money."

"What about it?"

"She won't be getting it anymore. I think she'll stick to Fratelli as long as he's got a job, and we know where he works."

Mendoza had surveyed his three detectives pleasedly, lounging back in his desk chair. "Sometimes the routine pays off. We haven't any record of the M.O. on the Bullock's job, but I wondered if somebody else had—I sent a query on to NCIC's computers last night. We have here the result." He tapped the yellow page on his desk blotter. "Two carbon copies. Last March in Philadelphia, last April in Pittsburgh."

"You don't say," said Grace interestedly.

"They decided to spend the winter someplace warmer, maybe," said Conway. "That's the hell of a long way off."

"And if they took anything like the Bullock's haul seven months ago, how come they needed more loot?" asked Palliser. He added, "Don't bother to tell me, I know. The pros can get rid of it faster than a dozen extravagant females. Gambling, women, dope, booze, name it."

"Nobody was ever dropped on for either job," said Mendoza, brushing his moustache thoughtfully, "which of course is why the record was still in the NCIC computer. But all the details don't always get sent to NCIC. It might be useful to hear what Philly and Pittsburgh can tell us." He picked up the phone. "Rory, get me through to Philadelphia P.D. headquarters." The call went through in five minutes; he was handed around a little, but finally got a Captain Royce of Robbery detail, who said he'd handled that one. *"Bueno,"* said Mendoza, and shoved the amplifier button. Royce had a heavy bass voice which boomed startlingly loud in the room; it was a very clear connection. "We've just had the same exact job pulled here. By what we got from NCIC. Did you ever get any leads on them at all?"

"What?" said Royce. "Is that so? It was the hell of a slick job—did you say Mendoza? They had the store's routine down pat, how the day's take gets handled—they knew just where to go and what time. They had to have some inside knowledge, but there wasn't a smell of a lead. All the security guards had records like new-fallen snow, and they'd all been at Gimbels for years. Nothing pointed to any of the regular personnel. None of our street informants knew a thing, and that was straight. For what it's worth, Mendoza, that said to me that maybe none of the gang is known—er—generally, on the street, if you follow me. It was a high-class job."

"Yes. So was ours. You never got a glimmer of an idea?"

"The hell I didn't," said Royce. "But it was just nothing, legally, and after all the city doesn't pay me to chase ghosts. We're always busy, and after a while it got stashed away in the unsolved file and I had to forget it."

"Yes, I'm a big-city cop too. What was the idea?"

"Well, after we'd looked everywhere else possible," said Royce, "we took a look at all the employees' records, and maybe I was just woolgathering but I wondered about this one woman. Employed as a salesclerk in the cosmetics department. One Marcia Wilmot. She only worked there for three months, and their personnel usually stay a lot longer than that. She quit her job two weeks before the job was pulled. Well, what could it say? I asked around, and there was nothing to say it wasn't all perfectly kosher. She told the other clerks that her mother had had a heart attack, she was going home to take care of her, even though she hated to give up a good job."

"Home being?"

"New York," said Royce.

"*Vaya historia*," said Mendoza.

"If that means what I think it does, the same to you in spades," said Royce. "It could have been absolutely straight. On the other hand, Wilmot was said to be a divorcée and nobody knew her maiden name. So try to look for her living with her mother in the Big Apple? And there really wasn't any reason to—it was just a handful of nothing. But I had a very strong hunch that she was tied in somehow."

"How well I know the feeling," said Mendoza. "That's all very interesting, *gracias*. Did you get a description, by the way?"

"Sure, for what it's worth. About thirty-five, medium height and weight, dark hair, brown eyes. Good-looking. She's not on record anywhere, at least under that name."

"And I hate to think how many brunettes answer to that. And she needn't have stayed brunette. But thanks so much."

He got less from Pittsburgh, where he talked with Lieutenant Wells. The job pulled at the Joseph Horne store had been another carbon copy, and Pittsburgh had gone through all the motions and come up blank. Yes, of course they had looked at the security guards, also at employees' records; but no employee had quit recently, they were all accounted for and not throwing money around.

"However," said Mendoza, putting the phone down, "it may offer us a small pointer, boys."

"You want us to wade through all Bullock's employment records?" asked Conway. "My God, it'd be a month's job."

"I have," said Mendoza, grinning at him rather wolfishly, "great faith in hunches, Rich. Even somebody else's."

"Shortcuts," said Grace meditatively. "The initials. Mary Webb or Margaret Willard or something. But she didn't show on the Pittsburgh job."

"Not out in the open."

"And we haven't checked back on all the guards yet," said Palliser.

"The routine does pay off. A good detective, John, leaves no stone unlifted—"

"Teach your grandmother," said Palliser resignedly. "All right, all right. I suppose we'd better get on with it."

As they stood up, Farrell poked his head in the door. "New body. The squad just called. Under some bushes in Lafayette Park."

"¿Qué es esto?" said Mendoza. He followed the others out; Hackett was just ripping a triplicate form from his typewriter. "So come on, Art—no rest for the wicked."

Higgins had done what there was to be done on Whalen. He typed up a statement from the answers they'd heard from Daniel, and took it up to the house on Portia Street. Daniel Whalen signed it, and gave him a more detailed description of the missing items.

"It wouldn't be any use your getting me to look at photographs," he said baldly to Higgins' suggestion. "I only saw them for a flash. We always keep the kitchen door closed, and I had no idea anything had happened—after Dave went out there—until I heard them run down the hall. I was here in the living room—I can't maneuver this thing very fast—and by the time I got to the hall door, they were just coming out of Dave's bedroom. All I can say is, they were both Negro, and pretty black, and young."

"I see." Higgins ruminated. There weren't many areas now where some Negroes didn't live, if there were still the solid black areas very much in existence. He didn't think, however, that there were many, if any, right around here. He asked Daniel.

"You forget, I don't get out and around, Sergeant," said Daniel bitterly. "But no, I don't think there are any right around here, for eight or ten blocks anyway. Dave and I had discussed moving—the crime rate up— but that's all over, and we'd never had any trouble, this is a quiet street. This was our old home, Father bought this house in nineteen thirty-nine when I was still in high school. We were comfortable, it was home. The *bastards!*" he cried suddenly, slamming one hand down on the arm of the wheelchair. "The *bastards!*" The cat Merlin jumped in his basket, startled at the sudden loud voice, and then sat up pretending not to have noticed, and yawned pinkly.

Higgins muttered awkward sympathy. There wasn't much anyone could say to him. He wondered how Daniel could manage about the funeral. The invalid sank back in renewed apathy after the little outburst, shutting his eyes. After a moment he said, "No—we've had quite a few Orientals moving in around here, but they seem to be mostly quiet, decent people."

"Yes," said Higgins, and suddenly for no particular reason thought of the Cambodian family who had handed Palliser the one link that had uncovered Larry Hoffman as Walt Robsen's killer, last August. Larry Hoffman's final court hearing was coming up on Tuesday; they'd have to cover it. None of them would much enjoy seeing Cathy Robsen, or Sergeant Bill Hoffman and his wife Muriel, again.

"Mrs. Meeker's been very kind," said Daniel, "bringing in food. But I must see about getting in touch with that service—meals on wheels, isn't it? I can't depend on—"

There probably wasn't a chance that a rumor of the Whalens having hidden cash in the house had called down the attack, when the killers hadn't come from the immediate neighborhood. And that crude a break-in was too common to be dignified with the name of *modus operandi*. But the routine sometimes rang bells.

He went back to headquarters and spent some time down in R. and I., where these days they had computers. He turned up three names, with addresses attached, which were not too near the Portia Street house but not miles away either: names of Negro males with records of the crude break-ins. Darren Scott, Rosemont Avenue: two years ago he'd broken in the back door of a house in Hollywood and offered violence to the widow who lived there, while stealing cash and jewelry. He'd been eighteen then, and had been handed six months' probation. Randolph Wiggett, Park Street: eighteen months ago he'd been caught by a hefty householder, ransacking an apartment after breaking in the back door. It had been his third felony arrest as an adult, and at one time that could have earned him a life sentence; these days, what he'd drawn was a one-to-three. He might be still inside. Dwight Early, Normal Avenue: six months ago he'd broken in a window in a house in Atwater, and been caught up to when a pawnbroker recognized stolen goods; it was his first arrest and he'd been given six months' probation.

[46]

Higgins went up to the office and found it deserted. He called Welfare and Rehabilitation on Wiggett and learned without surprise that he'd been paroled after six months in. He called the lab and asked if they'd got anything from the Portia Street place. He was reminded that they had other things on hand but eventually would get to processing what prints had been lifted.

He smoked a cigarette, staring into space, and got up reluctantly. There was half a day's legwork ahead of him and it would have been nice to have some company on it. "Where's the boss?" he asked Farrell.

"Oh, he and Art went out to look at a body," said Farrell, hardly looking up from his *Herald.*

Higgins went out and discovered that it was starting to rain again.

Mendoza stopped two feet away from the new body and said, "*¡Oye!* Now just where did this come from?"

"Probably just another O.D.—or D.T.'s," said Hackett after a cursory glance; he was thinking about the house in Highland Park. Seventy thousand was all very well, but well under the inflated value. That place in the next block had gone for eighty-five, he knew. Still, a bird in the hand—

"Oh, now, Art, you've been a detective long enough to know better than that. Take another look."

After another look Hackett said, "Oh. Yes, I see what you mean, Luis. Funny place for her."

The patrolman, Erickson, and the flustered-looking man beside him just watched them. Mendoza squatted over the body, not touching it.

Lafayette Park was a quiet little piece of empty greenery between Sixth and Wilshire, close in downtown. It wasn't much used as a park; it had few benches and no other amenities. The only building in it was the Felipe de Neve branch library. It was a peculiar place to find a body, and this was a peculiar body to be there.

It was the body of a woman, and not a young woman. She was lying on her back half under an untidy patch of shrubbery, just into the park from Sixth Street; she stared at the cold gray sky horridly, mouth half open. She was at least middle-aged and possibly older, by the wrinkled throat, the enlarged veins on the one hand visible. She had kept a middling good figure, neither fat nor scrawny. The cold morning light was merciless on the make-up grotesque now on the dead face: too white powder, green eye-shadow, pink lipstick; but in life she'd have looked just well preserved, carefully groomed. Her hair, unkempt now, had obviously been professionally waved and tinted a discreet beige-blonde. The nails on the hand were a very faint pink, and on the ring finger was a solitaire diamond set in yellow gold. Mendoza peered at that more closely and said, "Somewhere around a half carat. Worth something."

She was wearing a full-length navy wool coat with a fur collar colored white and gray. It had fallen open to reveal the dress beneath, a tailored navy knit sheath. It was pulled up slightly over her knees; she had on sheer nylon stockings and medium-heeled navy pumps. Her left arm was under the thrown-back coat; delicately Mendoza moved that, and said, "*Así.*" On her left ring finger was a rather wide gold wedding band.

"At least she ought to be easy to identify," said Hackett, following his thought. "She's no derelict."

"Anything but." Mendoza stood up and automatically brushed down his trousers. "All those clothes are good quality. Not the most expensive, nothing flashy, but good. That coat's nearly new. So are the shoes. She doesn't belong anywhere down here—how the hell did she get here?"

"Wait for the I.D.," said Hackett. He looked at the other two men. "You're the one who found her?" he asked the civilian.

"That's right." He was a rather weedy man about thirty-five, with a nervous Adam's apple; he had a silver-gray raincoat belted tightly about him. "My name's Jurgen, Karl Jurgen. Yes, I found her and called the police, but I never saw her before, I don't know anything about it. I'm on my way to work—I'll be late but of course it can't be helped—"

"How did you happen to be in the park?" asked Hackett.

"I cut across here every day, it's a shortcut. I get the bus up Sixth. I'm the desk clerk at the Sheraton West," and he gestured.

"Oh," said Hackett. Just as all the civic buildings had ended up in the heart of the inner city, a few other more-than-respectable edifices rubbed shoulders down here with the dingy old residential streets and business blocks; and that old and respected—and very respectable —hotel, the Sheraton West, was one of them.

"I knew I had to call the police—was she murdered?" He looked horrified and fascinated at once. "The library isn't open, I had to go back to Sixth to find a phone. But I never saw the woman before, I don't know anything about it."

"All right, Mr. Jurgen," said Hackett. "Just give us your address and you can go on to work." He gave it readily, Kenmore Street in Hollywood, and departed half reluctantly.

"I think," said Mendoza, "I'd like a doctor to see her *in situ.*" He got through to the coroner's office on the

[49]

radio in the squad, talked to Bainbridge himself. "Just to confirm a few deductions," he said to Hackett.

Bainbridge came out in person, curious. He was rounder and tubbier than ever, accompanied by the inevitable black cigar.

"You do come across them, Luis," he said, looking at the corpse. "No I.D. on her?"

"Not unless she's lying on her handbag."

Very gently, Bainbridge lifted the corpse by the middle. It came all in one piece, stiff as a board. "No handbag," said Bainbridge, and felt the jawline. "Oh, yes. Rigor fully established and just starting to pass off. But it was a sudden death, and that's apt to hasten rigor. I don't think she died here."

"Neither do I," said Mendoza. "Any guess as to how she died, Doctor?" There weren't any visible marks on the body.

"Not till I have a closer look—" Bainbridge was inspecting the skull, feeling with his fingers. "Um. Well, there you are, I think. See what shows when I open her up, but it feels like a depressed fracture—" His thumb was just behind her right temple. "She could have fallen down on the sidewalk and done that."

"And then picked herself up and wandered in here to die?"

"You are so quick," said Bainbridge. "I don't think she did much moving after she sustained that, no. And the fact that she *is* here, after all—"

"*Allá va,*" said Mendoza. "How long has she been here?"

"You're supposed to be the detective," said Bainbridge, "but I got caught without a coat yesterday too."

"*Exactamente,*" said Mendoza pleasedly. "It stopped raining about ten last night. And if she got here—was put here—before that, it wasn't long before. If she'd

[50]

been lying here even half an hour in that downpour, her clothes would have been soaked, and they're only damp. I'd say she got here between nine-forty and ten."

Bainbridge grunted. "I'd say the same thing, and furthermore I'd say that was roundabout the time she died. And it's going to start raining again any minute. Do you want to wait for photographs?"

"I'd rather have her clothes intact. Take her in." Mendoza bent over the body again and carefully felt in the coat pockets. The left one yielded a crumpled handkerchief and a dime, the other one nothing. "Damnation. Art, just to be thorough we'd better have a hunt for the handbag all around here. If X tossed it out further away, *adios*, it'll be long gone, but—"

"Tossed it out of a car," said Hackett.

"Proceed from A to B to C," said Mendoza. "By her clothes, her age, her grooming, she wasn't alone in the street down here—"

"Unless she was staying at the Sheraton West," said Hackett.

Mendoza smote his forehead. "*¡Mea culpa!* We'll ask. But barring that—and even if so—she wouldn't be on foot here at that hour of night. She was in a car. And a woman of her age never goes out without a handbag. The sweet young girls, yes—the billfold in the jeans— but not this woman. We'd better call out some help."

They called in, but Farrell was alone in the office except for Wanda. She came over amiably, another pair of eyes, and in the next hour they covered every foot of the park like bloodhounds, pushing under bushes; but no handbag turned up.

"Hell," said Mendoza. "But—there's something else. Art, you go over to the Sheraton West and ask, just in case. But the wedding ring—the manicure—the professional coiffure—she came out of a comfortable home, she wasn't a nobody. Quite possibly somebody's already called Missing Persons to say that Mother didn't come home last night. I'd better go and ask."

Hackett and Wanda went over to the hotel, but there wasn't a guest registered who matched the description.

And at Missing Persons, Lieutenant Carey said immediately they hadn't anybody like that reported.

"Yes," said Mendoza to himself. "There was that pretty little woman in the phone booth, not missed at once because she lived alone. That's probably it." He took himself out to a solitary lunch. Later, he phoned the lab to send a man to the morgue for her prints.

At five-thirty he was swiveled around in the desk chair watching the gray rain blotting out the Hollywood hills in the distance, when Scarne came in with a manila envelope.

"Higgins was deviling us this morning for what we got in that Portia Street place. Here's the report. Damn all. Plenty of prints, but they all belong to the dead man or the brother."

"What can't be cured," said Mendoza.

"Anyway, there's the report. Oh, and I got the prints off your latest body. Thank God for computers. They're not on file with us. I sent 'em to the Feds."

"Probably a waste of time." But of course the F.B.I. had the prints on file of a good many perfectly respectable people.

As Scarne went out, Conway, Palliser and Grace came trooping in; Mendoza went out to the communal office. "You look as if you'd done a day's work."

Conway snarled. "Do you have any idea how many employees Bullock's has? And we're looking for the ones who quit or got fired up to six months ago too. I said, it'll take a month of Sundays, and it won't give us a damned thing."

"And if you mention routine—" said Palliser. There was a smear of ink on his handsome straight nose, and his eyes look strained.

"At least I haven't been endangering my eyesight," said Grace cheerfully. "I've finished checking the guards, and we can forget about them. The outfit they work for is one of the biggest around, very high reputation, and they screen their men to hell and back. Also, all of the security men at Bullock's have been there for a good long time—seven, six, five years—Masters is the newest and he's been there two and a half years."

"It'll end up getting stashed in the dead files," said Conway wearily.

Mendoza slid a long hand up his long jaw. "Same as in Philly and Pittsburgh. I'd like to think not. Because I had a little feeling—"

"Hunch?" asked Grace.

"*No sé.* Just a little premonition that these slick operators—"

"Oh, you too?" said Palliser. "Another hit?"

"I just wonder," said Mendoza. "Philly in March, Pittsburgh in April. Maybe it's taken them this long to get rid of the estimated four hundred grand."

Sometimes Saturday night could get a little hairy in this part of L.A., but that night the rain seemed to slow them down, keeping people inside. Piggott and Schenke, sitting on night watch, didn't get a call until ten-thirty. They both went out on it.

It was a dairy store on Virgil, and Patrolman Bill Moss was soothing the victim, a pretty blonde who had been crying. She looked about twenty, and her name was Sonia Murphy. She said to Piggott and Schenke, still tearful, "I'm *sorry*, but it is, I wish to heaven they'd called me Sally or Betty or something because it sounds funny, but I can't help it if Mother's Polish, I've got kidded all my life. But that woman! I just can't believe it! Didn't, I mean. I don't like working at night, but I'm not usually alone, usually Mr. Knight's here, he's the manager, because he doesn't like the girls being alone at night either. I take three nights a week and Marge takes three, and usually I'm not here Saturday at all—but Mr. Knight's wife is sick, it's some kind of emergency operation, she just went into the hospital today and he called me to ask if I'd come in because Saturday's usually a good day—"

"Now, now," said Moss benevolently. "They just want to hear what happened. Like the old TV show, you know. Facts."

She looked at him blankly and they realized that she was too young to remember *Dragnet*. Not even reruns? "Oh, I'm sorry, I didn't mean to— But to think! To *think* I was relieved. I was almost going to close early, there hadn't been many people in on account of the rain I suppose, and I was just going to lock up and call Bob— that's my boy friend, Bob Boyd—to come get me and take me home, when *she* came in—and I was so relieved to see it was a woman! I was! And then she said, you all alone here, honey, and I said yes—and she got a *great big gun* out of her purse and pointed it at me and said she wanted all the money in the register! I thought I'd die! Honestly!" Sonia gulped. "And poor Mr. Knight losing all that money—of course I had to give it to her—"

"Calm down," said Moss. "Can you tell the detectives what she looked like?"

"Oh, *yes*. She was—" Sonia hesitated and finally

chose, "flashy. She had on a red pantsuit and black ankle boots and a big white plastic rain hat with a brim. It had y-yellow flowers on it. And her hair was a real brassy blonde, pretty long, down to her shoulders anyway, and she had a sort of—well, a *lot* of figure, if you know what I mean—"

"Stacked?" said Schenke dead-pan.

"I guess you'd say so."

"Any idea how much was in the register?"

"I'm not sure. The tab'll say. At least a hundred dollars."

"Well," said Piggott, "she's not doing so bad, Bob. That figures to about five hundred for two nights' work."

"Do you *know* her? Know who she is?"

"I only wish we did," said Piggott.

Surprisingly, that was the only call they had on Saturday night.

Nothing much was accomplished on Sunday. Mendoza came in very late; he wasn't supposed to be in on Sunday at all but he generally was, if not for a full day, and nobody would dream of mentioning Sunday Mass to him—he was a little touchy about getting back into the fold after a good many years outside it.

Yesterday Galeano had spent the whole day chasing down the heist man, who had turned out to be one Randy Becket, still on parole after a term for armed robbery. He felt he deserved a quiet Sunday.

When Mendoza finally came in, Higgins was waiting to bring him up to date on Whalen. "It's damn all, Luis, and we might as well forget the whole thing now. We'll never drop on them, to make a legal case." He told Mendoza what he'd got from records, the very thin leads. "I struck out on Scott, he's moved and nobody knows

where. I found Wiggett. He just got beat up by somebody's husband and he's wearing a cast on a broken
ankle. I also found Early. He could be, couldn't be—we'd
never prove it. Says he was at the movies Friday afternoon."

"It'll go in Pending," said Mendoza.

"Damn it. That poor damned Whalen—maybe it
sounds as if he's feeling sorry for himself, but you can
see the spot he's in—his whole life destroyed, because
the louts didn't care what they did for a little loot. He'll
probably have to go to a rest home."

"And I wonder," said Mendoza, "what will happen
to Merlin."

"M— oh, the cat." Higgins regarded him, amused.
Mendoza was a cat man. A long time ago there had been
a case—when they'd finally identified the corpse, Mendoza had been a lot more concerned about her starving
cat than he had been with the killer; and come to think,
that was the cat he had wished onto Art and his wife,
Angel; they were cat people too.

Mendoza called the lab; they hadn't had a kickback
from the Feds yet, on the lady in Lafayette Park. Of
course the Feds had computers too, but as Marx reminded him, they also had, as a rule, a long backlog of
requests for information. There'd be something eventually.

It was just sprinkling on and off today.

Glasser came in next and told him about Alice Engel.
"We ought to get the autopsy report tomorrow. The
bartender at Pete's says Fratelli's a regular, in two or
three times a week—puts it down pretty heavy. Funnily
enough, the place where he works—the Eagle Grill—
the owner says he never drinks on the job. Nobody at
Pete's remembers noticing him specially on Thursday
night, the barkeep says he was there but didn't notice

[56]

when he left or if he was alone. Nobody named Sam is one of their regulars. Of course, I haven't chased down anybody else who was in the place then—the barkeep parted with five names of regulars who were there."

"In fact, all up in the air," said Mendoza.

"So what do you think?"

"That you'd better wait for the autopsy and lab report."

Hackett wandered into his office about four o'clock to say that he'd been talking to other forces around the county about the blonde heister. "So far, no bells ringing . . . Luis?"

"*¿Qué pasa, compadre?*"

"Oh, hell," said Hackett. He thrust his bulk out of the chair—he had really been serious about the doctor's diet last month and was down to two hundred—and stood staring out the window at the silver curtain of rain. "The Hoffman hearing. Tuesday. Who do you want to cover it?"

"*¿Nada más?*" said Mendoza. "*¿Qué puede uno hacer?* What can anyone do there, Art? You were on it, me, George, John. We'd all better show up. You don't know what testimony the judge may ask for. At least it's not a jury trial, with the confession on record. And he's turned eighteen, he's a legal adult."

"And the judge," said Hackett abruptly, "is Fletcher."

"*Bastante.* The mills of the gods," said Mendoza sardonically.

"I just hope to God I don't have to testify. What I couldn't help saying—and Fletcher the bleeding heart looking sideways at that confession and talking about police brutality—"

"Cross the bridge when we get there," said Mendoza, and stabbed out his cigarette as if it was a personal enemy.

[57]

THREE

On Monday morning, with Palliser off, Mendoza came in rather late and was just glancing at the night-watch report when Bainbridge came bustling in, plunked himself down in the chair beside the desk, and brought out a fresh cigar.

"Business being a little slow for once, I did the autopsy for you myself." He laid the official report on Mendoza's desk. "Got her identified yet? Well, you probably will. She was somewhere in her middle fifties, and what's called well preserved. She'd lived an easy life, that is, never had to scrub floors or whatever. She'd never borne a child. What you want to know—it was a depressed skull fracture all right. I doubt if there was any weapon involved, what it looks like is that she fell, or was knocked, against some broad flat surface, and *kaput*. She might have died within five minutes or so. The indications are that she had a little struggle with somebody—there are bruises on both her upper arms, as if somebody had taken hold of her pretty roughly, and there's a fainter bruise on the left side of her jaw."

"Yes. And?"

"Well, she hadn't been raped and she hadn't been engaging in sexual intercourse. She'd had a meal about four hours before she died, which was any time between seven and midnight Friday night, but we decided to call it about ten. There was the equivalent of about three drinks in the stomach contents. I don't know what, I haven't done any analyses. If you're bound to know what her last meal consisted of, or whether she drank martinis or Scotch highballs, I can probably find out."

"Yes," said Mendoza. "Not much to go on until we know who she was. But thanks so much, Doctor. Maybe you'd better do those analyses, give us some details. What about her clothes?"

"I sent 'em to your lab." Bainbridge fished in his pocket and dropped the two rings onto the desk. "You never know what little detail may show up to give you some lead. I'll get to the analyses, probably get back to you sometime on Wednesday."

Mendoza didn't watch him out; he picked up the diamond ring. It wasn't a new ring, and quite anonymous, just a nice solitaire diamond in a Tiffany setting. The wedding band was just a wedding band—no engraving. Mendoza rummaged and found a paper-clip box in the top drawer, dropped them both in. If they ever identified her, and any relatives showed up. . . . A well-preserved lady of middle age. Whom nobody had yet missed, or Carey would have called. And nothing in from the Feds yet or the lab would have called. But a woman of this type would be bound to be missed sooner or later. Wait and see.

He picked up the report again and saw that the night watch, after a quiet Saturday, had had a hectic Sunday night. Three heists—two bars and a pharmacy—and a man dropping dead in an all-night cafeteria on Wilshire. He went out to the central office to see who was doing what. Landers and Grace had roped Conway into helping out on the paperwork on the Bullock's job. There were five witnesses due in on last night's heists to make statements and look at pictures, and that would occupy Glasser, Hackett and Galeano quite nicely. Higgins had gone out on the dead man: there'd been I.D. on him but Piggott and Schenke hadn't been able to raise anybody at the address.

Mendoza wandered back to his desk chair again and swiveled around to the window. It was raining again, and in southern California in November, that certainly meant another wet winter. His mind slid from the well-preserved lady to Alison's new-old *estancia*—certainly the right word for it; they'd been up there yesterday morning, and she was wild to make the move. It had certainly—if expensively—turned out an impressive place, high up in the hills above Burbank, with a spectacular view right down to the beach. Because the four and a half acres were outside the city limits in the county, the taxes were not all that bad. She had, of course, been having a field day buying new furniture, the house being four times the size of the place on Rayo Grande, what with the separate suite for Mairí. His red-haired Scots-Irish girl providing him with the set of feudal retainers. Mairí had arrived as a nurse for the twins, and turned into an honorary grandmother. And now there were the Kearneys—caretakers of the estate—and the new apartment for them created out of the old winery. But that was just as well—except that the Kearneys had a black cat named Nicodemus, and how he and El Señor were going to share even four and a half acres remained to be seen. And the matter of the ponies was becoming pressing. Ever since the subject had been first, and unfortunately, mentioned in their hearing, the twins had been demanding to know when the ponies might appear. And Ken Kearney the former rancher would know about ponies. Mendoza supposed there'd be some available, somewhere around. There were bridle trails in Griffith Park where you saw people on horses, so there must be stables somewhere. Yes, and Kearney casually suggesting a few sheep to keep the undergrowth eaten down; there'd only be landscaping around the house. A small stable for the potential ponies had been contrived out of an old shed up there, and there were plans for a riding ring; that had set the twins off again yesterday. "This where the ponies gonna live, when are we gonna get the ponies, Mamacita?" At least, since they'd been in nursery school, they'd got English and Spanish untangled. And there ought to be a good parochial school somewhere at that end of the valley. He wondered suddenly if the sheep would need a barn too. Now he thought about it, he'd never seen a real live sheep in his life. The things that girl got him into. . . .

Higgins had gone out on the necessary routine; cops didn't always deal just with crime. The paramedics had been called last night when the man collapsed in the cafeteria, and said it was probably a massive coronary; he'd been gone before he hit the floor. His I.D.—driver's license, Master Charge, Exxon gas card—said he was Earl Harper of an address on Genesee Street in Hollywood. They had looked around the cafeteria last night and found a car registered to him parked on a side street, and brought it into the police garage.

It was one of the unpleasant chores of the job, breaking bad news. The I.D. card in his wallet had said, in case of emergency notify Mrs. Marjorie Harper. The address was an old frame house, neatly maintained; Higgins parked in front, went up and rang the bell.

She was a plump, cheerful-looking woman, and she stared at Higgins on her doorstep—Higgins might as well have had COP tattooed on his forehead—and listened to him without a change of expression. She just stood there while he told her the facts, and her eyes started to glaze a little.

She said in a too-calm tone, "I never gave it a thought. Not a thought. He's usually home and in bed by eight, but he might've been delayed. Or gone on an errand. My daughter just brought me home a few minutes ago."

"You didn't expect him home last night?"

"Earl works the night shift," she said. "He's a male nurse at St. Vincent's Medical Center. Most nights he has dinner home, of course, but last night I was going out with my daughter to the theater, the Pasadena Playhouse, and we'd be late so I stayed over with her, she lives in Pasadena. Earl said he'd get dinner out before he went to work."

"I see," said Higgins. "I have to tell you it's mandatory to have an autopsy, unless he'd seen a doctor within ten days. You'll be notified when you can claim the body. His car— Are you all right, Mrs. Harper? Would you like me to call someone for you?" They were still there on the porch, the front door open.

"Thank you," she said politely. And then, suddenly, "But Earl can't be dead! He's only fifty-nine, he's never had a sick day in his life! You can't be talking about *Earl*—" And then she started to cry, and in the end he had to go in and call the daughter, and wait until she got there with her husband. The husband was equally incredulous and insisted on going to the morgue to

[62]

identify the body. It was, of course, Earl Harper. His son-in-law looked very shaken, and kept mumbling, "Fifty-nine, fifty-nine, and never sick in his life—my God—"

By the time Higgins got back to the office it was nearly eleven o'clock.

Glasser had just finished taking a statement from one of the witnesses to the pharmacy heist last night when Sergeant Lake brought two people in to see him. The man—small, gray and ferociously energetic—was Michael McNulty of the Board of Health, and the woman—large, florid and flustered—was Miss Florence Cook from the Aid to Dependent Children agency.

Glasser lifted a hand at Wanda across the office, and she came over at once. "Miss Larsen is with me on the case," said Glasser.

"Absolutely disgraceful!" said Miss Cook violently. "That house! Merciful heavens, that house! Our office was notified, of course, by Juvenile Hall—I understand the police had told them the children were A.D.C. subjects—and immediately I found the memo on my desk this morning—of course we are not open on Saturdays—I went to interview Mrs. Engel. I had *not* been to the house before, needless to say."

"Why not?" asked Wanda innocently.

"I beg your pardon?"

"Well, after all you're disbursing taxpayers' money to see that children are looked after properly," said Wanda, "and I should think you'd want to know something about their homes."

"My dear girl, we are extremely shorthanded at the office—such a heavy case load—if we attempted to visit personally every single applicant, we should never get through the necessary paperwork."

"Had you ever seen Mrs. Engel's children?" asked Wanda.

"Of course she did not bring them to the office when she applied—"

"Then you didn't even know they existed? She just said she had four children and no money, and you started handing her some?"

Glasser opened his mouth to shut her up, but too late. "My dear girl," said Miss Cook, "you must realize that our time is limited, extremely limited. With all the paperwork—"

"Taxpayers' money is also limited," said Wanda. Her eyes were very blue, and seemed to be shooting sparks at Miss Cook, who swelled for further speech. "But you saw Mrs. Engel—didn't it occur to you that she couldn't be a very satisfactory parent?"

"If I had ever dreamed of such conditions, naturally I—that house!" said Miss Cook.

"Simmer down," said Glasser to Wanda. "It's the bureaucratic mind. No entry. One way."

"What?" said Miss Cook.

"If anyone is *at all* concerned that any action is being taken," said McNulty, with an arctic glance at Miss Cook, "I can assure you that it is. Unlike some other civic agencies, the Board of Health does not automatically and arbitrarily withhold its services from the public on weekends. Two of my colleagues and myself examined the house on Darwin Street on Saturday, and gave the tenants a verbal eviction order at that time. In fact, I considered the danger of infection to be so severe—only three months ago we had several cases of typhoid in that general area—that I had the house sealed at once. I have not let the grass grow under my feet, I assure you, Sergeant—"

[64]

"Detective," said Glasser.

"—And I obtained a condemnation order this morning. It was when I had driven down there to post it properly that I discovered—" his glare was frosty— "this —er—Miss Cook on the premises. She had actually broken the seals on the door."

"I had to see Mrs. Engel! How did I know the house was empty? You hadn't left any signs on it. After what the matron at Juvenile Hall told me about the children—"

"My dear madam, you might have inferred that some authority had placed the seals. Now I am in a position to know that the police discovered the condition of the house on *Friday*—and you have taken no steps until this morning, to protect children nominally in your care. I, on the other hand, spent my entire Saturday afternoon and Sunday hunting down records to discover the owner of the property and informing them—"

"Who is it?" asked Glasser.

"Like several blocks of property in that general area, all that block is owned by a large realty corporation—there has, of course, been some talk of an urban renewal project—"

"Profiteers!" said Miss Cook. "Monopolists!"

"And the condemnation order is now posted," said McNulty triumphantly.

"But where is Mrs. Engel?" demanded Miss Cook. "I must locate her at once! She will be taken to court as an unfit mother—we'll need a warrant for that, of course—"

"Sorry," said Glasser, "you're in the wrong office for that. You'll have to go down to Juvenile and tell the story there. We'll try to find Mrs. Engel for you—we want to see her again too." When the two of them had gone out, he sat back and laughed.

"It's not that funny, Henry," said Wanda. "I'll bet I could walk into that office and say I had six kids and no husband or money, and they'd simply hand out the monthly checks."

"But we had," said Glasser, "better find out where Fratelli and Rose have flitted to. That place he works will be open at two."

Mendoza had just come out of his office, hat in hand, at a few minutes before twelve, with the intention of going out to an early lunch with whoever was unoccupied. Only Galeano was in the office, typing. Sergeant Lake was just coming in.

"Oh, you're still here, Lieutenant. You've got something new. Homicide down on Twenty-seventh." He handed Mendoza the memo-slip with the address.

"¡Condenación!" said Mendoza. But the homicides got committed—and discovered—around the clock. "That means you and me, Nick."

"Right with you," said Galeano. As they walked down to the elevator, Mendoza thought irrelevantly that Galeano was looking a bit younger and more cheerful lately; he'd lost some weight too—like Hackett he was inclined to put it on. Mendoza wondered if that had anything to do with that German girl Nick had fallen for in such an unlikely way: how was he doing with her? Everybody had thought amiable, stocky, dark Galeano was a confirmed bachelor at thirty-five. Still, thought Mendoza with a sudden inward chuckle, look at George Higgins. And as he pressed the elevator button, a small imp at the back of his mind said, *Or Luis Mendoza*, and he burst out laughing.

"Something funny?" said Galeano.

[66]

"Just human nature, Nick." Everybody had thought Luis Mendoza was a confirmed bachelor too, and a good deal older than Galeano or Higgins, and six years later, where that girl had got him: the twins, and now the new one (who would turn out to be another redhead, of course), that dog, and now a vast (well, for L.A.) estate, the feudal retainers, and now more livestock. What next, he wondered. But she'd said she was going to take up painting again, with a real studio. That might quiet her down a little; one never knew.

They made a dash for the Ferrari through the rain: not a downpour, but the steady kind of rain that brought a lot of water down.

The address on Twenty-seventh Place—this was one of the solidly black areas—was an old stucco house on a narrow residential street. It wasn't an affluent-looking block, but all the houses were well enough kept up, with strips of lawn and flower beds in front. This one was painted pink, and at the largest front window were crisp white priscilla curtains, visible from outside.

There was a squad parked at the curb, with Patrolman Barrett waiting in the front passenger's seat. Beyond the square front porch the front door of the house was open.

"What have we got?" Mendoza and Galeano ducked into the back seat of the squad.

"Something damned queer," said Barrett. "Rather you than me, try to figure it out. These two women are at home—they're sisters—and the doorbell rings, woman says she's selling something and gets let in, and a minute later brings out a gun and shoots one of them. A Mrs. Leta Reynolds. That's about all I got—the other one was pretty shocked and upset. There's a little girl there too. The other girl asked if she could call her mother and I said she'd better wait for you. She seems a pretty good type—maybe she's got over the shock enough to answer some questions. I left Ray with her." Down here they ran two-man cars.

"Queer isn't a word for it," said Mendoza. "We'll want a lab truck." They arranged for that; he and Galeano went up the front walk and into the house.

Patrolman Wiener was just inside the door, which led directly into a living room. He said, "The girl went into the bedroom. Wanted to get the kid away from the body."

"Understandable," said Galeano. This was a pleasant, homey room, with a worn American-Oriental rug on the floor, old-fashioned upholstered furniture in shades of green and beige, a real brick hearth. It was clean and neat, except for the body; and at first glance you might have thought Leta Reynolds was merely asleep.

She was a nice-looking young woman, chocolate brown, with neat regular features and a slim figure. She was wearing a dull-orange sheath dress and black patent-leather pumps. There was a gold bracelet on one arm, a gold wrist watch on the other. She was lying back on the couch, looking quite comfortable. There was a dark stain on her left breast—not a very big stain.

"She said she heard three or four shots—didn't realize what they were," said Wiener. "I'd guess a small caliber, twenty-two or something." He went into the hall. "Miss Corey, the detectives are here. They'd like to talk to you."

She came to the door of the living room. Wiener introduced them formally and she nodded. "I'm Melinda Corey." She looked about twenty; she was more handsome than pretty, with rather sharp features, a great knot of hair coiled on top of her head; she wore a smart dark-green pantsuit. "Please—we don't have to stay here?

I mean—" she glanced at the body, gulped and turned away.

"We'd rather not," said Mendoza. "There'll be some technicians here in a while."

"The kitchen," she said. "There's Lily—" She opened a door and looked into a bedroom. "You just stay there awhile, honey. Don't be scared at any noises—there's just some people coming to—to help Mommy."

"Will she be all right?" The little girl looked about six; she had big black eyes and neat pigtails tied with red ribbons.

"I think so," said Melinda. "I'll be back after a while." She shut the door and led them down the hall to a square kitchen big enough for a table and four chairs. There was a little stack of dishes in the sink. She sat down at the table and they sat with her. There was a big ceramic ashtray on the table, and Mendoza offered her a cigarette. She bent to his lighter.

"I don't believe any of this has happened," she said. "Half an hour ago—Leta saying she'd do the breakfast dishes—and then the doorbell rang—"

"We have to take it in order. We don't know much about it, suppose you tell it from the beginning. First, she was your sister?"

She nodded once. "Leta Reynolds. I suppose you want—some background. Whatever you call it. She was twenty-seven. She was divorced. This was—I mean, she and Len started to buy this house and she got it as a settlement and went on paying on it."

"Did she have a job?" asked Mendoza.

Melinda put a hand to her eyes. "If she'd just been at work! Any other day she would have been! But if she had been, maybe I'd have got shot. It doesn't make any sense. Yes. Yes, she worked at the Armstrong Photo

Salon, she's a retoucher. Usually, she'd have gone to work at nine o'clock, but she'd put in some overtime on those rush wedding pictures last week, and Mr. Armstrong told her to take this morning off."

"What about you?" asked Galeano. His tone was warm and friendly; she relaxed a little.

"I'm going to L.A.C.C., my second year. I came to live with Leta because it's closer for me—Mother and Dad live in Inglewood. I'm an education major. I've got a part-time job at the campus bookstore. Please, I'd like to call Mother. This will about kill them, there were just the two of us left, my brother was killed in an accident two years—"

"In a while," said Mendoza. "We'd like to hear just what happened, Miss Corey."

"I'll tell you everything I know," she said, "but it just doesn't make sense. Leta kept Lily home this morning, she had a temperature and it was so wet out—she's in first grade—she was, I mean Leta, going to take her over to the Sanfords' when she went to work. That's where Lily always goes after school, her best friend is Barbara Sanford and Mrs. Sanford keeps her till Leta gets home at five-thirty. I didn't have a class till one o'clock. We had a late breakfast, and Leta got dressed to go to work—she wanted to get the tank filled on the way—and I was in the bathroom, washing out some pantyhose and things. When the bell rang."

"Take your time. Did you see the woman at all?" asked Mendoza.

"About—two seconds," she said. "Just crazy. I heard Leta open the door and I heard them talking—just a couple of sentences—and I couldn't tell who it was, I thought it might be my girl friend Edna, sometimes she hitches a ride to campus—so I came down the hall to see. This woman was standing by the couch—a perfectly strange woman—and Leta was saying she hadn't much time to look but she liked Avon things. So I knew it was an Avon saleswoman, and I went back to finish my washing."

"Was she white or colored?" asked Galeano.

"Oh, colored."

"Could you tell us anything about her at all?"

She shook her head dumbly. "I've tried to think. It wasn't two seconds. I thought she'd probably pushed her way in, Leta sounded annoyed, and I thought she'd get rid of her easier alone. I think she was taller than either of us, bigger. Not exactly fat, but—bosomy. That's just the impression I remember. She was—I don't *know*. I didn't really look at her. She had on a blue raincoat. And she had a bag—a sort of briefcase kind of thing. It just crossed my mind, her samples in that." She paused. "Well, it couldn't have been twenty seconds later—I mean that—I'd just got back to the bathroom and started washing again, when I heard some—some little pops. It wasn't like a gun—I never knew a gun could sound like that. Not loud bangs, just pops. It startled me—I thought maybe Lily had upset something—and I went down the hall, and that woman was just going out the door. I only saw about half of her back—and the door shut, and I said Leta's name and then I saw her—on the couch—I thought she'd fainted, and then I saw the blood—and I just rushed to the door after that woman— but just as I got it open I saw a car pull out from the curb in front. It must have been her—just time for her to get to it. And I can't even tell you what make it was! The rain, and she pulled out fast. It was a white car, medium size."

"That," said Mendoza, "is a very funny little story. Did you discover your sister was dead then?"

"Well, I went right back to her, and I've had some

first aid, but I couldn't feel a pulse at all, and I was terrified—I thought she'd been stabbed—I never thought about those pops. But I saw she was— So I called the police. It was the first officer said she'd been shot." She shook her head. "I didn't believe it."

"So we come to some basic questions," said Galeano. "Did she have—"

"Any enemies?" she took him up. "That's crazy too. Of course not. We hardly ever went out except to see Mother and Dad. We were both busy. She wasn't dating anybody—she'd sort of got her fill of men with Len, she wasn't interested."

"What about Reynolds? Was he bitter about the divorce?"

She shook her head. "It was five years ago. They just drifted apart. They were pretty young when they got married, and Leta was always one for improving herself and learning new things, and he wasn't. He never finished high, couldn't get such good jobs, and then he got to drinking. I don't think he cared when she divorced him, and he never came around to see Lily. We don't even know where he is."

And that was all.

Marx and Horder were busy in the living room. "She wasn't here long," said Galeano, "by that story. But she could have touched the coffee table—the girl says she was near the couch."

"But apparently not sitting down," said Mendoza. "The Avon lady. A gun instead of samples. *Extraño.*"

"And I'll add one thing you already know," said Galeano. "This is a working-class neighborhood, there probably aren't many people at home at this time of day. And nobody who is home, a dreary rainy day, is gawking out the front windows. Nobody else heard the shots, with all the doors and windows shut. Nobody but

Melinda saw the woman or the white car."

"She seems like a nice girl," said Mendoza, rocking heel to toe meditatively.

"Doesn't she?" The morgue wagon was just pulling up in front.

They went back down the hall. Melinda had made herself a cup of coffee, and the little girl was sitting opposite her with a cookie. She eyed the strange white men solemnly.

"Miss Corey—"

She looked up wearily. "I haven't got up the courage to call Mother yet. Now what?"

Lily asked suddenly, "Are you gonna make Mommy feel better?"

At a loss, Mendoza was silent. It was the bachelor Galeano who gave her a friendly smile and said, "We'll try, honey."

"She fell down. That lady pushed her and she fell down."

Galeano squatted beside her chair. "Did you see it happen?"

She nodded. "I wanted to see who came in. But she went right out after she pushed Mommy."

"Did she push her with anything? Like a stick?"

"Please—" said Melinda. "She's only six."

Lily thought. "Just kind of—with her hand." She held out one hand, forefinger pointed.

Galeano stood up and looked at Mendoza. Both of them were thinking, plenty of little guns around, muzzle only a couple of inches long, the whole hardly bigger than a palm. And at that range she could hardly have missed.

But where was a handle to this random, reasonless thing?

They went out to the Ferrari, leaving the lab men

still at work, and Galeano said with a sigh, "All we needed. Unless it's a homicidal maniac picking victims at random, and there aren't many of those around, somebody had some kind of reason to walk in and shoot her. We'll have to talk to everybody she knew—the employer —find the husband. Neighbors. The parents. Some kind of lead ought to turn up. And I'm starving. Let's go have lunch."

"Ought to doesn't say it will, Nick. This is the queerest one we've had in awhile," said Mendoza.

Landers, Grace and Conway had got to the Personnel office at Bullock's about nine o'clock. "This is the damndest job we've had in a while," said Conway plaintively. "I didn't joint the force to shuffle papers all day."

"You were just after a uniform to impress the girls?" asked Landers. Conway, who was good-looking and as dapper a dresser as Mendoza, laughed.

"Anything for a change, I suppose."

The Personnel office had given them a little back room, a table and some chairs. The stacks of file-folders they hadn't examined were still high. Landers divided them into three piles, emptied the ashtray filled at the last session, and they got to work in silence.

It was tedious work; they had to look in several places on each employee's work record for the name, date of employment, type of employment, and termination if any. Bullock's updated these files only quarterly; at the next updating, the file of any employee no longer on the strength would be weeded out, but as of now there should be a few. And Bullock's had a lot of employees. They broke for lunch early, were back at it by a quarter of one, and it was nearly an hour later that Conway let out a whoop.

[74]

"Beginners' luck, boys." He shoved a file at Landers. "If that doesn't ring a bell! There you are, the initials too—the time, the place, and the loved one all together."

It was the file of one Mary Webster. She had been hired last April, had worked as a salesclerk in the bedding department, had quit her job in the middle of September. They looked at a few more items on the file. Mary Webster was five-five, Caucasian, had brown hair and brown eyes, weighed a hundred and fifteen pounds, and was twenty-nine years old. Unmarried. Her address was on Fountain Avenue in Hollywood.

"I think you've turned something, Rich," said Grace. "M. W. And the time—"

"Nearly six months?" said Landers. "She wouldn't have had to stay in the job that long to find out the routine on taking the money in."

"We'd better take a look anyway," said Grace. "Not that I think she'll still be at that address. Not if she's it."

It had stopped raining and was turning very cold. All three of them went up to Hollywood in Landers' Sportabout. The address on Fountain was a new garden apartment with a pool at one side, now drained and covered for the winter; in the cold gray light the brightly painted doors—scarlet, green, blue—looked garish. The apartment they wanted was on the second floor at the back; it had a bright orange door and surprisingly the nameplate said WEBSTER.

"So, coincidence," said Landers, pushing the bell.

In a minute the door opened and they faced a woman about sixty, with gray hair becomingly waved, plain crystal glasses. She was wearing a pink quilted housecoat and pink slippers. She looked surprised to see them.

"We're looking for a Mary Webster who used to work at Bullock's," said Landers.

She stared up at him—tall, lanky Landers with his

youthful face didn't look like anybody's idea of a cop—and said, "I'm Mary's mother." And then the tears welled up and began to spill down her cheeks. "I'm sorry," she said. "Was it something to do with the store? She had to leave without notice—and she hadn't been there long, she used to work at the valley branch of Robinsons' but when we moved here—it was nearer to drive. She'd only been there since April, but they were very kind about it, they paid her for the last two weeks. Was it a mistake?"

"I—" Landers was taken aback.

"Oh, I'm sorry, excuse me, but she—she was only twenty-nine, and since her father died five years ago she was all I had—such a good girl—and engaged to such a nice young man, they were going to be married at Christmas—how I'd have loved grandchildren, but she was an only child—hadn't been feeling well, so tired for no reason, but we thought, just run-down—vitamins—"

"Excuse me," said Landers, "I don't think—"

"And when she finally went to the doctor— It was a brain tumor. She just—wasted away. She—she died last Wednesday, the funeral was Saturday." Determinedly she gulped back a sob. "I'm sorry. Something to do with the store? That last check?"

"No, Mrs. Webster," said Grace in his gentle voice. "We thought there might have been a mistake, is all. How much was the check for?"

"A little over three hundred dollars." She looked anxious.

"Then there wasn't any mistake, everything's all right, ma'am."

Back on the street Landers said again, "Coincidence."

Hackett and Higgins had spent an annoying after-

[76]

noon chasing the heisters. Two of the witnesses looking at mug-shots had made two identifications, and they went out looking for them: Ray Reeves and Harry Fogarty, both with appropriate pedigrees. Reeves had moved, but a neighbor obligingly told them where his girl friend worked, at a drugstore on Vermont. They found her, and she told them Ray had moved down to Compton on account of getting a job there, on the maintenance crew at Compton College. He was going straight, really, she said, he wouldn't have done anything. It was then four o'clock and Compton was nearly twenty miles away even on the freeway, so they went to look for Fogarty.

They found him at his last-listed address in Boyle Heights, and he was belligerent. He admitted he'd just lost his job but claimed he was absolutely clean. He couldn't, however, prove it. He'd been home alone watching TV last night, he said.

They came out to the street; it was twenty past five. They were using Hackett's new car, the custom Monte Carlo he'd got at such a bargain, and in the dingy street in the gray light it looked like a circus wagon, brilliant iridescent lime-green with a saffron top.

Higgins said, "Hold a line-up tomorrow and see what the witnesses say? He looks good for it."

"He looks very good for it," said Hackett, "but we can't do it tomorrow, George. The Hoffman hearing."

"Oh, hell and damnation," said Higgins.

Hackett took him back to his car, said goodnight and drove home. For once the children were quiet and peaceful, and Angel told him the real estate woman would be coming tomorrow night with all the papers to sign.

"I want to do some sorting out—it's awful what you accumulate—but I think we'd just better set a definite date and *go*," she said. "It costs more but you can get the moving people to do all the packing. Say the end of the month—it'll be a thirty-day escrow. The only thing is, Mark will have further to go to school—"

"It will," said Hackett uncomplainingly, "be further for me too, my Angel."

"But all the nice unpolluted air, up that high," said Angel bracingly. "And *much* lower taxes, darling."

Higgins drove home—he was getting used to the new route now, up the Pasadena freeway—and found all his family there. After too many years of not having any family, he appreciated the one he'd acquired. It had been an upset and a muddle, moving to the new house, and things weren't straight yet. Mary wanted to paint all the bedrooms and panel the dining room, and Higgins wasn't very handy with tools. But it was a nice house, bigger than the old one, and the yard was fenced for the little black Scottie Brucie.

Steve Dwyer cornered him after dinner, while Mary and Laura were doing the dishes. "I want to ask you something, George."

Higgins put down his paper. "Well, what?" Steve was looking more like Bert all the time, and growing; he was up to Higgins' shoulder now, and Higgins was six-three.

"Well, I mean, I don't want to—I mean it was just something I want to *know*," said Steve, and his voice was lowered, and he cast a glance toward the kitchen where the two females were chattering.

"Well, what?" said Higgins again. Steve had evinced a faint sort of interest in girls the last few months; Higgins supposed he ought to have a belated man-to-man talk with him, but the idea was embarrassing.

"Well, look," said Steve. His round young freckled face looked rather desperate. "George, I know Mother wants to fix the place up, and paint and so on costs money. It's just, can't we sort of squeeze out enough to build a darkroom in the garage like I had? Because—"

Higgins began to laugh. Photography had always been Steve's first love, and evidently adolescence wasn't interfering with it yet. "We'll do it," he promised. "We'll fix one, Steve—running water, safety lights and all. Because one of these days you're going to be an LAPD lab man, you've got to keep your hand in."

A blinding grin rewarded him. "I just wanted to *know*," said Steve.

Glasser and Wanda had landed at the Eagle Grill just after it opened. Leon Fratelli was behind the bar. It wasn't a very fancy place, but it looked reasonably clean. There were only two customers in at that hour.

He said to Glasser's question, "Yeah, there were some guys come and said we hadda get out—an order of some kind. Why the hell, I said, we got a dictatorship, tell people where to go, get out, don't come back? Listen, I don't guess Rosie's the best housekeeper in the world, but it was damn cheap rent and what's it matter to anybody?"

"All we want to know is," said Glasser, "where have you moved? With Rosie? There are—um—some A.D.C. papers for her to sign."

"Oh. The money for the kids. That's good," said Fratelli. "Well, hell, rents most anywhere sky high, it's terrible. We ain't found a place. Acourse, it's easier not havin' the kids, I got to say that. Right now we got a room in a hotel on Temple, the Arcade. It's four bucks a night, we got to find some place else."

"You know," said Wanda, outside in the Gremlin, "what puzzles me, why does he stick to Rosie? He's not any prize himself, Henry, but she's a lot farther down."

"I don't think," said Glasser, "he'll stick to her much longer. She's getting past picking up the johns and rendering even token service."

"Those children," said Wanda. "My God."

"Yeah. Very unlikely that whoever fathered them was much better than Rosie. It says somewhere, man He made a little lower than the angels," said Glasser.

He went out helping on the legwork on the heists later, and it was five-twenty when he landed back at the office. Wanda was there, nobody else.

The autopsy report on Alice Engel had just come up. As expected, she'd been beaten, raped and strangled. Pubic hairs from the body had been sent to the lab. There was also a lab report which had come in earlier. Numerous latent prints had been lifted in the house. Five identifiable prints belonging to Leon Fratelli (record appended) from headboard of bed, chest in bedroom, chairs in living room; numerous prints belonging to Rose Engel (record appended) from both bedrooms, kitchen. The lab said the pubic hair belonged to a male Caucasian; if a specimen was obtained from any suspect, it could be matched for comparison.

"So what do you think?" asked Glasser. "You bucking for detective."

"Just what you're thinking, Henry," said Wanda. "The whole dirty thing is obvious."

"Yes," said Glasser. "Just for fun, let's see if the boss thinks we can get a warrant."

But it was five to six, and Mendoza had gone home a little early.

FOUR

WHEN MENDOZA CAME IN on Tuesday morning there was a manila envelope from the coroner's office on his desk with the night report. He slit it open: the autopsy report on David Whalen. There wasn't much in it: the weapon had been a long narrow knife with a serrated edge, and no special skill had been exhibited; he had been stabbed four times, and two of the blows would have been fatal alone.

He glanced at the night report; a nice quiet night for Matt and Bob, only a hit-run out on Alvarado. He heard Hackett and Higgins coming in, and took the autopsy report out to the hall with him.

"Damn it, Art, it's a Murder One charge. Even Fletcher can't hand him much less than— Morning, Luis, what've you got?" Higgins took the report without interest.

"I'll take no bets," said Hackett glumly, and Scarne came in behind Landers and Conway. It was Grace's day off.

"Morning," said Scarne. "I knew you were chafing at the bit on this one, Lieutenant, so I brought it up myself.

It just came through." He handed Mendoza the yellow teletype; it was the kickback from the Feds on the prints of the lady in the park.

"Ah," said Mendoza.

"Of course it may not help you much, it's a little out of date," said Scarne with a grin, and departed.

The prints were those, said the F.B.I., of Marion Barry Stromberg, and the reason they were on file with the F.B.I. was that back in 1943 Marion Stromberg was working for Lockheed Aircraft. "¡Ca!" said Mendoza. He passed the sheet to Hackett.

"Now that's helpful," said Hackett. "Thirty-seven years back."

"Well, it gives us a name," said Mendoza. He marched back into his office, the two of them on his heels, and got out the phone books.

"Oh, for God's sake," said Hackett. "There must be four pages of Strombergs, Luis, and in thirty-seven years some people get divorced and remarried—"

"Not everybody," said Mendoza. The F.B.I. computer had just turned up the name and the connection; no doubt on microfilm somewhere was a record of where Marion Stromberg had been living at the time, her marital status, her age and even description: the standard application form at Lockheed would have accompanied her prints. They might have to ask the Feds to dig for that, and how long it might take to unearth it God knew. "Use a little imagination, Arturo," said Mendoza briskly. "Barry sounds like a surname—her maiden name? Could be. So she was married then. A surprising number of people do stay married to the same husbands and wives." He riffled through the Hollywood book to the S's.

There were a good many Strombergs, all right. "What's your idea, set Jimmy to calling every one in the book?"

"Sarcastic," said Mendoza. "The little gray cells, *amigo*. If the lady in the park had been living in the midst of a loving family, she'd have been missed and reported by now. ¿*Cómo no?* So the probability is that she was living alone, which would probably mean that she wouldn't be listed under a former husband's first name in the phone book. Come on—" he shoved the Valley book over to Hackett. "Many hands make light work. Forget Central for now— I'll swear she didn't come from anywhere down here."

In the end, astonishingly, they collected only eight which Mendoza chose as probable-possibles. Out of a welter of Strombergs from the five county books, they rejected all those in Watts, Lynwood and Lennox; those were rather solidly black areas. Out of all the Strombergs listed only by initials, there were five M.B.'s and three M's, in Glendale, Hollywood, Studio City, Beverly Hills, West Hollywood, Huntington Park. "First cast," said Mendoza, looking at the list. "And don't tell me these are all male householders. A lot of single women use initials only to avoid the possible obscene calls."

"A lot of women living alone," said Hackett, "have unlisted numbers."

"And the phone company's bound to answer questions from the police," said Mendoza.

There wasn't much point in starting work on any of the cases on hand; the Hoffman hearing was scheduled for ten o'clock, at one of the smaller courtrooms in the Hall of Justice.

Hackett, Higgins, Palliser and Mendoza got there at a quarter to ten. It was a closed hearing; there wouldn't be any press. In the last row of folding chairs, over by one of the tall windows, Cathy Robsen was sitting. She had been subpoenaed, they could guess, just in case the judge wanted to question her. The men from Robbery-

Homicide hadn't seen her since last August. She looked older and thinner: still a good-looking woman, dark-haired, in the mid-thirties. Just before ten o'clock the Hoffmans came in: Sergeant William Hoffman of Hollenbeck precinct and his wife Muriel. Neither of them looked at Mrs. Robsen or the men from headquarters; they sat down near the front, on the opposite side of the aisle, and just waited, looking straight ahead. They had both aged ten years in three months. Muriel Hoffman, once the smartly groomed good-looking blonde, was haggard; there was a too-bright rinse on her hair, and she wore a rather dowdy black suit. Hoffman, a man as big and burly as Hackett and Higgins—another big man who might as well have worn the plain label COP— looked somehow shrunken. He was very correctly dressed in a dark suit, white shirt, dark tie; he was shaved and tidy; and he looked queerly like a corpse propped up there.

They all sat in silence, waiting for the bailiff, the attorneys, the prisoner and the judge to appear, for the ritualistic legal formalities to get under way.

Walt Robsen and his wife Cathy had been close friends of the Hoffmans; they lived within blocks of each other and had been friends for years, all much of an age —the Hoffmans with two boys, the Robsens with a boy and a girl a little younger. Robsen and Hoffman had both put in fifteen years as LAPD men. They had ridden a squad together as rookies, made rank together, shared an office at Hollenbeck division as detective sergeants, helped each other and given each other advice.

And it had been Robsen who had argued Hoffman out of the idea of building a pool in the back yard: the whole Silver Lake area was running down, property was losing value.

Larry Hoffman, in his junior year at high school, had wanted that pool. He was better at athletics than anything else, and on the swimming team. It was, of course, all Robsen's fault that there wouldn't be any pool. So he had taken his father's target pistol one afternoon, biked over to the Robsens' on Robsen's day off, and shot him dead while he sat alone over a book.

When Bill Hoffman knew about it, he had nearly killed him. Today he looked to be in tight control of himself.

The judge, Fletcher, was notoriously given to the standard euphemisms and platitudes of the left: thieves, killers, rapists, perverts were unfortunate victims of society, their undesirable behavior caused by poverty, divorce, racism. But there wasn't much he could do with a charge of first-degree homicide. Given a good fire-breathing defense attorney, he would doubtless have done what he could. But Larry Hoffman's attorney played it very quiet and careful.

He was a portly middle-aged man named Norman, and he made it clear from the outset that he was not there to plead for a minimum sentence, any lesser sentence than the offense merited, or to offer any excuse for that offense. He called the judge's attention to the psychiatric report, and just in case Fletcher hadn't read it, read it to him. The psychiatric evaluation, which for once seemed to make sense, found Larry Hoffman to be of normal intelligence, but an immature and egocentric personality prone to faulty judgment. He then read the signed confession to the judge and sat down.

Fletcher didn't want to question the Hoffmans, or Cathy Robsen. He wanted to know all about that confession and he questioned all the men from Robbery-Homicide at length, sending the others out of the courtroom while he questioned them separately. He was obviously annoyed at being unable to discover any discrepancies in the testimony.

All that time Larry Hoffman sat silent beside his attorney, head down, not looking at anybody. Hoffman never once looked at him; Muriel Hoffman did, once or twice, with an unreadable expression.

Fletcher adjourned for lunch, reopened the hearing at one o'clock, and to everybody's surprise handed down an abrupt verdict without any lecture attached. After complaining of the district attorney's uncalled-for severity in making the charge one of first degree, he admitted that under the circumstances he had no choice as to the verdict, or as to the sentence; it was a mandatory proceeding. The minimum sentence the charge carried was twenty years to life, and that was what he handed down, adding some unctuous phrases about the prisoner's youth and high chances of rehabilitation.

The bailiff took Larry's arm. Norman never looked at him again, but busied himself gathering papers into his briefcase. Larry vanished through the door at the rear of the court, and the Hoffmans stood up. The Robbery-Homicide men were in the aisle nearer the double doors, and as the Hoffmans approached, Hackett stepped toward them, hand out.

"Hoffman—"

Hoffman sidestepped and moved right past him, eyes remote; he marched straight for the door and through it.

Muriel Hoffman spoke his name, but he gave no sign that he heard. She said to Hackett simply, "I'm sorry." Her eyes went to Higgins, Mendoza, Palliser. She said, "You were all kind. I'm sorry about Bill. It's just, you see, he's so ashamed. He won't even talk to any of the men at his own station. If he'd just—talk it out—even go out and get drunk—I wouldn't worry so about him." She looked anxious and strained. "I'd better go after him—damn it, I wish he would get drunk," and that was half to herself. She hurried up the aisle; she checked as she came past the row where Cathy Robsen was sitting, and they exchanged one grave long look. Perhaps there was too much those women had to say to each other for any of it to be said at all.

"And with that out of the way," said Mendoza, taking Hackett by the arm, "we shall now play detective and trace down Marion Stromberg."

"I still say—"

"The eternal pessimist. *Sé bueno, hijo mio,* and see what perseverance and imagination can do." In the Ferrari, he lit a new cigarette and got out the list from the phone books. "Huntington Park, now," he said. "I don't think so. A solid old area, but blue collar, and a black tide rising. Whereas that new coat with the real fur collar—mmh, yes. Ambrose Avenue, Hollywood—very possible. Also Beachwood Drive." Mendoza knew his city backward and forward. "Arriba Drive, Monterey Park—also possible. Beverly Hills, no. That coat, the shoes—Bullock's, not Magnin. Glendale. Oh, yes. An unpretentious town, but solid money in some parts."

"You're going by the clothes?" said Hackett. "And the fact that she worked at Lockheed during the war so she was living here then. She could have been living in New York ever since, and come out here to visit a cousin, been seen off at Union Station and run foul of a suitcase snatcher who knocked her down before she got on the train. That place is deserted before and after trains come and go."

[87]

"Thank you. One of the porters tidied up the station by dumping her in Lafayette Park?"

"There aren't any porters anymore. Menial work. Or she could have been living with a relative named Zilch, in Zilch's house, and she hasn't been missed because Zilch is on a trip."

"With human people, anything is possible," said Mendoza. "Let's try going by the probabilities." He switched on the engine. "Glendale is a very definite possibility, we'll try there first."

However, the M. B. Stromberg on Valley View Road, Glendale, turned out to be at home; he was a garrulous pensioner eager for company, and they got away with some difficulty.

The apartment on Ambrose Avenue in Hollywood was on the way back from the valley, so they tried there. Nobody answered the door; Mendoza tried the apartment across the hall, and raised a red-nosed thick-voiced young woman home from work with the flu, who told them irritably that Miss Stromberg worked at the phone company. Yes, she knew her. May Stromberg.

"Seen her recently?" asked Mendoza.

"I saw her come in last night, why? I'd forgotten to get the mail, I was downstairs when she came home." She wasn't curious, preoccupied with her own troubles; she shut her door sharply.

"Beachwood Drive," said Mendoza. "Now that's the right sort of place, Art, for that coat—and the solitaire diamond. Not at all fancy—solid unobtrusive worth. Let's have a look at Beachwood Drive."

"You always had an imagination," said Hackett.

Beachwood Drive curved up into the hills above Franklin Avenue; there were no new houses up there; it was a quiet area of solid old places dating from the thirties. It was a place of upper-middle-class gentility:

conservative. The houses on this block sat on standard city lots, fifty by a hundred and fifty, with lawns in front, curving walks, bordered flower beds, separate garages at the end of cemented driveways.

The one they wanted was a good-sized Spanish stucco with a red tile roof. The overhead door on the double garage was raised; no car was inside. Mendoza pushed the doorbell five times; there was no response.

"I don't think anybody's out gardening in this temperature," he said, "but we'll look." Down the drive, they looked at an empty neat back yard with a rectangle of lawn, trees, flower beds. Mendoza walked briskly back to the sidewalk and up to the house next door, which was French Colonial with a long wing to one side. The door was opened by a tall thin woman looking to be in the sixties, with a mass of curly white hair.

"We're looking for a Marion Stromberg," said Mendoza. "Would that be the Mrs. Stromberg next door?"

She looked him over carefully. "What's your business with her?"

"My God," said Hackett, "don't tell me."

"Marion Stromberg does live next door?" Mendoza brought out the badge, which agitated her considerably. She demanded to know what police wanted of Mrs. Stromberg, apologized for being suspicious.

"But when a woman lives alone, with so much crime going on—what do you want with her? I've been just a little worried that I haven't seen her around just lately, I usually do, but then— Police coming and asking—"

"You haven't seen her lately. Tell me, is Mrs. Stromberg about fifty-five, medium height, medium weight, smart dresser, tinted blonde hair?

She lost some of her high color. "Why, yes. Yes. Something's happened to her, and you—oh, my heavens. What's happened to her?"

"We have an unidentified body downtown," said Mendoza gently. "It looks as if it may be this Mrs. Stromberg. Could you tell us about any family, someone who could identify her?"

"There isn't any family," she said. "You'd better come in, it's freezing out. I'm Mrs. Caldwell. Sit down. Oh, my heavens! There's nobody at all—they never had any children, she was all alone after Dr. Stromberg died. That was about five years back, he was some older than she was." She looked shaken. "They'd lived next door since nineteen fifty-nine, the year after we moved here. My heavens. What happened to her?"

"She was found dead on the street," said Mendoza.

"But that's awful—dropping dead, a heart attack or— But you didn't know who she was? She'd have had identification in her handbag—there'd have been her car—" She put a hand to her mouth. "I had been just a little concerned. Not seeing her around. Not that we were close friends, but we were always—friendly. I've got a big family, I'm out a good deal, and she wasn't. Always very quiet they were, even when he was alive —they never went out much. But I'd see her nearly every day, leaving to drive to market, or we'd be taking the trash out at the same time on Mondays—and I hadn't seen her in a while, and the garage door's been up, she always closed it when she came home." She was looking very distressed. "Why, she was a good ten years younger than I am—I can't get over it."

"Isn't there anyone—possibly the husband of some friend—who could identify the body?"

"I don't know at all. She had a few good friends, there was a Jean she'd mentioned, and a Paula—but I couldn't tell you their last names. But I could tell you if it is her. I wouldn't mind, really. Not a very pleasant thing to have to do, but I've seen bodies before—I was with both my parents when they died, and my husband. And we want to be sure it is her. Do you want me to come now? I'll just get a coat."

She was a common-sensible old lady, and practical; she said to Mendoza on the way to the car, "I can show you where she hid a spare key to the house. She told me in case of fire when she was away. Not that she ever was away much, it was just in case." This was one of many occasions when Hackett deplored Mendoza's predilection for sports cars; he hunched on the jump-seat uncomfortably on the way down to the morgue.

Mendoza took her into the cold room; when they came back she was looking sick and even more shaken. "It's terrible to see someone like that. She always kept herself up so well—not flashy, just smart and nice. Oh, dear, this has upset me." She sat down heavily on the bench along the wall. "Seeing her like that—and nobody knowing who she was—I suppose somebody stole her handbag, the car too very likely. But it seems queer."

"We'd like to find out about it," said Mendoza. "What can you tell us about her, Mrs. Caldwell? Her routine, her friends, her interests?"

She shook her head. "Not very much. We lived next door to each other all those years, but aside from saying good morning or whatever—as I say, I've got a big family. She was—just quiet. She didn't go out much. She had charity meetings of some kind, I think it was, a couple of times a week. She called them her good deeds. Just a few times, I happened to be in the yard when she was leaving, she'd say off to do my good deed for the week. She wasn't interested in gardening and she didn't play cards. I suppose she read a lot. She'd go out to market a couple of times a week."

"Her husband was a doctor?"

"An optometrist, not a real doctor. But he had his

own office on Hollywood Boulevard for years, I guess he made a good living. She must have been pretty well off, not a lot of money but plenty—I know she owned a house she rented. She was—well, what my mother used to call a real lady. Kept herself to herself, you know, but she was friendly too and, well, nice. Just not very social."

That seemed to be about all she could tell them, but the house might tell them more. They went back to Beachwood Drive and she showed them where the key was hidden—not a very safe place—under an empty flower pot on the counter in the garage. They thanked her and she retreated into her own house a little reluctantly.

They unlocked the front door and went into Marion Stromberg's house. Whatever had happened to her, for whatever reason, it hadn't happened here; that was immediately obvious. The house was immaculately clean, museum-like in its orderliness. The very slight film of dust, from her five days' absence, they could guess she could not have tolerated. The furniture was old, some of it antique, solid and good furniture, the rooms tastefully arranged. It was all conservative and a little colorless, but with an atmosphere of elegance. Nothing, obviously, had been disturbed in the large living room, formal dining room, kitchen with its spacious built-in nook, the two front bedrooms with a bath between, the smaller den at the back of the house. They found an address book on the desk there, containing only a few names: one entry was that of a legal firm. There was no correspondence around, or none she'd kept. In the desk drawers were neat files of canceled checks, receipts for bills.

"Not much use getting the lab up here," said Hackett. "We'd better get the plate number and put out an

A.P.B. for her car." Mrs. Caldwell had told them that she had driven a light-blue Buick Skylark about five years old.

"Yes," said Mendoza vaguely. He stood in the middle of what had obviously been Marion Stromberg's bedroom—closet full of good clothes, double bed made up with an expensive quilted spread—and looked around. He said, "A very sterile existence, wasn't it? So quiet. Such a lady."

"You," said Hackett, "have exercised the famous crystal ball quite enough for one day. It's five-forty-five. And we've got inquests coming up, on Whalen and the Engel kid, to slow us down further. Tomorrow is also a day. Let's go home, boy."

Galeano came into the office at a little after four, feeling frustrated and mystified. He had got out and around today, on the Reynolds thing, and had got absolutely nowhere. Galeano had worked a lot of homicides, and in his experience if you took a good hard look at the victim, his associates, his areas of being, something usually showed to point the way. Here there was just nothing. He'd never run across such a bunch of honest, respectable, high-minded people in his life, and damn what color they were.

Herbert Armstrong, who owned the studio where Leta Reynolds had worked, was horrified and grieved. She'd been a fine girl, an excellent retoucher. At that job, she'd had no contact with the customers, of course. All her friends were the same type she was; and by inference their associates. Young women, some married, some not, in ordinary jobs, or just at home as housewives. Her parents were the same: the father was a skilled machinist at a plant in Inglewood. All Melinda Corey's friends were respectable hard-working citizens. The only fellow she occasionally dated was one Lee Ballard, who was a law student at U.S.C.; his father was a member of a very reputable legal firm in Santa Monica. It didn't seem that Leta Reynolds or her sister had known anybody who'd ever had so much as a drunk-driving ticket. Leta went to work, came home, took care of Lily. Quiet girls, both she and Melinda.

The parents could give him a lead to the ex-husband; they were barely acquainted with the family, who lived near them in Inglewood. Len Reynolds was said to have been living up the coast in Ventura for three years, where he had a job with the post office. That seemed to put him out of the picture, seventy miles up the coast. Besides, everybody said he hadn't been mad about the divorce, and that had been five years ago.

There was nothing to take hold of, damn it. Even the Avon business—there wasn't any listing in the phone book on that. Some door-to-door selling scheme, he didn't know much about it.

He was also curious about the Hoffman hearing, and Lake gave him the word on that when he came in. "At least it's something, but he'll be eligible for P.A. in seven years."

Glasser and Wanda were in sole occupation of the office. "Saved by the bell," said Glasser. "I've got an arrest warrant to execute—it just came through—and I've also got an old-fashioned prejudice against exposing lady cops to possible violence. She was hell-bound to go with me."

"I've been on the case," said Wanda, annoyed.

"Ah-hah. I've got a little hunch that Fratelli could be a mean character when he's riled. I'd rather have Nick to back me up, thanks."

[94]

"Any time," said Galeano absently. "Either of you know anything about this Avon business? I couldn't find a listing in the book."

"Oh, it wouldn't be in the yellow pages," said Wanda. "It's direct selling—no offices. Mother had an Avon area once, but it can be a lot of work. Why?" Galeano told her, and she was intrigued. "I hardly think a real Avon lady—but I see you have to check. That is a funny one." She looked in the Central book, and found a number for Avon Sales Products. Galeano tried it, but the phone rang nine times without an answer.

"Come on," said Glasser. "I want to get this bird booked in before end of shift."

Galeano went out with him. It was nearly dark, and had turned even colder. "We'll have to take your car," said Glasser.

"That kiddie-car of yours—you just don't like transporting prisoners."

"I didn't pick it out," Glasser reminded him. He had, as a matter of fact, won the Gremlin in a drawing.

They got into Galeano's car, and Glasser told him, "It's the Eagle Grill over on Fourth."

They had to park double in front, and went in in a hurry. Fratelli was just serving the two men at the bar; about ten others sat around at tables. Glasser went up to the end of the bar and said quietly, "All right, Leon, I've got a warrant for your arrest. Come on out."

Fratelli stared at him. "What? You can't arrest me— I didn't do nothing—damn fuzz—"

"Come on," said Glasser. He was four inches shorter than Fratelli and probably forty pounds lighter, but unless he had to he wasn't going to pull a gun in here, in a crowd like this.

The same thought was passing through Galeano's mind. He flipped up the pass-through at the end of the bar and went past Glasser; he was the bigger man. "Let's do what the man says—don't make it hard on yourself." He took hold of Fratelli's arm.

Fratelli roared and shook him off, and brought up a fist like a ham, staggering Galeano back against the shelves of glasses behind the bar. Momentarily blinded —the fist had caught him square on the left eye— Galeano swore and groped, saw Fratelli swinging again with a bottle in his hand, and grappled with him. Glasser crowded in from behind; in the narrow space behind the bar, they struggled impotently, Galeano hanging onto one of Fratelli's wrists grimly. He heard the crowd beginning to mutter about the fuzz. Then Glasser's hands were over his and he heard the cuffs snap together.

"All *right!*" said Glasser crisply. "That's enough, Leon." But with the cuffs on, Fratelli suddenly quieted down. He walked out to the car meek as a lamb. Glasser asked, "You all right, Nick?"

"I'm O.K. But I think you'd better drive, I seem to be bleeding some."

They booked Fratelli in at the central jail, and stopped at First Aid. Fratelli was wearing a big fake-diamond ring, and had caught Galeano a jagged cut with it. The nurse in First Aid washed it, told him he was going to have a beautiful shiner by tomorrow, and applied a neat dressing. Glasser passed on the message for the jail doctor; he was to get a specimen of Fratelli's pubic hair and send it over to the lab, please. "You sure you're O.K. to drive home, Nick?"

"I'll be O.K.," said Galeano. But he wasn't going home. At this end of the day, he needed a shave and there was a little blood on his shirt, and his right knuckles were raw where he'd got in one good one on Fratelli's jaw. But damn it, if she would think about marrying him—and he thought it was going to be all right—she'd have to get used to him as he was. After he dropped Glasser off in the lot, he drove up to the restaurant on Wilshire where Marta Fleming worked.

She spotted him right away when he came in, and as soon as she'd emptied her tray she came over to the single table by the window. "Nick, what has happened to you? You are hurt much?" Her dark eyes were concerned.

"Just a fellow resisting arrest—nothing much." He smiled at her; he thought it was going to be all right, but he was being careful. She was convent-bred, and of a very conventional middle-class German family, and her husband hadn't been dead a year yet. Not until January. But she'd go out with him, let him take her to dinner at quiet places. And there were a couple of hopeful signs, he thought. She was thick as thieves with his mother, the pair of them prodding him to attend Mass regularly, persuading him to go on that diet.

He grinned up at her. "You can bring me a steak. I've earned it. And a bourbon and soda first."

"The calories," she said severely. "So you have earned it. One. But rice with the steak, no potatoes." Her tawny blonde hair was pinned back under the uniform cap, but when they went out somewhere she let it loose.

"That's my girl," he said; but he said it to her back as she hurried off.

Landers and Conway had finished going through the employee records at four o'clock, and had drawn a blank. There were no other significant initials or dates.

"I said from the start, a dead end," said Landers.

But Conway had got interested in this very slick

operation. "All right, so there had to be inside information from somewhere. It didn't have to be an exact copy of the jobs in Philly and Pittsburgh. Look, why the hell should that same gang be all the way out here? If you ask me—people get around these days, and all sorts of people—it's likelier it was somebody who was there then, read about those jobs. Now here, and needing some ready cash, thinking about all the loot to be had in one fell swoop—the hell of a lot more than he'd get on any other kind of heist. Look, Tom—"

"And just happening to run into three eager accomplices at the nearest bar?"

"Hell," said Conway, "if he had the inside dope, he could hire three thugs to help out nearly anywhere." Landers admitted that. "Look, Tom, are any of those guards unmarried? If so, has one of 'em maybe just found a new girl friend? Men get talking about their jobs—even security men—if they're with somebody they think they can trust."

Landers said doubtfully, "Well, it's another idea to toss around. The lab report was no use—all the prints in the elevator belonged to the guards, and no prints in the van at all. And the rope was an ordinary brand you can buy at any hardware store." He massaged his jaw thoughtfully. "You know," he said, "one of the guards said something about the ground-floor man going around checking to be sure all the customers are out. I wonder—somebody like that, lurking behind counters long enough to see what was going on with the money bags? Seeing all the take from one or two departments going to the same place, he could guess it was all going there. And then all innocent going up to a guard, 'Is the store closed? I didn't realize,' and getting let out."

"Yes, but," said Conway, "the rest of it, up on the eighth floor—"

Landers got up suddenly. "That freight elevator is numbered," he said. "Come on, Rich. Let's try something." He led Conway out to the regular employees' elevator that went all the way down, and took it down to the seventh floor. Here, at this side of the building, were Infants' Wear, Children's Wear, Ladies' Lingerie, Fabrics, Luggage. He led Conway as far as that, and stood looking helpless and inquisitive until a clerk bustled forward.

"May I help you, sir?"

"I—er—left an umbrella in the store yesterday. In one of the rest rooms, I think—I was waiting for my wife—" A slander on Phil, who never kept anyone waiting.

The clerk was instantly helpful. "It may have been turned into Lost and Found, sir. If you'll go straight down this aisle through Ladies' Lingerie, you'll find an elevator to take you up—it's the ninth floor."

"Oh, thank you," said Landers. He led Conway back, found the dead-end aisle, and there was the elevator. It was labeled, To 8TH AND 9TH FLOORS ONLY. LOST AND FOUND 9TH FLOOR. They got in, and he pushed the button for 8. The elevator rose smoothly and stopped; the door slid open. They were at the other end of the hall from the Personnel offices. Facing them, just slightly down to the left, was a double-doored elevator clearly marked 3; up the other way were signs along the hall: TO ACCOUNTING—TO PERSONNEL.

They looked at each other, and Conway uttered a wicked word. "So easy when you know."

Landers shoved him back into the elevator. "They must, said everybody, have been hidden somewhere until just the right minute." He sent the elevator up to the ninth floor. The door opened on a rather dark corridor and a sign: LOST AND FOUND, with an arrow

[99]

pointing ahead. They went halfway down the corridor, past doors with frosted glass tops labeled PURCHASING, MAIL, CATALOG. Across from the last was a door which opened horizontally across its middle; a man was in there with his back to them, whistling cheerfully. A sign tacked up beside the door read LOST AND FOUND—OPEN MON.-FRI. 10-5, SAT. 10-7.

The man turned. "Afternoon. You looking for something?"

"I think," said Landers, "we've found it, thanks."

Grace called the office at five o'clock to ask the result of the Hoffman hearing, and Lake told him. "I tried to call you about two o'clock."

"Oh. We were," said Grace, "at the County Adoption Agency."

"Any luck?" asked Lake. The Graces had one much-loved adopted baby, little Celia Anne, twenty-one months old, and were hoping to acquire another.

"Not so far. All the red tape."

Mendoza came home, ruminating gently about Marion Stromberg. He garaged the car next to Alison's Facel-Vega (at least the new place had a larger garage with room for Mairí's car) and went in the back door. Cedric the sheepdog was slurping water from his bowl on the service-porch and looked up happily, waggling his rump. Nobody was in the kitchen, but various good smells indicated that dinner was on the way.

In the living room, Alison was curled in her armchair perusing *House Beautiful* with difficulty, almost completely covered by all four cats in a complicated tangle. She sat up, scattering cats, and said, "I never heard the car—you're late, *enamorado*—"

He just had time to kiss her before the twins came to pounce on him. "Daddy, Daddy, I was so good in school today I got a gole star from Miss Turtle—" Terry.

"Thirkell," said Alison automatically.

"That's nothin', Daddy, she's just teacher's fav'rite, she could get a gole star for nothin'—" Johnny.

"Anything," said Alison.

They had to tell him all about school, and demanded promises to be read to before bed. They hadn't quite outgrown Grimm; they could read for themselves now, but — Time! thought Mendoza. Yesterday they had been crawling babies. Suddenly, they were personalities.

"Now, my lambies," said Mairí from the door, "let your father have his dinner in peace, and a dram before." They'd have finished their suppers an hour ago. "Will you want to come see wee Luisa take her bottle? Time enough for stories later."

"Ooooh, *yes*—" They were fascinated with the new one, and scrambled to follow her.

"You can bring me some sherry," said Alison. "It'll take six minutes to do the ham in the microwave, and everything else is ready." Inevitably pursued by El Señor, Mendoza poured him his half-ounce of rye, got his own drink and the sherry, and went back to the living room.

"Shut the door and come here quick," said Alison excitedly.

"*Mi corazón*, I'm always willing, but wouldn't the bedroom be more—"

"*¡Imbécil!*" said Alison with a giggle. "Listen, Luis —don't dare say a word, but Ken thinks he's found some suitable ponies." She had easily fallen into saying Ken and Kate; the twins had even begun to say Uncle Ken. The Kearneys had grandchildren of their own and liked the species. "It was in some ranchers' magazine, an ad. You know he's looked all around here, what stables there are, and hasn't found any for sale. But he called this afternoon and said these sound like the very thing. A pair of Welsh ponies, seven years old, used to children and gentle. It's a ranch up the other side of Santa Barbara, and he said if we want him to he'd call the man to hold them until he goes up to look at them. Of course I said yes. What we thought, they could stay there until we're moved, and Ken can bring them down for Christmas."

"Mmh," said Mendoza, who by this time had settled in his armchair and pulled her comfortably into his lap. "And how much is the pair of ponies going to cost?"

"Well, six hundred for the two of them. With saddles and bridles," added Alison hastily. "Ken said he'd drive up tomorrow and if they're as good as he thinks he can clinch the deal."

"Qué bien," said Mendoza.

"So," said Alison, "now tell me about the Hoffman hearing."

He did, absently. "Hoffman looks like hell. What his wife said—" He told her that, and she nodded soberly.

"It must feel like—the most terrible kind of betrayal, Luis. If one of your children does something very wrong, it'd be on your shoulders too."

"I hadn't thought of it like that, but maybe that's so, querida. An extension of oneself—hard to see them as separate personalities, is that what you—"

"No," said Alison. "Not exactly. Don't you see, not just Sergeant Hoffman—all of them. How can they ever possibly trust anyone again?"

[102]

"Yes, I see," said Mendoza. "I hadn't thought of it that way either."

Jeff Dillman, sitting in the dispatcher's slot down in Communications, automatically picked up the indicated phone and said, "Police Department, may I help you?" The clock on the wall clicked and the minute hand jumped to mark exactly ten o'clock.

"Will you please send a squad to—" Also automatically Dillman scrawled down the address given, before his mind registered something a little queer about that: "squad"; the ordinary citizen asked baldly for cops.

"Would you repeat that, sir? What's the complaint?"

The address was repeated carefully. "The front door is unlocked. You will also please inform the night watch at Robbery-Homicide of this call. Immediately, please."

"What?" said Dillman.

"Do you have that address? Please repeat it."

"Yes, sir, I've got it. What's the c—"

"Thank you," said the very calm male voice, and broke the connection.

That, Dillman thought, was queer. He got on the radio, consulting the big colored map of Central territory on the wall in front of him. By time and area, Moss in X-19 was closest, and he relayed the call crisply. Investigate unknown complaint.

But, Robbery-Homicide?

He thought about it, and a minute later called up there.

It had been a quiet night so far for Piggott and Schenke. Sometimes the day watch left them jobs to do, suspects to hunt for; but tonight they'd just been holding down the desks.

When the call came up from Communications at ten-five, Piggott took it, noted down the address. "O.K., but what's it all about?" Communications didn't know. "What's with this, Bob? Funny—a citizen calling in on a regular line asking for us."

Schenke said, "Say that address again. Just inside our territory, Silver Lake—most people would have called Hollywood. That address rings a bell. Let's go see."

They got there at ten-twenty-five. Moss was just pulling up to the curb in the squad; he'd got caught in a traffic jam on Silver Lake Boulevard, an accident.

There were lights on all over the house, a nice house with a steep terrace in front. The porch light was on, and the first thing they all noticed was the nameplate on the door: HOFFMAN.

Everybody in LAPD knew that name.

They went in and looked and Moss said, "Oh, Jesus Christ."

Hoffman had made a very precise job of it. The fourteen-year-old boy had been shot, probably in his sleep; he was in bed in a back bedroom. Muriel Hoffman had also been shot in bed, in the master bedroom. Bill Hoffman was sprawled across her body, and his Police Positive was still in his right hand.

There wasn't any suicide note anywhere, but on the coffee table in the living room was a brown manila envelope carefully addressed by hand to Mrs. Catherine Robsen.

"I think we'd better call the lieutenant," said Piggott.

FIVE

It DISRUPTED THE ROUTINE slightly.

Wednesday was Hackett's day off, but he came in. He and Mendoza got to the Robsen house not much after nine o'clock; they wanted to get to her before the press did, and the press would be on this early today. Nobody at LAPD would have relayed the news, but there had been neighbors out last night, people who had heard the shots, looked out to see the squad.

Cathy Robsen listened to them numbly, only once putting a hand to her eyes. "He was insane," she said. "It drove him insane. He'd been so proud of Larry. I'd only seen Muriel once since— And he wouldn't let her call me."

"There was a bottle of sleeping tablets on the bathroom counter, empty. It looked as if he'd got her to take them—maybe in a bedtime drink—so she was knocked out when he shot the boy first."

"Yes," she said. "I suppose they'd both—been needing sleeping tablets lately. Poor Mike." She looked at the manila envelope on the coffee table.

Bill Hoffman had made a neat and careful holograph

will, leaving everything he owned to Cathy Robsen.

"I don't want their things," she had said to it sadly.

There wasn't much to say to her. "There'll be an inquest—just the formality. You needn't appear. And we'd just as soon you didn't talk to the press."

"I've no intention of doing that. The sooner everybody can forget all this the better."

Mendoza nodded at the envelope. "You'd better take that to a lawyer—he's named one as executor. A holograph will is legal in California."

She just nodded. "And, oh, God, the children," she said. "They'd hear, of course, even if I didn't tell them. Better to tell them. They're fifteen and thirteen—old enough to understand, don't you think?"

"Is there any relative at all?" asked Hackett. "Somebody will have to make arrangements."

"Neither of them had any family." She looked at the will. "You said, a lawyer mentioned there. Could I ask him to take care of that, I wonder." And after a silence, "Bill was insane, you know. He might have wanted to die himself—since it happened—but unless he'd been insane he'd never have killed Muriel and Mike too."

On the doorstep, Hackett said a little savagely, "And I wonder if this is going to help Larry acquire any more maturity." Some helpful soul over at the jail, where he was awaiting transport to Susanville, would be sure to see he got a *Times* with the story—probably on the front page.

Galeano kicked that around with the other men some: the hell of a thing, but they had cases on hand to work. This Reynolds thing was wild; and the Avon connection, he realized after what Wanda had told him, was doubly wild. But you had to clear the extraneous out of the way, tie up loose ends as you went; and it had entered in.

The address for Avon Sales Products was on Los Feliz in Hollywood. He got there about nine-thirty; it was one of the newer, violently modernistic apartment buildings. The woman who answered the door was fortyish, fat, unexpectedly businesslike: Mrs. Agnes Winniger. She was both horrified and highly amused at his story. "I wouldn't think," she said, "it was really one of our representatives, you know."

"But the point came up, and I have to check, you can see that."

"Oh, I suppose so. Good heavens, the things that happen—" She was, it appeared, the district supervisor for Avon for the whole area. He was rather staggered to learn that there were some hundreds of Avon ladies in Los Angeles alone. But, she explained, they covered the areas close to their own homes. She could check the nearest representatives to the Twenty-seventh Street address.

There were two possibles, a Mrs. Burns, a Mrs. Polk. Thirtieth Street and Brighton Avenue. Galeano drove back downtown and tried Thirtieth Street first. Mrs. Burns was a tiny black woman, highly indignant at being approached by police. When she finally answered questions, she told him that on Monday morning at eleven-thirty she had been at her daughter's apartment in Leimert Park babysitting her grandchildren, and three people in the next apartment could tell him so. And when it came to police coming down on respectable decent people and nosing into private lives, all she could say— Galeano thanked her hastily and got away.

Mrs. Polk, at a single house on Brighton Avenue, was more cooperative, if indignant that the fair name of Avon had got into a murder case. "I saw that in the paper —what an awful thing! That poor young woman—and it said she had a little girl too." She had, she said, been at home all Monday morning, doing laundry and ironing. She was a tall, heavy woman, medium black, with large hands and muscular arms. Of course the thing was ridiculous, but it had to be cleared away. He called, and Melinda Corey was home. Mrs. Polk put on a coat and they drove down to Twenty-seventh, and Melinda said, "No, that's not the woman."

"I should think not," said Mrs. Polk genially. "Walking in and shooting people." She was quite grateful to Galeano for the chance of seeing the murder house and meeting the victim's sister. Galeano drove her home again.

Mendoza and Higgins landed at Federico's on North Broadway for lunch, and ran into Landers, Conway and Palliser. They did a little talking about the Hoffmans, and then Mendoza heard about the interesting discovery Landers and Conway had made at Bullock's. Palliser was enthusiastic about it.

"And that," said Mendoza, "is interesting all right. With a little unobtrusive snooping and some native intelligence, anybody could have acquired that supposed inside information. Possibly. But—" he leaned back in his chair and emitted twin streams of smoke from his nostrils— "it sounds a little casual, for the cool professional way the job was done." He grinned at Conway. "Sure, you might drop into any bar below Fourth and pick up a few men ready to do a little hired strong-arm work the wrong side of the law, but ten to one they'd be fairly unintelligent louts. The boys who pulled this one were pros —quick, cool, efficient, every move planned. I've got a hunch, Tom, that your hunch is wrong. And ditto for Rich's. You might possibly have guessed right as to how the information was collected, but for my money these jokers are the same gang who pulled the jobs in Philly and Pittsburgh. And there's no line on them at all." He swallowed the last of his coffee and put out his cigarette. "Whereas I hope some poking around on Marion Stromberg may yield some fruitful ideas. Come on, George, let's do some productive work for a change."

Marion Stromberg's address book gave them places to start asking questions. Mrs. Caldwell had recalled a Jean and a Paula, said to be close friends; Mendoza and Higgins started out with Mrs. Jean Grant at a handsome house on a quiet street in West Hollywood. Mrs. Grant was very much the same type and age as Marion Stromberg: well groomed, intelligent. She was startled and shocked to hear about Marion. "My God," she said. "Oh, that's dreadful, to think of her—" Mendoza hadn't gone into details. "Why, she was a year younger than I am. It makes you think—" But she was no fool, and when he began to ask questions she asked some herself. "It wasn't natural, a heart attack or something, when you're asking about— What's all this about, anyway?"

Higgins, who along with Hackett considered that the boss had a tortuous mind and tended to complicate things unnecessarily, said bluntly, "She was banged on the head and died of it, Mrs. Grant. Last Friday night. We'd like to find out how it happened."

"Oh, my God. Marion. Marion of all people. That's incredible."

"Why?" asked Mendoza. "Why of all people, Mrs. Grant?"

She made a helpless gesture. "Marion was so—retiring. Quiet. She didn't go out much. She was careful. I mean, if she was driving at night the doors were locked, and she'd never have let a stranger in the house—anything like that."

"We don't know a great deal about her," said Mendoza. "We're trying to piece together what might have happened."

"Well, anything I can tell you, but the last time I talked to her was last—I mean, a week ago last Monday."

"How long had you known her? You considered yourself a close friend?"

"Yes—" she hesitated. "I suppose Paula Ogden and I were about her closest friends. We'd known the Strombergs for, oh, twenty-five years—my husband's an optometrist too, we met first at some association dinners. When Fred was alive it was a little different—they used to go out more, to the theater, to restaurants—but they weren't ever awfully social. Of course she missed him terribly, it left her so alone. He had a heart attack in his office, died instantly. But you said, she was just found in the street—I can't imagine what—"

Mendoza asked more questions, and a picture began to emerge. Jean Grant, Paula Ogden (whose husband was a teacher at U.C.L.A.), a couple of other women, had occasionally met for lunch, shopping; visited each other's homes casually. In other days, the couples had entertained each other, and other people, at dinner parties now and then— "But nobody does entertain much now, the way we used to—" And since Marion's husband had died, she didn't have people in, except casually. All the other women had families, grown children, concerns and interests in life to keep their days full. "Oh, she did miss Fred. Never having children, it either drives you apart or makes a marriage closer. But what I can't understand is how she happened to be alone somewhere at night. The only place she went at night was the Arcadia."

"And what," asked Mendoza, "is the Arcadia?"

She gave a sharp sigh. She was a dark woman, rather too thin, and at the moment looked her full age. "I know it was very noble and good of her—I expect more people ought to do something like that—but those places give me the creeps. The convalescent homes. Old people sitting around waiting to die. You see, her mother was there—for a couple of years before she died. It was then Marion got interested. She said so many of the old people in places like that hadn't any families, or sometimes the families never came to visit them, and they just waste away from lack of attention. The nurses haven't time for anything but the necessities. I gather there are a few people, from religious groups I suppose, go visiting those homes like that—Marion had been doing it ever since her mother was there. Going in a couple of nights a week, getting the old people playing card games, or having a special little party if there was a good rerun on TV, or just to talk to them—she said it was pathetic, how so many of them just needed to talk, be listened to sympathetically. She kept on going there even after her mother died."

"I see. Where is it?"

"Out on Vermont somewhere. It was good of her," said Jean Grant listlessly.

They saw Paula Ogden at an older house in Santa Monica, and she was the same general type, if blonde and flightier. She'd known Marion forever, they'd been in high school together, she said. She couldn't believe it, about Marion. She asked a spate of questions Mendoza parried, and was led on to elaborate the picture. Of course Marion had been lost without Fred, but she'd seemed to have settled down and been happy enough. Jean had always said Marion should have done something with her life, she'd been smart at school, and she'd had a job at Lockheed during the war, that was just after she and Fred were married and he was overseas. But Fred didn't approve of wives working, even when it turned out there wouldn't be any children. They'd always lived a very quiet life; for one thing he was what was called saving, they didn't spend much money, it was only the last few years before he died, maybe when his investments were doing well, that Marion had had really nice clothes, begun to buy things for the house. And of course Paula wouldn't know what to do without her two darling poodles, she always had dogs though she couldn't abide cats. But Fred didn't like animals in the house; they never had any pets.

She told them about the Arcadia and how really unselfish and wonderful of Marion it was, to be so kind to the old people, but after the times she'd gone to see her aunt in one of those places she couldn't have borne it, but then she'd never been good with sick people.

"She must have been on her way home from there, and somebody got into her car to rob her—or maybe somebody was hiding in her car when she came out. That could happen, couldn't it? To think of Marion getting killed like that—but the awful things that happen every day—"

The last time she had talked to her was on the phone, Friday morning. Just to chat. Marion had said she might go out to dinner, even if it was raining. "She did pretty often, it's not much fun alone, but she said it was such a nuisance cooking for just herself, and she liked a nice restaurant."

"Did she say where she might go?"

"No, but probably the Brown Derby or the London Grill, she liked those."

They came out to the Ferrari, and Mendoza lit a cigarette—the Ogden house had been devoid of ashtrays —and stared at the Santa Monica foothills dark against a gray sky. It was another cold overcast day. "Do you pick up any nuances, George? Those two women were about her closest friends. They're sorry, they're incredulous at her getting murdered, but we don't get the floods of tears."

"She doesn't seem to have been a very—intimate kind of woman," said Higgins. "Sort of colorless. Reserved?"

"Mmh. Possibly kept at the level of the dutiful meek hausfrau by the masterful Fred. Well, let's go and see if she was cheering up the old people on Friday night."

As they turned onto Santa Monica Boulevard, Higgins said, "I can't say I buy the idea that anybody jumped into her car. And on Vermont, heading for home, she'd be traveling on a well-lighted main drag, until she turned on Franklin, and that's pretty well traveled too. As for the other idea, anybody with any sense locks a car, leaving it somewhere after dark."

"*Conforme.*" Mendoza stopped at the first public phone booth and consulted the Hollywood book for the address. It wasn't very far down Vermont, just below Sunset. It occupied almost an entire block: a low, tan, stucco building with venetian blinds at every window.

In the long narrow lobby tiled in imitation white brick, there was a counter with a frosted glass window closed across it, a hall running away to the right. In a wheelchair near the door a very old man sat slumped over the linen band binding him to the chair; he was shaking with palsy. The place was silent as a tomb; nobody seemed to be around. Mendoza rapped on the window; it half-opened and a fat woman in a white uniform said, "Sorry, the office is closed."

Mendoza displayed the badge and economically stated their business. "Oh, my goodness!" said the woman—nurse, aide, office girl?—and her red cheeks got redder. "Mrs. Stromberg! For heaven's sake! Why, she was just here on Thursday! Oh, wait till I get Miss Dowling—just a minute—" The window shut with a bang.

[113]

A couple of minutes later she reappeared from the corridor leading up to the right. "I just buzzed her—she'll be right down. I can't believe it, poor Mrs. Stromberg, the police coming—"

"You knew her well?"

"Well, she'd been coming two nights a week for nearly seven years, most of us on this shift knew her, of course. Like Miss Retzinger and the Good Samaritans, only they don't always come on the same nights. Some of the R.N.'s didn't like it, thought it was a nuisance, but— Oh, Miss Dowling! Would you believe it, Mrs. Stromberg's dead—murdered!—and the police are here about it!"

Miss Dowling was a big angular woman in a white uniform with a cap perched low on her bulging forehead. Conspicuous on her left breast was her little gold R.N. badge. She had sandy-red hair and a broad cheerful face. Just now it looked astonished. "Murdered!" she said.

"Last Friday night," said Mendoza.

"For the Lord's sweet sake! I will be eternally damned," said Miss Dowling. "That sweet little woman. What was it, a burglar?"

"We don't know. Was she here on Friday night, do you know?"

"No, she was not. To tell you the truth, we were wondering what happened to her last night—she was always here Tuesdays and Thursdays right on the dot, about six-thirty. And I'm not one of the R.N.'s who didn't like these people coming," she added good-humoredly. "Here, let's sit down—I'm on my feet enough as it is." There was a vinyl-upholstered banquette built on two sides of the lobby; they sat down there and she brought out a package of cigarettes from her breast pocket, bent to Higgins' lighter. "You look like a cop all right," she observed briefly, "if he doesn't." She might have been

[114]

thirty or sixty, energetic and self-confident. "You know, a good many of these poor old souls—and ninety percent of the patients in any place like this are the old people—are put down as senile because they've lost any interest in life. I could tell you—people here whose families never come near them, think they're half dead and won't know the difference. Well, they do. It'd surprise you what a change it makes in them when someone drops in to play a little card game with them, bring a special treat, home-made cookies or fudge—just to talk to them, listen to them. The L.V.N.'s are run off their feet, haven't time to give them any personal attention. They perk right up, look forward to these people coming in—and damned few people do come, you know, realize the need is there. Write the old folk off, they're no good to anybody any-more, shut 'em away and forget 'em. But a patient's a patient as long as there's a heartbeat." She twinkled at Mendoza. "Some of us appreciate the ones who care and do take the trouble. But what in God's name is this about Mrs. Stromberg?"

"If she wasn't here Friday night— These other people you mentioned. She was friendly with them? Who are they?"

"Oh, yes. They've all been coming for years. Mrs. Stromberg the longest—we had her mother, Mrs. Wallace, here for two years before she died—she was a nice old lady. Miss Retzinger's mother has been here nearly five years, she's quite helpless with arthritis but her mind's still sharp—and Miss Retzinger's got interested in some of the other patients. The Reverend Whitlow and his Good Samaritans—" she uttered a short laugh— "well, the man means well, and it doesn't seem to make much difference to the old dears who's listening or being sym-pathetic, so long as it's somebody. He has his own church, some nondenominational one, the Holy Shepherd it's called, and some of the church people call themselves the Good Samaritans, visiting the sick, you know."

"Did Mrs. Stromberg seem just as usual on Thursday night?"

"Certainly did to me, but then she wouldn't know she was going to be murdered, would she? There wasn't anything on TV the old dears would enjoy, but Miss Retzinger had brought some cookies and candy—diets be damned," said Miss Dowling, "it's about the only pleasure they have left—and Mrs. Stromberg got a game of rummy going, and they had quite a merry little party in the lounge, up to about nine o'clock. We do close down early—they usually left about nine."

"Well." Mendoza stood up. "Where could we reach Miss Retzinger?"

"At the branch library on Santa Monica—she's the children's librarian there. I wish you luck on finding out who killed Mrs. Stromberg—a real sweet little woman she was. I can't get over that, I can't indeed—but then none of us can know what end we'll come to."

"There isn't anything else I can tell you," said Melinda Corey.

"Maybe there is." Galeano had asked the L.A.C.C. registrar what classroom she'd be in, and waited to catch her at the lunch break. It was too cold to sit on one of the benches outside, so they were in an empty classroom. The straight wooden chair with the tray arm on it was too small, and Galeano was uncomfortable.

"I don't know what." She was staying on at the house, she had said this morning, and her mother had taken Lily, but she'd have to let the house go; the payments were too high.

"Did your sister recently, or ever, have an argument

[116]

with somebody—trouble over anything? Come on, everybody does sometimes. Little things." What was in his mind was that other funny case last August, where a very small thing had triggered off big trouble. But in any case, as Mendoza said, what constituted a motive depended on who had it; and with this thing looking as nutty as it did, it was very possible that a real nut with an irrational motive had done it.

"Nothing that would make anybody—"

"You don't know. Tell me about anything."

"Well, it's silly, but she did have an argument with the salesclerk at the Children's World shop uptown. That was last week. Leta was furious. She'd got some hair ribbons for Lily, and gave the girl a ten, and the girl gave her change for a five and wouldn't believe her about the ten. Leta called the manager and all the good that did her was, they told her when the register was cleared, if there was an extra five they'd call her. Well, naturally the clerk wasn't going to admit a mistake. She probably sneaked the five out of the register later. But Leta couldn't afford to lose five dollars. Everything so high, even if she was making a good salary— And sometimes it was like pulling teeth to get the support payments from Len. He was supposed to pay her a hundred a month, and lots of times it'd be late."

"Yes," said Galeano. "That's the only recent thing you can think of? All right, something else. You told us she wasn't interested in getting married again, but she was a good-looking girl. Had anybody made a pass at her, annoyed her any way like that?"

She shook her head. "When she first went to work for Mr. Armstrong, she thought she might have some trouble with him like that. He started acting kind of fatherly and silly, patting her arm and calling her pet names—you know the way a man that age acts when he wants to make a pass. It was a good job and Leta didn't want to lose it. She just let him see, in a nice way but making it pretty plain, that she didn't like it, wouldn't stand any nonsense, and he quit it. She never had any more trouble from him."

"Oh, really," said Galeano. He remembered Armstrong, seen briefly, as a dignified light-skinned Negro about fifty, austerely dressed and looking like a solid citizen. But if he was given to making passes at girls half his age—

She hadn't anything more for him. And of course, though they'd been living together, they wouldn't have told each other about every single incident happening in the course of every day.

He sat in the car thinking about Leta Reynolds, and he didn't see how the five dollars could really tie in. Not unless the salesclerk was nutty as a fruitcake, and if she was she wouldn't be holding down a job, would she? Well, go and look at her. But first, he got out of the car, walked half a block to a public phone, and looked at the book.

Herbert Armstrong was listed at an address in Leimert Park as well as at the photographic studio.

He drove over there and pulled up in front of the house. This was one of the solidly black areas that was also affluent; a lot of professional people lived here, as they did in View Park, the next area over. Jason Grace and his wife had a nice house in View Park. There were elegant big houses in both locations, some quite expensive places. The house where Armstrong lived was a two-story colonial with a brick chimney, an expanse of lawn in front.

Galeano got out of the car and went up to the front porch, pressed the bell. He thought, this is damned silly. Suppose they had a maid, or one of the kids answered the door—if they had kids—but if they had, they'd likely be grown and away. But they might have a relative living with them— Damn it, he thought, I don't even know that he's married. He pressed the bell again.

Unhurriedly the door opened. He said, "Mrs. Sidney?"

"Why, no, nobody of that name lives here."

"Oh, excuse me, it's the address I had."

"No, I'm sorry. I'm Mrs. Armstrong, just my husband and myself live here."

Galeano muttered an excuse and hastened back to the car. As he drove off he was thinking. Mrs. Herbert Armstrong was a tall, heavy-bosomed female who matched Melinda's description at least cursorily. And if Herbert was given to dalliance with young women, she was probably aware of it. And she might on some occasion have seen Leta Relynolds at the studio without Leta seeing her—or possibly Leta just didn't remember her. And if she had evidence that Herbert was playing around again, she might have jumped to the conclusion that his playmate was Leta.

It was *possible*. Anyway, he wanted Melinda to take a look at Mrs. Armstrong.

She'd be home about four. Take her over there, get her to ring the bell, pretend to be selling something?

He headed back for the station automatically, parked in the lot, and on the front steps met Glasser coming out. "Well, good, you can come be a witness," said Glasser. "If you're not nervous of meeting Leon again." Galeano felt his eye absently; it had certainly developed into a colorful sight, and he'd been conscious of a slight ache in it all day.

"What for?"

"The lab just called. The doctor sent over some of Leon's pubic hairs this morning, and it's just a matter of looking through a microscope. Somebody finally got around to it, and it's a match for the hairs from Alice Engel's body. Nice evidence, but it's always nicer if we can spell it out for a judge."

"That thing."

"Come on, I'm escaping from Wanda. I have an old-fashioned prejudice against talking about sex in front of an unmarried girl." Galeano grinned at him; Wanda was probably a little—just a little—tougher than Glasser thought. There was a little whisper on the grapevine about those two; he wondered how Glasser really felt.

They took the Gremlin up to the jail, and presently Fratelli was brought to them in an interrogation room. He looked neat and clean enough in the tan uniform, but he hadn't been allowed to shave and a heavy beard stained his jaw. He looked at them with a scowl and Glasser told him to sit down.

"You might as well tell us about it, Leon. How you killed Alice. We know it was you."

"I never done a thing like that. I told you how it was, it was that dude brought me home. He seemed like an all-right guy, but it must've been him did that. He said his name was Sam."

"No, Leon, there isn't any Sam," said Glasser. "It was you."

"I never did no such thing."

"Listen, do you understand anything about science? Scientific evidence? The lab boys can take a hair from your head and compare it to another and prove it's the same, from the same place. You get me? Just the way they can match shoes to footprints."

"Yeah?"

"That's right. And you may remember that the doctor detached some hairs from you last night, not from your head."

[120]

"He hadn't no right—crazy thing to do—I thought first off he was a nut—"

"And now the lab boys have compared them with hair found on Alice's body, and what do you know, Leon, they're all yours. There wasn't any Sam. You did that. We can prove it in court. Suppose you tell us how it happened."

He sat there thinking. He looked at his hands spread out on his knees, and he said, "That's for real?"

"For real, Leon. You ever do anything like that before?"

"No! No, I never," said Fratelli violently. "That's true on the cross. I never. I dunno why it happened—I don't. I—I—I'd been mad at Rosie—I tell you how it was—" He took a long breath and held it.

"Yes? Go on, tell it."

"Rosie—she's no good anymore, see. Getting to be more of a lush every day, she's drunk alla time. No good to me. What kind of john's gonna look at one like that? And she ain't int'rested in turning tricks no more. I'd been mad at her—and then she goes off 'n' the kids are hollerin' for somethin' to eat—damn it, they ain't my kids—"

"She says one of them is," said Glasser.

"Well, I guess. I got fed up."

"But were the kids?" asked Galeano gently.

"What? Oh, sure, sure, I got 'em some hamburgers. I went out for some drinks, there wasn't nothin' in the place. I went to that bar, an' after I had a few drinks I felt better, see, I felt O.K. I wasn't so mad at Rosie, except like I say she's no good at it no more an' I hadn't had none in a while. I got back home O.K., an' the kids had shut up and gone to sleep. Alice was asleep there, I saw her when I went to the john. I—well, I tell you, I just dunno what put it in my head. Musta been crazy just awhile. I just got to thinkin', how maybe it'd feel—to do it to a kid—like that. I never thought about nothin' like that before. But I kept thinkin' about it, and after a while I—I—I went in there. I never meant to *hurt* her—honest, I never."

"Just what did you think it would do to a nine-year-old?" asked Glasser coldly.

"I—never thought. An' I started—doin' it—and she commenced to holler and scream and that made me mad, I'd just started—and I grabbed her just a second to make her keep quiet—I never meant to hurt her," said Fratelli hopelessly.

"That's enough," said Glasser. He opened the door. "You can have him back." As they walked down the hall he said to Galeano, "Such a dirty job, Nick, dealing with such dirty people."

"But there are always more of the do-right people around, Henry. We just don't see as many of them as other people do," said Galeano seriously.

Mendoza and Higgins came into the office at four-thirty. Lake looked up from his paperback as they came past the switchboard and said, "Two things, Lieutenant. You're supposed to call the coroner's office. And a funny thing happened about an hour ago—" he picked up a small brown paper bag and handed it over. "This pawn-broker came in with that. Either he's the most honest man in the world or he's covering up something else. He said when he took a look at the latest hot list he thought he recognized this stuff. He took it in last Saturday for five bucks. He's got a shop over on Second."

"Call for Diogenes." Mendoza was amused; pawn-brokers weren't usually so obliging. He upended the bag, and there was the little loot from the Whalen house:

the old Waltham railroad watch, the Masonic ring, the cameo pin. He turned it over in his palm with one finger. Five bucks. Seventeen bucks they'd got altogether. And a man's life.

"Hell," he said, "pure formality, but we'll have to get Dan Whalen to identify it."

Higgins had passed on into the office, and now came back. "I called the coroner's office. The inquest is set for Friday." Yes, officialdom would want to get that one over, let everybody forget it.

There were inquests set for Dave Whalen and Alice Engel tomorrow.

"What've you got there?" asked Higgins. Mendoza told him. "Funny." He yawned. "I could run over there now."

Mendoza hesitated. He was feeling a little stale; and he wanted to think about Marion Stromberg. Better see her lawyer tomorrow. He dropped the few items back in the bag, and Conway came in towing a big black fellow and said, "Good, somebody's here. Another possible suspect in that other bar heist, who'd like to sit in?"

"George can help scare him better," said Mendoza. He dropped the bag into his jacket pocket and started out again, and thereby changed a couple of lives.

It was just threatening to rain again; hadn't actually started. He bypassed the freeway and went up Sunset, thinking absently about the various things they had on hand—actually a lighter caseload than usual, but that was the natural curve after the end of the summer heat, as tempers cooled with the temperature. And all they knew so far about Marion Stromberg—just what the hell had happened to her? The sweet little woman? As for Leta Reynolds, that was even wilder. Nick had been working that; talk to him tomorrow, see if he'd come to any conclusions.

Portia Street wasn't very long. Even some time before he got there he was aware of a column of black smoke rising off to the right; and when he turned on Portia, there it was ahead—two fire trucks, an ambulance, an excited crowd milling around. It was the Whalen house.

He angled in behind the ambulance and got out in a hurry. The hoses were playing steadily; there were crackling flames engulfing the whole right side of the house—the bedrooms and kitchen there. He groped for the badge, running up to one of the firemen standing by the first engine, hand on a valve.

"What's happened here? I'm on police business— with the householder—" And as he said it, he saw the canvas-covered mound in the street, between the two engines. The man turned and he saw the legend *Assistant Chief* on the helmet-badge.

"You're too late then." They had to raise their voices over the play of hissing water, the shouts of the men to each other, the excited voices of the crowd turned out to watch. "The paramedics tried, but he was gone. Suicided with the kitchen gas—but something sparked her off, probably the pilot light."

Mendoza stared at the angry bright flames. Seventeen dollars and two men's lives, he thought. A hand caught his arm; he turned. Mrs. Meeker, the Whalens' next-door neighbor, had recognized him. "Oh, oh, isn't it terrible!" she cried. "Poor Dan—he couldn't go on—"

A voice in Mendoza's mind said suddenly, *Dave always had to have a cat*. Not Dan. Dan had been pre-occupied with his own troubles. "Mrs. Meeker," he said loudly, "is Merlin out?"

Her shocked mouth gaped at him, and then she shrieked. "He's always in—cold weather—doesn't like—"

The wicker basket was in the front room. That side of the house hadn't caught yet, but there must be a good

[124]

deal of smoke. Mendoza was on the front porch in three seconds. He heard an outraged shout behind him, "Where the hell d'you think you're—"

He yanked off his jacket, balled it around his right arm, and knocked the window in with three hard blows. Great billows of smoke rolled out at him. Holding his breath, he clambered over the broken edges of glass into the room. He couldn't see, but he remembered the general location of the hearth and, remembering to bend low under the smoke, he groped over there. Wickerwork under his fingers, a furry inert body—

And his mind said, *Not another innocent, for nothing.* He seized the cat Merlin in one arm and groped back to the window. Outside, he ran back to the engine.

"Oxygen—"

"Well, for God's sake, a cat!" said the assistant chief. "Hey, Dick! Com'ere with that tank!"

In two minutes, Merlin stirred and sneezed. He struggled up groggily in Mendoza's arms and uttered an indignant attempt at a serious feline cussword.

"Oh!" sobbed Mrs. Meeker. "Oh, thank God—poor Merlin, poor boy—oh, how brave of you, are you hurt? Oh, give him to me, I'll love to have him, darling Merlin —I never saw anything so brave—"

"I'm quite all right," said Mendoza. Except, of course, for his suit jacket; he'd paid two hundred and fifty bucks for this suit three months ago.

But, looking at Merlin slowly recovering catly dignity in Mrs. Meeker's arms, he felt a warm satisfaction.

Piggott was holding down the night watch alone; it was Schenke's night off. Middle of the week, it was a quiet night. Piggott, sitting there alone, was thinking about the Hoffmans. He was, he hoped, a good practicing

Christian, and alone there in the big office, he did a little praying for Bill Hoffman, who had once been a good man and a good cop.

He didn't get a call until ten o'clock, and then it wasn't anything to go out on. It was a Sergeant Costello of the Glendale force, and he sounded tired. He said, "I'm going home to bed now, but you pass this on to your day watch, hah? That Bullock's job—we just had a real carbon copy here, at Robinsons'. We'll want to get together with whoever worked your job, see what got turned. You know if they got any leads?"

"We're nowhere on it," said Piggott.

Costello just said, "Hell," in a discouraged voice, and rang off.

At the end of shift, in the chill night, Piggott drove home to the apartment on Sycamore Avenue. He came in quietly, not to wake Prudence, and for just a minute stood in the living room looking at the lighted tank of beautiful tropical fish. And a very queer thought took hold of him, that God must love most other creatures much more than man, they were so much more beautiful. That it wasn't the animal creatures who had thought up racial and religious hatred, wars, political persecution, terrorism, the sordid and random and mindlessly violent crime.

But that wasn't anywhere in the Bible. He undressed quietly in the dark and got into bed beside Prudence; she stirred, muttered, "Matt," and went to sleep again.

SIX

NEARLY ALL THE MEN came in about the same time on Thursday morning, bunched in the same elevator: Palliser, Landers, Grace, Conway, Glasser, Galeano. Sergeant Lake was just settling in for the day, plugging in the switchboard for direct calls where, overnight, the desk downstairs had relayed. "Morning," he said, and there was a small grin on his sober mouth. "Did you notice the boss made the *Times*?" Hackett and Wanda came in together; it was Higgins' day off.

"What?" said Palliser.

"I don't think he's going to appreciate it much," said Lake seriously. He offered them the morning *Times*. In the lower left corner of the front page was a very candid close-up shot of Mendoza holding Merlin while a fireman administered oxygen. He looked very sternly noble, and the billows of smoke rising behind him made an effectively dramatic background. VETERAN P.D. OFFICER RESCUES PET, said the headline. The story started out, "Lt. Luis Mendoza of the Robbery-Homicide office forgot official duties today to save the life of a pet cat, forgotten in a fire which all but gutted a modest home on Portia Street. This tragic and heartwarming story came to light—"

"Oh, my God, he'll have a fit," said Hackett. "We didn't hear about the cat. He'll be fit to be tied. I wonder where the hell they got the picture."

There were a couple of lab reports in; Lake handed them over. "And some of you'll be heading for Glendale." He gave Piggott's note to Palliser.

"I knew it!" said Palliser. "By God, I had the feeling they were going to make another hit! Of all the gall—no details, but it's got to be the same gang. Hell's fire, and we've got just nothing at all—" He huddled with Landers and Grace.

Even in this usually monotonous job, surprises came along; Hackett read the first lab report with some astonishment. He'd nearly forgotten that two-week-old corpse found in the derelict house last Friday; it had looked like an O.D., and he seemed to recall that there'd been an autopsy report confirming that, heroin overdose. Now here was a kickback from the Feds on his prints, and it seemed he'd been one William Wilfrid Edgard, with a homicide warrant out on him in Indianapolis. Everybody got to California sooner or later, thought Hackett. There was also that pawnbroker to see, about the little loot from the Whalen house; but first he put through a call to Indianapolis to tell the force there they could stop looking for Edgard.

The other report was from S.I.D. ballistics, on the gun in the Reynolds case. There ought to be an autopsy report sometime today. Galeano read it, and got on the phone. "Listen, this ballistics report. I never heard of this damn gun—a Bernadelli automatic? What the hell is it?"

"They're not as common as some others," admitted Scarne, "but I've seen a couple of others. We found the ejected shells, by the way, but there aren't any prints on them. It's an import, Italian made. Takes .22 short ammo. It's a little bit of a thing, about four inches long—useless sort of gun, but of course at short range—"

It had been very short range. "I'll be damned," said Galeano. "But it's not a rarity—there are some around?"

"Sure. Couple of big East Coast importers deal a lot in Italian stuff. This one's been made for twenty years or so."

About then Mendoza called in to say that he was going directly to see that lawyer, would be in later. The inquests on Dave Whalen and Alice Engel were set for ten o'clock, in different courts. Palliser, Landers and Grace had taken off for Glendale.

Galeano went to catch Melinda Corey before she left the house. She agreed to try for a look at Mrs. Armstrong this afternoon. "But it seems awfully far-fetched."

"Are you sure you would know the woman?" he asked "For sure?"

She pressed her lips together. "I know I said I only saw her for about two seconds, Mr. Galeano. But I'm sure. There's a sort of picture frozen in my mind—her at one end of the couch and Leta standing facing her. I can't describe her, but I'm sure I'd know her if I saw her."

Galeano wondered. A waste of time—could she really be sure? It was nine-thirty; he headed back downtown for the Hall of Justice to sit in on the Whalen inquest. Glasser would cover Engel: the evidence on Fratelli would have been passed on and all the evidence would be offered on that one, which would take longer. On Whalen, the jury expectably returned an open verdict, persons unknown.

Hackett went down to the pawnshop on Second

Street, on the track of the pitiful little loot from the Whalen house. The pawnbroker was a thin dark young man with very steady shrewd dark eyes in a narrowly handsome face; Hackett thought he'd hate to try to put a lie over on him. His name was Weingard. He said, "No offense, Sergeant, but in this neighborhood it doesn't help the business image much, police dropping in often— reason I brought the stuff over. Sure, I can tell you who brought it in. Kid by the name of Pete Jackson. They live in the neighborhood, up on Roylston. His mother gets rid of the welfare money a little faster than usual, she's got a good old Longines watch she hocks now and then —saves up to get it back for next time."

"Know anything about the kid? He ever been in trouble?"

Weingard shrugged. "He is now, isn't he? He tried to offer me some merchandise I saw right away was shop-lifted—cheap costume jewelry, and he didn't even have the sense to take the tags off. That was a couple of weeks ago."

"Well, thanks very much," said Hackett. Against all the odds, were they going to drop on Whalen's killers after all? The mother's name was Marie, Weingard said; he had the address from the times she had pawned things with him.

It was a ramshackle old apartment building, and she had one of the back apartments giving on an alley. She wasn't particularly distressed at a police sergeant asking questions; there was a subtle aura of muscatel about her even at this hour. She looked pure African, thick lips and woolly hair and glistening black skin. "Pete?" she said. "I don' know where he'd be. Not at school—he don' like school much. He usually comes home at night."

Hackett went back to the office and told Lake to put out the word to their street informants that they wanted Pete Jackson. He'd also ask Piggott and Schenke to try to pick him up, if he came home tonight.

"Well, there you are," said Palliser. "It's the same pros, and there just isn't anywhere to go on it."

"Except," said Landers, "that the same thing holds true for this set-up—anybody wandering around the store could have found out enough to make the intelligent guess."

"Only did they?" wondered Grace. "It's six of one, half dozen of the other. Could also have been the inside dope."

Landers laughed sharply. "At least it won't be us pawing all through the employee records, if that's the route you want to go."

They had met the Glendale men—Sergeant Costello, Detective Dahlman—at the Robinsons' store that had been knocked off last night. It wasn't nearly as big a store as Bullock's downtown, and they wouldn't have got as big a haul, but it would amount to a nice take even so. Maybe all department stores had much the same arrangements; this one resembled Bullock's in miniature, with its administrative offices on the top floor. Here there was only one freight elevator: other than that, it was the same arrangement: registers closed out, money bags taken up to Accounting, then taken to the bank night drop by two guards.

The store was in a pleasant small shopping plaza, with smaller shops around it but at a little distance. They were now sitting on a couple of stone benches facing the front of the store, smoking and kicking it around.

"I don't think much," said Costello, "of that little idea you got from the boy in Philly." He was a stocky blue-chinned tough. Dahlman was younger, quieter,

[131]

competent-looking. Glendale had a pretty good force, if a small one.

"Neither do I," said Palliser, "but it's all we've got to hand you."

The operation had gone off the same way: four masked men in the Accounting office just as the store was closing, the staff and security guards tied up. "I'll tell you another way it was one Goddamned slick job," said Costello morosely. "They'd have taken a bigger haul in the Galleria, but they played it safe."

"What's that?"

"Big new shopping center—well, a few years old—over on the other side of town. There are bigger department stores—The Broadway, Buffums', Penneys'. But also a lot more lights, and restaurants open after the stores close, and more people around. They played it safe and hit here."

"The accountants," said Dahlman, "are saying around seventy thousand."

"And we had another thought on that aspect," said Landers. "The Bullock's people said three hundred G's, which seemed fantastic—of course they deal in a lot of expensive stuff, furs, cameras, furniture—but when we had second thoughts and asked, it wouldn't have been that much in cash. A lot of the take isn't actual take—just transference of credit with Master Charge, Visa, Bullock's own credit cards. And there'd be a certain number of personal checks. They finally said, more than half of all transactions would have been like that. But even so, it was a good haul."

"So say it's the same here, and it probably is," said Costello. "*Auuggh!* People thinking of the paper as money—robbing Peter to pay Paul. Say it was half cash. They'll just have dumped all the checks from both jobs, burned them somewhere."

"So we go through the motions," said Dahlman, "checking the guards, the employees? I buy your idea, Landers, anybody could have spotted that routine with a little snooping. Ask me, the security wasn't so damn tight either at Bullock's or this place."

They sat in silence for awhile; nobody had any more ideas. The Glendale lab, of course, was dusting for prints and looking at the rope used; they would probably turn up the same results the lab downtown had. Or rather, the lack of them.

The lawyer's name was Duane Earnshaw, and he was a large genial man about sixty. His practice was obviously successful; his offices were on Fairfax Avenue in a low, modern, single building. He had two partners and the front office boasted three glossy, youngish secretaries.

He had been conventionally sorry and surprised to hear about Marion Stromberg. He said he and his wife had been socially acquainted with the Strombergs. He volunteered information, and none of it was of immediate use to Mendoza. Stromberg, he said, had been a shrewd investor: stock, real estate. He had left her around two hundred and fifty thousand soundly invested, a couple of pieces of rental property. Marion Stromberg had made a will after his death, which still held: she had divided the estate between a second cousin of hers back in Illinois and her husband's niece. "The only relatives either of them had, a very fair thing to do," said Earnshaw.

"You say you knew them socially. What did you think of her, Mr. Earnshaw—as a person?"

Earnshaw sat back in his large expensive desk chair and lighted a cigarette. "Well," he said a little perplexedly, "they were difficult people to know, Lieutenant. My wife didn't care for either of them, and it

[133]

had been a very tenuous acquaintanceship—we never saw them often. Dr. Stromberg didn't seem to have any particular interests at all, you couldn't get him talking on politics, sports, any subject you could name. He was a colorless sort of fellow, all business, and she was the same. I must say she surprised me a little, after he died—she had quite a good business head, she was a more intelligent woman than I'd thought. But—well, colorless is as good a word as any."

"Yes," said Mendoza. By all they'd heard, a sterile sort of life; but if she'd never known anything else, possibly she hadn't realized that. "What about this niece? Were they close at all?"

"I doubt it. She said—" Earnshaw thought back—"when she made the will, she thought it was only fair that Mrs. Dunn should share the money, being Fred's only relation and it being Fred who'd made the money. The Dunns live in Santa Monica, by the way."

"Well, thanks very much." Mendoza stood up. He had gone to the house on Beachwood Drive before coming here, and rummaged; in a photograph album in the den he had found a studio portrait of her taken, he thought, about five or six years ago; he'd wondered why. Or was it older, had it belonged to her mother? She hadn't had a face that changed much with time; he thought anyone would recognize it who had seen her lately. It wouldn't do any harm to get it into the *Times*; maybe it would jog someone's memory, who had seen her last Friday night.

The Brown Derby, he thought, getting into the car. Or the other restaurant. Unfortunately, the staff who would have been on duty at the dinner hour on Friday wouldn't be on until this afternoon. Catch them then.

He stopped at the *Times-Mirror* building, saw a subeditor and passed over the photograph. He walked into the Robbery-Homicide office at ten minutes to eleven.

Lake was reading a paperback at the switchboard. Hackett was on the phone, and nobody else was in. He went into his office and found the morning *Times* neatly spread out on his desk blotter.

Hackett grinned as a wounded roar rose from the inner office. "*¿Para qué es esto? ¡Diez millones de demonios desde el infierno! ¿Y ahora qué?* Goddamn it, of all the gall—and who the hell wrote this guff—"

Hackett strolled in. "Pretty picture," he said. "You look quite romantic, Luis—just a little reminiscent of Barrymore playing Hamlet three sheets in the wind."

"And where in hell they got that picture—" Mendoza flung himself on the phone book. "The fire station—damn it, there wasn't any press there—Jimmy!"

He called the fire station on Sunset, got the assistant chief, and fired off furious questions. The assistant chief was amused. "Why, Lieutenant, we always carry a camera in case of getting records for the arson squad— when I saw what that was yesterday, I told Tony to get a few shots. He must have peddled that one to the *Times* for human interest value—not supposed to do it, of course. I thought it was kind of nice, myself. You so concerned for that poor little kitty-cat."

"You can go to hell!" snapped Mendoza. He sat back and brushed his moustache back and forth irritably. He was still fuming when Galeano came in and told them about the Whalen inquest. "What about Reynolds? Have you got anything on it?" Galeano started to tell him about that, and Lake came in with a new call.

"It's a double homicide. Coronado Street."

"Oh, for God's sake," said Mendoza, getting up. "One thing after another. Come on, Art."

It wasn't quite as cold today, which could mean that it was building up to more rain. They took the

Ferrari and Mendoza got on Beverly, driving a little faster than usual. Coronado crossed there just below Rampart, and as they turned the corner they saw the squad sitting about halfway down the block. This was a residential street, the houses old in this part of the city; it was a middle-class block of comfortable places, nothing fancy. The house where the squad car waited was an old California bungalow flanked by others very similar; it was painted white with green trim. A lawn in front was brown with winter.

Patrolman Yeager had two people in the back of the squad. He got out as Mendoza and Hackett came up. "My week for looking at bloody messes," he said gloomily. "These people just found them. Mr. and Mrs. Coons. That's their car." It was an ancient Chevy parked in the drive. "They're old friends of these people—Mr. and Mrs. Jackman, Brian and Jessie Jackman. They hadn't seen them in a month or so, and landed here about half an hour ago, found the door unlocked, walked in and found them. They're pretty old, and it was a shock—they had to go back to the main drag, find a phone and call in." They were walking up to the house.

There was a screen door sagging on its hinges; the inner door was wide open. They went in to the expectable living room of this kind of house, old-fashioned furniture, a worn flowered rug, rather fussy curtains. It was a combination living-dining room, with a built-in sideboard with glass doors at the far end, an old round, oak table there and chairs. The room was dusty and dim, the house facing north, but it looked fairly neat.

"The kitchen," said Yeager behind them. They went through the dining area to a swinging door propped open. The kitchen, as usual in a place of this vintage, was large and square. There was a square painted table to one side with a pair of matching chairs. And the kitchen was not neat.

The table had been shoved crookedly against the wall, and one chair had fallen over on its side. There were dishes on the table with food on them and two pans on the stove. A large bowl had been upturned on the floor and lay in pieces among the remains of whatever it had held. And sprawled on the floor, lying against one another, were two corpses, a man's and a woman's.

"This didn't happen yesterday," said Mendoza. The food was congealed and moldy; the blood on the floor and the bodies was long dry and brown. The heat was on in the house, a gas furnace most likely, but the thermostat was turned low and the bodies had not suffered much change except discoloration.

"We'd better turn the lab loose first," said Hackett.

"And I want a doctor's opinion about time, right now," said Mendoza. "By all the blood, they were knifed."

"You better take a look in the bedroom," said Yeager.

In silence they followed him down a cross hall. There were two bedrooms. The front one was the larger; it held an old-fashioned bedroom set, double bed, large dresser with a mirror fixed over it, another chest of drawers.

"*¡Por Dios!*" said Mendoza. On the mirror, crudely drawn in what looked like black paint, in letters three inches high, were the two words IDLE WERSHIPERS!

"I'll be damned," said Hackett under his breath.

On the dresser, just below that, stood a small china statue of the Virgin. There was a crystal rosary on the dresser tray, and a framed lithograph of the vision of the Virgin at Fatima on one wall. Mendoza backed out and went down to the living room again, looking around. On a table in front of the window was another china statue of Our Lady of Carmel, and in an open-shelved curio cabinet in one corner were several other religious figurines—St. Francis, St. Anthony, St. Michael.

"You see what I mean," said Yeager.

"I do indeed." Mendoza led them both out, got in the front seat of the squad and called in for a lab truck, talked to the coroner's office. Hackett got into the passenger seat. Mendoza swung around and introduced himself abruptly to the silent couple in the rear seat. "This is Sergeant Hackett. Now I know you're considerably upset by this and we don't want to make things any harder for you, we'll let you go home as soon as we can. But you understand, we'd like to know something about Mr. and Mrs. Jackman."

They nodded at him dumbly. They were over the first shock, though she had been crying. They were very old people, perhaps in the late seventies. He was a tall, gaunt, bald man with stringy jowls and faded-blue eyes; she, a short, heavy woman with a round face, neat gray hair. "What d'you want to know?" he asked.

"About any family, for one thing."

"They had a son and daughter," said Mr. Coons promptly. "Bill Jackman, he's a pharmacist, works at a Thrifty up in Hollywood, he's married and they got a couple of grown children. The daughter's Mrs. Helen Burley, her husband manages a chain market, they live in Burbank." He was shaking just a little. "Awful to die like that. Awful. Some maniac."

"You'd known them a long time?"

"Forty-five years. Brian and me worked together all that time. On the maintenance crew at Hollywood High School. We was about the same age, he was just a little older. Retired fifteen years ago. He was eighty, you know. Jessie just turned seventy-nine last week."

"I take it they were Catholic." They looked surprised, nodded. "Very religious? Tried to convert people?"

"Why, no, sir." They hadn't seen the scrawled words on the mirror. "Just good, decent, religious people. They didn't talk about it much. Bill usually drove them to church, Brian wasn't let to drive anymore."

"I couldn't come see Jessie on her birthday," said Mrs. Coons suddenly. "I was laid up with a cold. I'd baked a cake for her this morning—we live in Culver City, don't get out much now—" She began to cry again.

"Well, that's about all for now, thanks," said Mendoza.

"I don't know," said Mr. Coons with slow dignity, "that I just feel up to driving home. I don't expect they'll renew my license again."

In the end, they called up another squad; Yeager drove the old people home in the Chevy, and rode back in the other squad.

A doctor came out from Bainbridge's office and annoyed Marx and Fisher who were busy in the kitchen. Coming out, he said to Mendoza and Hackett, "We might pin it down closer at the autopsy, or maybe not. They were killed either late Sunday or Monday. I think. Both of them were stabbed repeatedly—tell you more about the knife after the autopsy. They wouldn't have put up much of a fight, especially if he caught them off guard. They were pretty elderly, and the woman was heavy. But I think they were sitting at the table when they were attacked. The dishes—food on the table—"

"Yes. Not an utter stranger just crashing in," said Mendoza. He looked up and down the block. Another working-class block, with not too many neighbors home during the day. But the kind of area where people stayed put; the Jackmans had probably lived here for many years, and most of the people on the block would

know them—each other. He said that, absently, to
Hackett. "There's not much we can do here pending
the lab report, but talk to the family—ring doorbells and
talk to the neighbors. Had there been any trouble
around here lately, prowlers or— Had they mentioned
anyone bothering them? And let's hope the lab turns
something." He used the phone in the Ferrari to call
the office; Palliser, Landers and Grace had come back,
and he filled them in, told them to come down here
after lunch and start the legwork. For a start, he and
Hackett tried the house next door, but got no response.

"And you know, Luis, what you just said—not necessarily so. They were old. They may have lived here for
years, but few people that age are still living alone in
single houses. I'd bet most of these places have changed
hands, and there'll be younger people around, younger
than they were anyway. There must be some people at
home along here, but you notice nobody's come out to
ask about the squad cars, ask about the Jackmans."

"True," said Mendoza. They tried the house on the
other side, and as soon as the bell rang, the door opened.
They showed the badges.

"I saw the police cars, I wondered what had happened." She was a little, thin, middle-aged woman in a
shabby cotton dress.

They told her, and she put a hand over her mouth
and her eyes held terror. "Oh!" she said. "Oh! Those
poor old people—"

"Did you know them, Mrs.—"

"Burroughs, I'm Amelia Burroughs. No, sir, we just
moved here last week. We don't know anybody here."

"Do you remember hearing or seeing anything unusual along here, last Sunday or Monday?"

She shook her head. "Is that when—? I was out about
an hour, up to the market, on Monday. No, I didn't. And

my husband wasn't here Monday, he was at work, he drives a bus for the city."

They went back to the car. "And you know, Luis, as cold as it's been, everybody's had doors and windows shut. And it was raining on Monday," Hackett reminded him.

Mendoza conceded that ringing doorbells along the block might be a waste of time.

Mr. Coons had told them which Thrifty drugstore it was where Bill Jackman worked. They drove up there, not looking forward to breaking bad news. But at the pharmacy counter, a white-smocked middle-aged man stared at the badges and asked, "What do the police want Bill for?" They explained, and he said, "Oh, my God! Jesus, that's awful. And I don't know what to tell you—my God, they're not here. They're all over in Arizona. Yuma. Bill's youngest granddaughter got married yesterday and they all went over for it—Bill and his wife and son and his wife and kids, Bill's sister and her family. Bill's daughter, that's the bride's mother, she and her husband live in Yuma. And my God, I can't think of her married name—her first name's June—I don't know how you'd reach them. My God."

"The Coonses might know," said Hackett to Mendoza.

"I'll take you back to your car. You'd better go and ask. I think this one is going to be a bastard to work," said Mendoza.

Galeano said to Melinda, "Now take it easy. All you have to do is take a look at her. Forget about pretending to sell something—that's not such a hot idea, she might be interested. Just ring the bell and ask for Mr. Smith, say you've got the wrong address."

"I still think this is awfully far-fetched," said Melinda. "She'll think it's funny, the same thing happening twice."

"So let her." The garage door was up and there was a car inside; she was at home.

"Well—" Melinda got out of the car, which he had parked three houses up. She had on a blue pantsuit today, and a short leather jacket over it. She closed the car door and started toward the Armstrong house at a brisk walk. Galeano watched her up the front walk; she pushed the bell. After a wait the door opened, and she spoke to the woman inside, backed away, started back to the car. It was just starting to sprinkle.

She got into the car and said, "No. She's not the one."

"You sure?"

"I'm sure. The woman who killed Leta was a lot younger. Big and busty, but younger."

"Well, it was just an idea," said Galeano.

The maître d' at the Brown Derby looked at the badge with raised eyebrows, listening to Mendoza. "I'm very sorry to hear about Mrs. Stromberg," he said quietly. He was a short, stocky, dark man with the restless eyes of the experienced waiter. "She'd been coming here for a long time. She and Dr. Stromberg used to come in at least once a week. They were very nice people."

"I'd like to know if she was here last Friday night."

He thought. "Yes, she was. Since Dr. Stromberg died, she used to come in oftener. She had said to me, it was boring, cooking for herself. She'd be here for dinner two or three times a week. Yes, she was here Friday, I'm sure. There weren't many people in that night—Friday is a good night usually, but the rain kept people in."

"Do you remember what time she was here?" The restaurant was open but at this hour of the afternoon not many people were here. No one was in the restaurant section at all: set-up tables waited for diners to come. There were half a dozen people in the bar off to the right. They were standing in the square foyer, with the cashier's desk to the left, a corridor leading beyond that with a discreet sign indicating the rest rooms; just down from the door to the bar was a public phone on the wall.

The maître d' thought. "It was fairly early, I think. She usually came early. I'm almost sure she was sitting at Doris' station. Let me get her." He went into the restaurant section and came back a few minutes later with a slim blonde girl in a waitress' yellow uniform. She was looking very shocked.

"Mrs. Stromberg!" she said, hardly acknowledging the maître d's formal introduction. "Why, that's just awful. She was such a nice lady."

"You knew her pretty well here?"

"Oh, yes. She came in a lot. The others said, especially since her husband died— I've only worked here two years. We'd all waited on her, different times."

"She was here last Friday night?"

She was studying Mendoza now, interested in a detective. She nodded. "Yes, she was. I was a little surprised she came out in all that rain, but she did. She was at one of my tables."

"Do you remember what time?"

"It was about six-thirty when she came in. Around there."

"Did she have a drink before dinner?"

"Oh, she always did. Just one. A daiquiri."

"Remember what she had for dinner?"

"I think it was the beef stroganoff. It might have been shrimp scampi—those were about her favorites, but I think it was the stroganoff. She always had salad instead

[143]

of soup, thousand island dressing, and she never wanted dessert."

"That's very good," said Mendoza. "Did she talk to you much—then or any time, I mean?"

Doris thought that one over. "Well she was always nice. Pleasant. But if you mean she talked about herself or—well, personal things, no. Some people do—our regulars, I mean. Mrs. Stromberg was just—nice. She always left a good tip, too. She wasn't dressed as smart as usual Friday, I suppose on account of going out in the rain."

"Remember what she was wearing?"

"A navy knit dress, sort of plain, and a navy coat with a fur collar. She had a bright-red handbag," said Doris.

"What time did she leave?"

"I'd say it was eight o'clock, maybe a few minutes after. She didn't hurry over her drink, or dinner either, and of course there wasn't anybody waiting for a table so it didn't matter. It might have been later when she actually left," said Doris, "because she made a phone call."

"Oh, she did? How do you know that?"

"I saw her. Look, she was sitting at that table right there—" She pointed at one of the first tables beyond the foyer. "When she left, I came up and collected my tip, but I didn't start to clear the table right away because I had to get the drinks for another party. I did that, and I went back to clean up Mrs. Stromberg's table. It took me, oh, a couple of minutes, you know, putting the plates on a tray and the used napkin and wiping off the table, and setting it up again with a place-mat and silver. And while I was doing that, I saw her come across the foyer and go to the phone."

"Mmh," said Mendoza. "She went down to the rest room to powder her nose and put on fresh lipstick, and by that time you were busy at the table."

"That's right. She was still at the phone when I took the tray out to the kitchen."

Mendoza thanked her absently. Now where the hell had Marion Stromberg gone after that, last Friday night? In the rain? And whom had she phoned? Go right down the names in her address book, and he had a hunch right now everybody would say, not me.

A colorless sort of woman. But someone had felt strongly enough about her, over something, to take hold of her roughly, knock her around some.

And where the hell was that Buick Skylark? There had been an A.P.B. out on it since Tuesday night.

He drove up Alexandria to Sixth slowly, uncertain where he wanted to go; and then he accelerated and turned on Western, up to Santa Monica. Of course there wasn't a parking place anywhere around the library, and he had to park on a side street two blocks away.

He found Miss Leila Retzinger busily shelving books in the children's wing. She was a little brisk dowd of a woman, with bright brown eyes, sallow skin and a quick high voice. She looked at him with her head on one side and told him that Miss Dowling had called her. "What a very terrible way to go. But I understand it was quick. Perhaps it is even worse to linger on for years in misery and loneliness. But what can I tell you about it, Lieutenant?"

"You saw her on Thursday night. Did you talk much with her at all? Did she happen to mention anything about her plans for the next day?"

She again put her head on one side exactly like a little brown bird and said, "Why, no—there wasn't any occasion. After all, we are there to give attention to the patients, not to talk to each other. Mr. Whitlow—I refuse to say Reverend, for his is not an established church and we have always been Episcopalians—would insist

[145]

on prayers, but after that we got them settled down at card games, and I was talking to Mrs. Pinckney a good deal of the time, and then Mrs. Morgan. Mrs. Stromberg was across the lounge with Miss Romney and Mrs. Peterson. I scarcely exchanged a word with her, I'm afraid. If I had known it was the last time I should see her— She was such a nice woman."

Mendoza went back to the office and got Bainbridge on the phone. "Well, I thought you'd forgotten about it," said Bainbridge. "Yes, I did the analyses. Stomach contents, beef, sour cream, mushrooms, rice, lettuce, asparagus. The alcohol was rum."

"As indicated," said Mendoza. "More than one drink?"

"Definitely. About the equivalent of three."

"Thank you so much," said Mendoza.

Hackett, Palliser and Landers came in and Hackett said, "The Coonses came through with the name and I called Yuma. General consternation. They all drove over, and they'll be back some time tomorrow, late. But we're not going to get anything from any of the neighbors down there, Luis. Most of them at work all day. The people on the other side of the Jackman house, we heard from a woman across the street, own a deli up on Virgil. They were friendly with the Jackmans, just casually, and I saw them, but they don't remember anything unusual happening on Sunday and of course Monday they were gone all day. I think anything we turn on this'll be from the lab."

"Yes," said Mendoza sardonically. "All we can logically infer is that X attended the public schools, as indicated by his misspelling. I'm going home, boys." It was five-thirty, and raining steadily.

As Mendoza stood up and reached for his hat,

Sergeant Lake's voice was raised in the hall outside. "Just a minute, ma'am, you can't—oh, damn—"

A pretty, little, elderly woman appeared in the doorway. She was pink-cheeked, white-haired, beautifully groomed; she came tripping in on stilt heels; she radiated warmth and joy. "Dear Lieutenant Mendoza! Ah, you sweet brave man! I simply had to come—it was providential that we had our regular meeting this afternoon and we all agreed I must contact you—I am the secretary, of course—dear Lieutenant, we have made you an honorary member unanimously—"

Mendoza took a step back and dropped his elegant black Homburg.

"—Of the West Hollywood Cat Lovers' Association. We should all be so honored and delighted if you would come and tell us all about your own dear kitties—I know you must share your home with some lovely kittums. Such an inspiring picture, we all agreed! Risking your life for a dear little kitty!"

Mendoza said icily, "As far as I am concerned, madam, a cat lover is another cat. I am not interested—"

"And I simply had to bring you a copy of My Book—" she pressed a little volume insistently into his hand. "Poems to my dear kitty pussums—I had just a few copies printed for special friends—I do hope you'll like my little efforts. And you must come to one of our meetings, my dear man—"

"I am not—"

She shook her finger at him merrily. "My card is there, and we shall so look forward to seeing you at our next meeting! I've marked the date for you—you'll find us all friendly—don't be shy! Now I won't interrupt your busy schedule, but do come!" She tripped out and down the hall.

Hackett began to laugh. He bent double, gasping.

Mendoza retrieved his hat. He put it on slowly, pulling it just to the correct angle, and brushed his moustache back and forth. Hackett subsided into his desk chair, giggling. He said, "Tell 'em—about El Señor and his rye—sorry, just struck me funny—"

Mendoza said distinctly, "God damn eternally the man who invented cameras," and stalked out.

Mairí had gone out to the market and brought the *Times* home that afternoon. "Well, for heaven's sake," said Alison, "I wonder where they got the picture." They had heard about Dan Whalen, the fire, and Merlin—largely on account of Mendoza's suit jacket, which was past reclamation.

"And wasn't it just like the man, never mentioning what a terrible blaze it was—guidness to mercy, see all the smoke there," said Mairí.

Alison suddenly dissolved into mirth. "Now the man might have been killed!" said Mairí. "Well you know it!"

"I know—only he wasn't— But Mairí, it *isn't* Luis—not really a good picture of him—b-but it's exactly like an old still of V-Valentino yearing at Vilma Banky or some other vamp—" Alison went on giggling, looking at it.

The twins came home on the private school bus, and rapidly became obstreperous, quarreling and noisy—it was raining again and they couldn't go out to play. The trouble with babies, thought Alison, was that they turned into children. She cuddled Luisa Mary—a perfectly contented peaceful mite of life, quite easy to cope with, but a couple of years from now. . . .

When the phone rang around five o'clock, the twins were settled down having supper.

"I'd have called before," said the slow country drawl

of Ken Kearney, "but I got hung up some. Carburetor trouble on the way up here, so I was late getting in. But I've got it fixed up O.K. What I wanted to tell you— the ponies are fine. Just what we want. They belonged to this fellow's kids—Lew Ford, he's got a spread here, very nice, herd of Herefords—and the kids outgrew 'em. They're worth the money, a very nice pair, and I clinched the deal. He'll be glad to keep them till next month. But what else I'm calling about—you know what I said about some sheep. Well, Ford says he knows a fellow a few miles north might have some to sell—you know, it's mighty hard to find any sheep right around L.A. I thought I might kill two birds with one stone—see what they look like, and if they're O.K. I can rent a U-Haul and bring them right down, put 'em up there."

"But we're not moved in," said Alison. "Would they be all right up there alone?"

Kearney's laugh was hearty. "Right as rain. We just want 'em for eating down the weeds. I'll call you back, let you know how much he wants."

Just as she put down the phone, she heard the Ferrari, and rushed to tell Luis about that.

He said, "The sheep. And what next? And I suppose you saw that—that photograph—"

"No comment," said Alison. "Where on earth did they get it?"

"Never mind," said Mendoza. "I need a drink." But then, of course, the twins discovered he was home and came running.

Hackett came home and Angel told him it was all arranged. They'd definitely be moving at the end of the month, a short escrow, and it would cost about seven hundred dollars. Hackett was aghast, but she said they

[149]

wouldn't move again for a long, long time, if ever, and it was such a nice house.

"Yes," said Hackett. "Well, I hope we don't have to get a loan from the bank."

When the night watch would be on he called in. "Matt? I meant to leave you a note, but it slipped my mind. Look, would you check on this Pete Jackson. . . ."

SEVEN ━━━━━━━━━━

ON FRIDAY MORNING, with Glasser and Galeano off, the night watch had left them a couple of things. That was one of the annoyances of the job; new things were continually coming up to work, while old cases waited to die natural deaths.

Piggott had found Pete Jackson at home; he was waiting in jail to be questioned, but they could only hold him twenty-four hours. There had been a new heist while Piggott was taking him in; Schenke had just noted on the report laconically, "By description, the blonde bomber again." It had been a liquor store. There were witnesses coming in to make statements this morning. There was also something more serious. Just before the night watch closed down, a squad car had called in. Moss reported coming across a nearly naked woman on the street, lying half on the sidewalk, in the middle of a block on Eleventh; she was unconscious and seriously injured. He'd got an ambulance and she'd been taken to the emergency ward at the General.

Palliser and Landers went out on that, to see what the hospital could tell them.

Conway, talking with Galeano yesterday, had got interested in the Reynolds thing, and was looking over all the back reports on it. That inquest was called for this morning; he and Wanda would cover it.

One of the witnesses on the heist came in at eight-fifteen, and Hackett started talking to him.

Mendoza passed on the gist of the Jackman killing to Higgins. "We should be seeing the family some time this afternoon." It was the better part of three hundred miles over to Yuma. "They may be able to give us some lead." He was formally very dapper in a dark suit; he would be sitting in on the Hoffman inquest this morning.

"That's offbeat all right," said Higgins. "Somebody—and somebody way off his rocker—with a prejudice against Catholics—"

"But," said Mendoza, "why these particular Catholics, George? At this particular time? There must be a lot of Catholics to hand right around there—and a lot of other places. That old couple were living restricted lives, Jackman not driving anymore. They probably got out very seldom, except with the family. Who singled them out, and why? What triggered it?"

Sergeant Lake came in and said, "There's a female just come in who says she knows something about the Jackmans. Mrs. Anna Guttierez, lives down the block from them."

"*No me diga,*" said Mendoza. "Fetch her in. Any news welcome."

She was in the forties, plump and still pretty, and she didn't subject them to any Latin emotion, though she was obviously distressed. There was no accent on her English; a good many Mexican families had been here longer than some Anglos had; but her choice of words said that she habitually spoke another tongue. "Mrs. Duvane phoned and told me," she said without preamble. "About the Jackmans. The Duvanes live next door—she said the police came to their delicatessen yesterday."

"Oh, yes," said Mendoza.

"I knew them." Her big dark eyes were sorrowful. "It's a terrible thing. But she said you were asking about Monday, and I saw them that day, I thought I must come and tell you. So I called Mr. West and told him I will be late. I work at the Goodwill office, but only three days each week."

"What time on Monday?" asked Mendoza interestedly.

"It was about twelve-thirty. They were good old people. I didn't tell you, I live across the street and down a little. Not every time I go to the market, but sometimes, I would go and ask if I could do any shopping for them—save them trouble. That's why I went across on Monday. They said no, they would be shopping the next day. But then—they were fine. Just like always."

"That's very helpful."

"They had just been eating lunch, Mrs. Jackman was washing the plates. They were fine. So if they were murdered that day, it was later. I thought the police would wish to know."

"We do indeed, we're very grateful to you for coming in. . . . That pinpoints it very nicely, doesn't it?" he said when she had gone out. "More than we could have hoped for. They were just starting a meal when the killer arrived, so that must have been dinner. The family will be able to tell us what hours they kept. And I said off the top of my mind, it wasn't an utter stranger, but it could well have been. The back door was unlocked. They were elderly and slow. He could have walked right in on them and got busy with the knife before they could get up. I hope to God the lab has something—they always take their time. We probably won't get an autopsy before Monday." He stabbed out his cigarette, looked at this watch and swore. "I've got to be at that inquest—not that there'll be anything to it. Short and not so sweet." He got up and yanked down his cuffs, reached for his hat.

At the hospital Palliser and Landers talked to a Dr. Sanders, who was a veteran of the emergency ward but could still be shocked. He hunched his shoulders and grimaced at them; he was a young man with tired cynical eyes. "My God, talk about the city jungle," he said. "What's been happening to that poor damned girl— I just came in, but I talked to Aarons and the nurses, and saw the chart. It looks as if she's been held prisoner somehow—"

"What?" said Palliser, startled. "Our report said she'd apparently been thrown out of a car after a beating."

Sanders nodded. "She may have been, but it was just the latest thing. By the condition of her wrists and ankles, she's been bound with wire for long periods of time. She's been tortured too—there are burns all over her, probably from cigarettes, and some nasty razor cuts—not deep enough for serious injury, just to inflict pain. She's been raped repeatedly, by all the laceration, both normally and anal. The latest injuries are the most serious—she's got both legs broken—one a compound fracture—concussion, and severe deep wounds in both thighs and buttocks. I understand one of your cars spotted her in the street—well, she couldn't have been there five mintues or she'd have been dead by the time the ambulance got there. The femoral artery was severed and she'd lost half the blood in her body by the time she was brought in."

"My good God," said Landers. "I suppose it's silly to ask if she's been conscious, identified herself."

"Let's say unrealistic," said Sanders dryly. "No. We hope she's going to make it, but we're not saying for sure yet. Of course we've pumped blood into her, and started I.V. feedings—that's another thing, she's been pretty well starved and dehydrated. And she was filthy —obviously hadn't had an opportunity to bathe in some time. That, and the wrists and ankles, made us deduce she'd been forcibly confined somewhere."

"There wasn't anything on her at all?"

"Four things," said Sanders. "One of them may be some help to you. You can see her if you'd like." He led them down to the nearest nursing station, picked up an envelope from the desk. "She was wearing rags of stockings and one shoe—it's a fairly new shoe from Leeds." That was a middle-priced chain shoe store. "And this." He shook the envelope and a bracelet dropped into his palm; he handed it to Palliser. It was an inexpensive gold-toned bracelet, and it was marked shallowly with a name; some department stores sold these as novelties, the costume jewelry not really engraved, but cheaply incised with an electric stylus. In rather shaky script, the letters on the I.D. bar of the bracelet spelled out *Linda Carr*.

"I'll be damned," said Palliser. "That's a break."

They had a brief look at her, motionless in the hospital bed, nearly buried in bandages. Her face hadn't been touched; she was a very pretty girl, a creamy-skinned blonde, and she didn't look much more than twenty.

Without having to discuss it, they took the I.D.

bracelet back to Parker Center and up to Missing Persons, and Lieutenant Carey had a look at their current files. When he came to the right one he said, "Oh, yeah, the name rings a bell now. We never followed it up because it looked to us like a voluntary take-off, and she's over twenty-one. She was reported missing about three weeks ago by an Arnold Sorenson. Listed as her employer. Haines handled it, and he had a look, but he thought she'd probably just taken off with a boy friend or on her own. Don't tell me it's turned into a case for you?"

"You'd better pray it doesn't," said Landers, "or you and Haines may be up in front of Internal Affairs for sloppy police work."

"What's the address?" asked Palliser.

It was on La Brea Avenue: a low-priced chain restaurant, Denny's. Sorenson was there; he was the manager. He was a big pear-shaped man in the forties, with thinning brown hair and myopic blue eyes behind horn-rimmed glasses. He heard what they had to say, and took off his glasses to mop his eyes, and said, "Oh, my God, my good God. I was afraid something had happened to her, but I never suspected anything as bad as that. I knew she wouldn't have just walked off the job without telling me. She'd only been in California six months, she needed the job, and she's a good steady responsible girl."

"Why did you report her?" asked Palliser. "Why not her family?"

"Because she hasn't got any," said Sorenson simply. "She's an orphan, she was raised in some church orphanage back in Illinois. She's only twenty-two—hell, gents, I've got a daughter her age, I wouldn't feel so easy about Lori being out on her own like that! But Linda's steady. A good girl. I knew she hadn't just walked away."

He had worried about it, he said, for a few days before he reported her missing. He'd got one of the other waitresses who knew her to go with him to her little apartment, and it looked as if most of her things were there, that she hadn't taken any clothes.

"How'd you get in?" asked Landers.

"Jimmied the door," he admitted. "My God, what could have happened to her? I used to worry about her getting on the bus that late, but she'd rather take second shift because she didn't like getting up early. I know there are a lot of violent kooks around, but to think of— God."

He could tell them when he'd seen her last. The restaurant was open from 6:00 A.M. to 10:00 P.M. A crew of waitresses and chefs came on at six and a second crew at two; Linda was one of the waitresses on that shift. The other girls would say the same thing: they didn't know her intimately, maybe, she'd only been working here four months, but the girls got along, they all liked Linda. Of the other girls, four of them, all but one had cars, and Ellie's husband always called for her. It was a Thursday night, a month ago last night. They'd closed the place up, and left mostly together; Ellie's husband had been early. The rest of them had gone out to the parking lot at the side, and Linda had said good-night and started across the street to get the bus. "She wasn't nervous about it," said Sorenson, "but I was. That's another thing, you see, she's from a small town, not a city anyway—she doesn't know what the city can be like. Is she going to be all right?"

"They don't know," said Landers.

"Oh, my God."

"We'll want to talk to the other girls. Ask about boy friends and so on."

"She doesn't have one," said Sorenson. "She a pretty strait-laced girl. She dated one young fellow she met in here, a few times, but she said he was too handy, know what I mean, and she gave him the push."

And maybe the young fellow had wanted to get back at her. Or maybe she'd just run into a violent kook.

They went out and looked at the bus-stop across the street. This was a fairly main drag but they were all business blocks this far down La Brea; there wouldn't be many people around at that time of night, and not so much traffic. The cross street was a narrow one, old residential. The arc lights were high above the intersection. They didn't have to discuss it. She might have been, almost certainly, the only one waiting for a bus here most nights.

"Hell of a thing," said Landers.

She'd had an apartment up on Berendo; the rent, Sorenson said, was up next week, and what about that? He could keep her things for her until she got better; it was mostly clothes. Palliser and Landers started up there to look at it, and Palliser said grimly, "Carey's Mr. Haines doesn't use much imagination, does he?"

"He probably didn't give Sorenson a chance to talk," said Landers. "Let's hope she comes to and tells us what happened."

On account of the witnesses in the liquor store coming in to make statements—"Who argues with a dame waving a gun around?" they both said expectably—Hackett and Higgins didn't get over to the jail until eleven o'clock.

Pete Jackson was brought to them in the bare tiny

interrogation room. He was sixteen, and looked younger; he wasn't very big, he had the same pure African features as his mother, a woolly cap of hair, and he looked a little scared.

"All right, Pete," said Hackett, and he laid out the few little pieces on the table. The old Waltham railroad watch's crystal had been broken when Mendoza knocked out the window, but it was all recognizable. "We know where you got this, but we'd like to hear the story."

Pete looked at the things and said, "Where'd you get that?"

"From the pawnshop where you took it. It was on the list of stolen goods." That went over his head; he didn't know anything about that. "We know where it came from and how it got there, so suppose you tell us the middle part."

Pete looked at him blankly, and Higgins said, "You're getting a little too fancy, Art. Look, boy. You snitched this from a house after knifing a man. There was somebody with you. Who was it?"

Pete looked sullenly at the table. "I don't know nothin' about it."

Both of them had dealt too long with utter stupidity to feel impatient. "We'll sit here until you tell us," said Higgins not unkindly. "We know everything but that, and you're going to be up in front of a judge for it anyway. Wouldn't you like to take him with you?"

Pete thought that over for a long painful minute, and then he said, "That ain't fair."

"That's right, but how do we know who he is unless you tell us?" asked Hackett cheerfully.

After another long minute's thought, Pete said, "It was his idea."

"Whose idea?"

"Bobby Porter. We needed some bread. Ma never

gives me none, she need all she get for the wine. But we dint set out to rob nobody, we was just ridin' around. Bobby, he sort of borrowed his brother's heap. An' we needed some bread, so he says hey man s'pose we knock off a house. So we did."

"Why did you pick that place?"

"We dint," said Pete succinctly. "Mighta been any place along there. We parked inna next street over an' come through yards. We tried one place but we couldn't get the door open. Bobby had a switchblade an' I had a big ole bread-knife, but we couldn't—"

"So you'd thought of knocking off a house before you went riding around?" asked Higgins.

"Uh. Yeah. I guess. That place, we got the door open. We dint know there was anybody there. Man come at us yellin' somethin', we just cut him a little bit, make him stop—an' I wanted get out then but Bobby made me help him rob that stuff. An' the guy's bread. He hadn't but twelve bucks."

"So tell us where Bobby lives," said Hackett.

"Di'mond Street."

It was all they needed, and they were slightly tired of Pete. They handed him back to the jailer, went back to the office and applied for the warrant, and went out again to look for Bobby. He too was probably a minor, and the worst that could happen to them was incarceration until they turned twenty-one, and probation. That wasn't much retribution for Dave and Dan Whalen. At least the cat Merlin still had a good home.

The Hoffman inquest was very official and brief. There wasn't a jury. The evidence was read into the court record and the coroner's representative handed down the expectable verdict, willful homicide and suicide while the balance of mind was disturbed. There were only two reporters there; the rest had all known how it would go. The Hoffman case was over—ended. Except for Larry Hoffman; and you could wonder how it might affect him, for better or worse or not at all. The egocentric personality.

The *Times* had run a brief story and the photograph of Marion Stromberg on its second page this morning. Unless Mendoza had asked for it, that murder probably wouldn't have got much mention at all if any; there wasn't enough newsprint to report every murder that occurred in L.A., and some murders were just naturally more interesting than others.

He got back to the office at a little after eleven o'clock, and Sergeant Lake said, sounding rather annoyed, "You've had nine phone calls about that thing in the *Times*. The secretary of the Western Cat Fanciers' Association wants to interview you for an article, and so do two people at a thing called Pet Pride. A sixth grade teacher in Montebello wants you to come lecture her class on kindness to animals. A P.R. man at a local agency has a great idea how to spot you in a TV commercial, and the rest of the citizens just called up to gush about your heroic act. The first three said they'll call back."

"*¡Ca!*" said Mendoza, also annoyed.

He disliked the routine, but it was always there to be done. He laid Marion Stromberg's address book on the desk and methodically began to call every name listed. There weren't all that many; and along with the names of personal friends, she had listed alphabetically the service companies she had dealt with: TV repairs, plumber, electrician, tree service, gardener, beauty shop. Indiscriminately he called them all, missing a few; he broke for lunch, came back to try for those he'd missed.

At two o'clock he was sitting back thinking about it, and in reflex action had got out the cards from the top drawer and was practicing stacking a poker deck. Domesticity had ruined his poker game, but he still thought better with the cards in his hands. Possibly one reason that Luis Rodolfo Vicente Mendoza was a reasonably good detective was that essentially, as Hackett had told him, his mind had all the deviousness of a criminal mind to start with.

The essential question, of course, was where the hell the woman had been between eight and ten on Friday night. And without much doubt they would know that if they knew who she'd phoned from the Brown Derby, but that was past praying for. Nobody she knew—and he hadn't missed many—had seen her or talked to her on Friday. Or, of course, said they hadn't. But all her female friends—acquaintances—the same kind: there hadn't been enough real feeling there for any animosity, had there?

But she had gone somewhere, alone or with someone, and had at least two more drinks. And where the hell her car had got to. . . .

Hackett and Higgins came in at two-thirty and announced that they'd finally run Bobby Porter to earth and had him stashed in jail. Hackett was still typing a report on that when Palliser and Landers came in and laid the new case in front of Mendoza. There wasn't, of course, anywhere to go on it, much to do, until and unless Linda Carr regained consciousness and told them what had happened to her. Landers said, "We want to talk to the girls on the same shift with her. Hear about the discarded boy friend. But on the face of it, it looks as if she was snatched off that bus-stop bench that night. All I say is, I don't think it was at random."

"I never said it was," said Palliser.

"You will both make detectives yet." Mendoza was shuffling the cards in his long strong hands, cigarette in mouth-corner. "If she'd just been snatched, mauled and raped, and left in the street, I'd say it was the random thing. But keeping her prisoner for a month—¡ay de mí!—I think it had to be a personal motive. No, there's not much we can do unless she can tell us about it. Have you checked the hospital?".

"She's still unconscious," said Landers.

"Jase and Rich," said Higgins through a yawn, "got interested in that Reynolds thing at the inquest and are going back over all Nick's reports. I think they're working it from scratch."

And then Lake came down the hall and said that Mr. Jackman was here, and stood back to let him pass into Mendoza's office.

Hackett and Higgins sat in on it.

"I don't think I've grasped this—this ghastly thing yet," said Jackman. "My sister didn't feel up to coming in—she has a slight heart condition, and you can guess how upset she is. God! Mother and Dad—they wanted to be independent as long as they could, and they got along all right, with our help, of course. And of course we checked up on them frequently. They were both well and fairly active, there was a market in walking distance, and Dad liked to have a garden. It was on account of this wedding, all of us away, that it wasn't discovered before—one of us always phoned them every day." He took off his glasses to polish them. He was a big man going bald, in a slightly shabby gray suit.

"When did you see them last?" asked Mendoza.

"It was a week ago today. I usually drove them to church—we all attend St. Mary's on Melrose—but we were leaving early Monday, busy packing and so on, and we skipped church on Sunday. Helen—my sister—had seen them on Saturday."

"Then we'll want to talk to her eventually. Had they recently mentioned any trouble or disturbance, Mr. Jackman? Prowlers, threatening phone calls?"

"Good Lord, no, why?"

"Had they said anything to you about running into any prejudice against your church?"

He stared. "In this day and age?" Mendoza told him about the message on the mirror, and he was incredulous. "Medieval," he said. And then, "But why—Mother and Dad?"

"Exactly," said Mendoza dryly. "Any number of Catholics around. We hope our laboratory will pick up something useful—fingerprints for choice. I suppose all of the family has been in the house at one time or another. They'll want your prints to compare. And I'd like you to look over the house and see if anything's missing."

"Yes, certainly. The—the bodies—"

"There'll be an autopsy, that's mandatory. We'll let you know when you can claim them."

"Yes."

"Tell me about their habits. When did they usually have an evening meal?"

"Well, since Dad retired they never had much for lunch. A sandwich. Then they'd have dinner about five o'clock."

"That pins it down to about five on Monday, then." Mrs. Guttierez had been providential. "Let me see if the lab is finished with the house," said Mendoza, "and you can look it over. I'm sorry to ask you, Mr. Jackman —it's not in a very pleasant condition—but it has to be done."

"Yes, all right," said Jackman shortly. "They owned that house since nineteen forty. I grew up there—Helen and I. God, this is. . . ."

Mendoza got S.I.D. and Horder answered. "Oh, yeah, it's all yours, Lieutenant. We left it sealed. We've picked up the hell of a lot of prints, some made in the blood. Also footprints. He walked in some of the blood, and the house being shut up and the bodies not found for four days, they'd dried as clear as a good moulage. We got some dandy pictures. It's a size nine, medium width, and it was a moccasin-type rubber sole."

"That's progress. So you'll want the family's prints for comparison?"

"I don't think we need 'em. When we've got prints in the blood, that identifies X pretty damn plain. The writing on the mirror, by the way, was black spray paint, the kind used on wrought iron. I can hunt down the brand for you if it's necessary."

"The wonders of science. Good. If you should come across a match for the prints in our files I trust you'll let us know."

"Oh, the dishes. There was a casserole of some kind with tunafish and mushrooms in it, and canned peas, and tapioca pudding."

"That doesn't matter now, but thanks. We can go to the house now if you'd like, Mr. Jackman." Mendoza put the phone down.

"I suppose I'd better get it over," said Jackman thinly.

It was still trying to make up its mind to rain again, chill and gray. Mendoza disliked being driven, but in case Jackman passed out on them they thought they'd better all go; they took Hackett's new Monte Carlo, and they were so used to the thing by now that it never occurred to them that Jackman might find it garish.

He didn't pass out on them. He looked around, looked at the lettering on the mirror and shook his head. The kitchen had looked only a little worse when the bodies were still there; there seemed an impossible amount of the dark brown that had been blood, and while the lab men had taken most of the spoiled food for analysis, they had left their chalk marks where the bodies had been, generous amounts of fingerprint powder all over everything.

Jackman just said, "God," again. "I'll have to get this —cleaned up somehow—before Helen sees it."

"If you'd just have a quick look for anything missing." Mendoza doubted very much that the killer had stolen anything here, but they had to know. Jackman started through the house; they heard him opening and shutting drawers, and presently he came to them in the living room and said heavily, "There's nothing gone that I can see. Of course there wasn't anything very valuable to steal. You—are finished in the house? I've got a key, of course. I suppose—I can hire somebody to come in and clean."

When they came out, Mendoza said, "*Un momento*, Art. I'll be three minutes." It was a dark afternoon, and there were lights in the house next door. He went up to the porch and rang the bell. In a moment little Mrs. Burroughs came to the door, and said, "Oh, it's you."

"Just one question for you, Mrs. Burroughs. What time were you at the market on Monday afternoon?"

She said, "Why—" and a man came up behind her, a round-shouldered middle-sized man in shabby clothes. "This is my husband, he's off today. It's the police officer I told you about, Harry."

He nodded at Mendoza. He looked tired, not just at the moment but as if it was a permanent state, and he was defeated by life in general. Mendoza reflected that driving a city bus was not likely to be a euphoric career. "Awful thing next door," he said.

"What happened," she told Mendoza, "I was starting to get dinner, and I remembered I was out of coffee. There was time before Harry got home, it's only a block up to the market. I left about half-past four and as long as I was there I went on and did a little shopping, it was about twenty of six when I got back."

"That's exactly the answer I expected," said Mendoza. "Thanks so much."

Tonight Bob Schenke was holding down the night watch alone; it was Piggott's night off. Friday night was usually quiet, and he had an interesting book; he was annoyed when he got a call at nine-fifteen.

It was a block of stores out on Wilshire, five store-fronts in the same building, and Patrolman Paulsen was in front of the end one, with a little crowd of people around him. He came to meet Schenke and said, "There are two bodies, sir, and it looks funny—"

"What?" said Schenke. Well, sometimes things came along fast and furious, but it was rather surprising, the first week of cold weather when the pace usually slowed down.

"One of them's the cleaning woman, and the other one I'd guess is the store owner. Those are the cleaning people," said Paulsen, who was rather a new rookie. "They clean all these places here every Friday night. They've got a van out back. It's the Service-Kleen Company. When the rest of them were finished, they came to get this woman—girl. Consuela Rivera. She was cleaning in the music store there. And they found her —them. Say they didn't hear a thing, but the building looks pretty solid."

Schenke said, "I'll take a look."

The five stores, or shops, housed a tax service, a woman's dress shop, an answering service, a health-food store, and the music store. SANFORD-NEWTON MUSIC, said the sign on the window. The front door was open. "They did that from inside, sir. They came in the back from the alley."

"Damn," said Schenke. Stupid civilians. He went in. The music store was long and fairly narrow. The lights were all on. At the right side in front was a cramped office space closed off with wood-and-glass partitions, and in the doorway of it was crumpled the body of a man. He was a thin man about forty-five, in neat sports clothes; he had a little black moustache. He was lying half propped up against a tall steel filing case just outside the office door. His jacket was pulled up under him and the corner of a billfold showed in that hip pocket. Schenke prodded it out delicately and opened it on a driver's license for Richard L. Sanford of an address on Poinsettia in Hollywood. He walked up the store, past racks of records and tapes, counters and shelves bearing sound equipment, tape recorders, stereo components, and past a door at the back labeled EMPLOYEES ONLY, came to a store-room and the two rest rooms side by side. There was a back door onto an alley, standing ajar. The second body was just outside the door of the women's rest room. It was the body of a very pretty young woman, and most of her clothes had been torn off, were lying scattered around. She was lying on her back with her legs spread apart and knees slightly flexed.

Schenke read the story almost at a glance. He looked out the back door. The narrow alley, with a white van parked a little way down, was between the block of stores and the backs of apartment buildings on the next street. He looked at the girl again. She had a mass of black wavy hair, a warm olive skin. Pity, he thought. About twenty-five.

He went back outside and called in to the lab. Nearly every bureau at LAPD worked round the clock; the felons kept weird hours. Duke was there, said they'd be up. Schenke went over to the silent little crowd huddled together. "O.K., somebody tell it from the start." There was a man and three women; the women all looked older than the girl; the man was tall and thin, in a white jumpsuit.

"Yes, *sir*," he said. "I'm Clarence Stiggs. We're from Service-Kleen, we hit this block every Friday night—you know how cleaning services do? Well, the jobs are all bunched together like—one office building or line of stores like this. We been cleaning here about three years. We do these places, and then we go on to another bunch of stores on Beverly. Tomorrow night we—but I guess that don't matter." He swallowed nervously. The women, looking scared, herded together silently.

"Go on," said Schenke.

They usually landed here, Stiggs said, about six-thirty. They met at the Service-Kleen office on Melrose, and all the crews—dozens of crews, he said, it was a big business—took the vans to the jobs. Here, each of them cleaned one place. It didn't take very long, about two hours. They dusted, vacuumed carpets, cleaned the bathrooms, put up new toilet paper and paper towels. By about eight-fifteen they'd be finished, meet at the van out back. But Consuela hadn't showed, and after a while he went in the music store looking for her. He found her. He called the police from there.

Schenke nodded. "None of you heard anything? Heard her cry out—any sound?"

"No, *sir*. If I'd heard her scream or anything I'd have gone to see what the matter was, naturally. But I was up in the tax office, other end. And some of the time we was running vacuums."

"O.K.," said Schenke. "You'll all have to come in to make statements. Tomorrow if you can make it. The Robbery-Homicide office at headquarters. Do you know Miss Rivera's address?"

One of the women volunteered, "It's Mrs. It's Boyd Street."

"O.K. You can go now, but don't forget the statements." They dispersed reluctantly, heading down the side street for the alley. The lab truck slid up to the curb behind the squad car, and Duke's lanky figure got out of it.

"What have you got?"

"Open and shut," said Schenke. "But likely, unless you can give us something concrete, we'll never know who or make a legal charge."

He thought he knew exactly what had happened here, even before he called Sanford's wife to break the news—if there was a wife. The store owner here late, maybe working on the books. The killer either having spotted the girl before, working here (those apartment back yards) or just coming along the alley while she was working at the back. Coming in and attacking her. And the girl making some sort of noise, loud enough to reach Sanford, not loud enough to reach the other stores. The killer knocking the girl right out. Running up front— Sanford had probably called out—to deal with Sanford, who was in the doorway of the office. The lights wouldn't have been on then—he'd bet the stupid civilians had done that. And knocking Sanford down, unaware he'd killed him against that sharp-cornered filing case. Going back to rape the girl.

He didn't need to spell that out to the lab men Duke

and Parry. They'd seen a lot of homicides and rapes too. But at the sight of the girl, Duke stopped and said gravely, "Whee!"

"Yes, she's stacked, but she's also dead," said Schenke, slightly shocked.

"I didn't mean that kind of whee," said Duke. He looked at Parry. "Have we got everything we need?"

"I'll go look. I expect so. You and Scarne have been on the kick long enough."

"You," said Duke to Schenke, "go back and write the report. We'll call the morgue wagon—in about three hours. They can't have this one for a long, long time."

"You're going in for necrophilia?"

"Oh, my, what long words you use, Grandma. No, we're going to print the body. Such a nice naked body."

"What the hell?" said Schenke. "You can't get prints off—"

"Oh, yes, we can," said Duke. "Now. A smart lab cop in Florida figured out a way, just a little while back. Pretty simple in a way. You have to use a fiberglass filament brush, lifting tape naturally, and Kromekote cards—140 by 178 millimeter—it's kind of like photographic printing paper—"

"I'll take your word for it," said Schenke hastily. "I'll go and write the report. After breaking the bad news."

The report was waiting for them on Saturday, with Landers off, Lake off and Farrell sitting on the switchboard. "No rest for the wicked," said Mendoza. The autopsy report on Leta Reynolds was in, but didn't tell them anything they didn't know.

Palliser called the hospital. Linda Carr was still unconscious, but they thought she was responding better.

There was nowhere to go on the female heister. The Bullock's job was tacitly filed away.

Hackett had seen enough homicides to read between the lines of Schenke's report; Mendoza passing it over to him, he passed it on to Higgins. "Bob got hold of his wife, I see." Before she had broken down, she had told Schenke that Sanford had stayed at the store late to work on the books. He and his partner, Frank Newton, owned two music stores; Newton ran the other one. Just a coincidence Sanford was there when the rapist walked in on the girl.

Higgins laid the report down and swore roundly. "All the legwork, hunting the rapists out of records! And try to pin one down legally!"

Farrell buzzed Mendoza. "Say," he said, "I meant to say I saw that shot of you in the *Times*. Evidently some other people did too. I've got a Dr. Adam Fuller on the line who wants to talk to you. He's the editor of some magazine called *The Cat Fancy*, which strikes me as sounding backward, and he wants you to write an article about saving that cat in the fire."

"No," said Mendoza. "I'm not here. I'm investigating the murder of a *Times* reporter. I wish to God I was."

"Well, all right," said Farrell. "But if you want to know, I think it was sort of heroic at that. I like cats myself." He sounded embarrassed, and rang off abruptly.

"*¡Por mi vida!*" said Mendoza.

"Look," said Hackett reasonably, "the legwork's always to do, George. If it wasn't rapists, it'd be heisters. We're waiting on the lab, on the Jackman thing. We might as well start the damn routine on the new one."

The phone rang and Mendoza picked it up. "Mrs. Robsen," said Farrell noncommittally.

"I just wanted to let you know," said Cathy Robsen,

"that the funeral's set for Monday. The chapel at Rose Hills. I—sort of got together with the lawyer on it."

"Thanks for letting us know, Mrs. Robsen."

"It doesn't matter," she said, "if none of you can make it. They're not *there.* I just thought I'd let you know."

"Yes, thanks." Mendoza relayed that. "Damn it, I'll have to go."

"It's raining again," said Higgins, looking out the window as drops began to hit the glass. "Damnation."

The phone rang. "Yes, Rory?" said Mendoza.

"I've got your wife now."

"I'm sorry to call," said Alison, "but I thought I'd better ask. I've been rather an expense to you lately, *mi marido favorito.* Ken just called. He's found the sheep. He wants to get five, and they're sixty dollars each. They're Suffolks, and they're what he calls wethers, if that means anything to you."

"*Nada absolutamente.* That's three hundred on top of the ponies. All right."

"Think how pastoral they'll look on the hill," said Alison. "They're such gentle creatures, Luis. Meek and mild."

Later on, Mendoza was to quote that to her bitterly. At the moment he said only, "Well, in for a penny, in for a pound. He'd better get the sheep."

Both the Landerses were off on Saturday. "I ought," said Phil, "to be getting at the laundry—changing the bed."

"There's time. You been thinking about what I said, being a fulltime wife?"

"We can't afford it," said Phil.

"They give you a leave of absence for maternity."

"And then we'd have to pay a babysitter. If we do, I'd rather make it permanent, Tom. Just quit and stay home. Only, could we make it?"

"We'll take a look at the accounts later," said Landers.

"I hope," said Hackett, "you've polished up the crystal ball?"

Mendoza stood in the hall of that colorless, faintly elegant house on Beachwood Drive. He said, "Damn it, she must have been something more than the correct, conventional, cardboard character we've heard about."

"Some people are just like that, Luis."

"On the surface. Most people have something underneath."

"Where else can you look?" Hackett sighed. He had been following Mendoza around for an hour. It was four o'clock, and the rain was steadily drumming down. Mendoza had been wandering around the house, apparently sniffing for the essence of Marion Stromberg. He had looked through drawers in the kitchen, the den, the bedroom. At her meticulous files in the desk, receipts neatly boxed. He had contemplated her cosmetics in the bedroom and the bathroom: sniffed her colognes: Emeraude, Rive Gauche, Aphrodisia. Looked at the piles of neat nightgowns, lingerie. She'd been a fastidious woman.

Mendoza said, "Where the hell is her car? It ought to have been spotted by now."

"In somebody's garage," said Hackett.

"I wonder." Mendoza wandered back to the living room and stared at the reproduction Renoir on the wall over the couch. And then suddenly he said, "Methodical—oh, my God, of course—"

"What have you thought of now?"

"Only the last few years she'd had really nice

clothes," said Mendoza. He started down the hall. "*Natu-ralmente*. All the clothes in her closet are winter things. She'd put summer things away carefully." He went into the second, smaller, bedroom, opened the door of the walk-in closet. It was full of clothes—warm-weather clothes, dresses, sleeveless tops, light-colored slacks. "Ah."

"What do you expect to find?"

"I haven't the slightest idea." Mendoza started to go through the white handbag hanging on the door. It was empty except for some loose change. He started to go through the pockets of the clothes. Not even used handkerchiefs rewarded him, until he took down a loosely knit white cardigan. In the right-hand pocket was a slip of folded paper; he brought it out.

"What have you got?"

"A phone number," said Mendoza. "Just a phone number. Nothing to say whose."

EIGHT ═══════════════

"SO I'M WOOLGATHERING," said Mendoza. Ensconced back in his desk chair with the cards riffling through his hands, he had just requested the phone company to trace that number for him.

"Not necessarily," said Hackett. "Looking under every stone." He shifted his bulk, that was not quite so bulky as it had been, and put out his cigarette. "I ought to go and do some honest work."

The phone rang, and Farrell put Mendoza through to somebody at the morgue, who plaintively asked to know whom should be informed that the Stromberg body could be claimed. "Hell," said Mendoza thoughtfully. The lawyer was the only answer. He gave them the name and address, and then got Earnshaw at home. Earnshaw readily agreed to take care of the arrangements.

Conway, Grace and Wanda came in, and Grace said, "We'll put a difference of opinion to you. The Reynolds case—a wild one. We've been looking back at the evidence, what there is, and Rich—"

"I just say it's fairly obvious," said Conway. He sat down in the chair beside Mendoza's desk, his cynical gray eyes squinted against smoke from his cigarette.

"The husband. Who do we look at first, a husband or wife gets murdered?"

"I thought the husband was supposed to be up in Ventura," said Mendoza.

"What the hell is seventy miles?" Conway brushed the miles away with a gesture. "I think Nick slipped up a little. Look." He had a 510 report in his hand. "What did the sister say? Bright little Leta was always improving herself and learning things—the husband wasn't. We've been talking to her parents, they were dead set against the marriage because Reynolds wasn't very smart or ambitious. She was a big cut above him, and she probably let him know it. That was the reason for the divorce. Wouldn't he resent it, her patronizing him? You bet."

"He might have then," said Grace. "But this is five years later, Rich. And who do you think the woman was?"

"You're just thinking too complicated," said Wanda. She sat down in the other chair and crossed her neat legs below her uniform skirt. "What I say is that this Melinda couldn't possibly recognize the woman. She admits she only saw her for about two seconds, and hadn't any reason to notice her at the time. She couldn't possibly be positive about anyone. I think it's very possible Nick's right and it could be that Armstrong woman."

"And I'll go along with that," said Grace. "At least I think we'd better talk to her. See what she looks like."

"All I say is—" began Conway.

Mendoza shook his head at him. "I don't buy the husband either, Rich. If we can make any guess about Reynolds, it was an irrational motive. Nothing very realistic. Nick got that far."

Farrell came in and said there was a Frank Newton

to see him. Mendoza looked exasperated and put the cards away. Conway, Grace and Wanda drifted out, and Hackett said, "Preserve patience for the civilians, *compadre.*"

"Waste of time," complained Mendoza. Newton came in and looked around the office, at the two of them, with a faintly apologetic air. He was a big man with somewhat florid good looks, curly graying hair, a strong nose, a mobile mouth; he wore a natty sports outfit. He said, "I suppose I'm intruding on you, I don't know one damned thing about this damned— I couldn't believe it when Sylvia finally got me awhile ago—Dick murdered! Dick! And that cleaning woman—my God, Dick and I've been partners eleven years! I came to ask you, if it's not a secret—how the hell did it happen? Why?" At an invitation he sat down abruptly beside the desk.

"It looks as if it was just a coincidence that Mr. Sanford was there when the girl was attacked," said Mendoza. "One of those things, Mr. Newton."

"God," said Newton. His eyes were somber. "Of all the Goddamned bad luck. I couldn't believe it. Sylvia never got hold of me till an hour ago—I got in a hot poker game down in Gardena, never got home till two A.M., and today I've been down in Laguna with my ex-wife, we're sort of thinking of getting together again." He ran distracted fingers through his hair. "I suppose you know your business, but how in hell do you hunt a wild man like that? How d'you know where to look? Doesn't seem to me you'd have a chance in hell. I talked to him Thursday, just business, and if I'd known it was the last time— Good thing we can't know things, I suppose." He lighted a cigarette. "We ran two stores, you know—I manage the other one, over on Sunset. I can't get over the damned bad luck, him just happening to be there at night—"

"We hope the lab may give us something concrete to point to somebody," said Hackett. "Fingerprints possibly. Were you in the Wilshire store much, Mr. Newton?"

"What? Oh, maybe once a week. We'd interchange merchandise, if somebody wanted something he didn't have and I did—why?"

"You'd better let our lab have your fingerprints for comparison, if you don't mind."

"Com— Oh, I get you. Sure," said Newton.

"And any employees—did anyone else work in the Wilshire store?"

"Yes, he has—had—a clerk, Susan Adams. She's been off sick with the flu all week. When I talked to him Thursday he was kicking about it, he was run off his feet there all alone. It's a damn good thing," said Newton suddenly, "she didn't walk in to open up this morning— Sylvia'd never have thought to call her. I don't know her address, but it ought to be somewhere in the files—I can look it up for you."

"If you'd do that, please." Mendoza stood up. "It's about the end of our day, Mr. Newton, if you'll excuse us. We'll hope to come up with something on it."

"Oh, sure, sure. God, I hope you do—I hope you get him." He was apologetic again. "I know I'm just wasting your time. Where do I go to get my prints taken? Anything I can do to help—"

Hackett told him how to get down to S.I.D., and after he'd gone phoned down to tell them he was on the way. Farrell had already left. Mendoza picked up his hat and they went out together.

For once Mendoza got in early on Sunday. There had been two more heists overnight, one at a bar, one of a couple getting off a bus late on Olympic Boulevard. Everybody was out on the legwork, hunting for the heisters and the rapists from records.

The phone company had come up with the trace on that phone number. It was registered to Ronald Truepenny at an address on Ardmore in Hollywood. "*¿Y qué es esto?*" said Mendoza to himself. Five minutes after he'd come in he went out again, and drove up to Hollywood in the very slight rain.

It was a garden apartment built around a pool. He walked around the rectangle of front doors facing on the pool; halfway around he found TRUEPENNY in a name slot, and shoved the bell. He shoved it four times before a bleary-eyed young man with an unshaven face, clutching a bathrobe around him, opened the door. He looked at the badge in astonishment and said, yawning, that he'd never heard of Marion Stromberg. "Crack of dawn, cops coming," he said. "Sherry, you know a Marion Stromberg?"

A pretty red-haired woman in a fleece robe came to join him. "I knew a Mary Stromberg in school. For heaven's sakes, a cop? You?"

"Your phone number was among her effects."

"Oh. Well, we only moved in here last month. Took over the phone. Couldn't tell you who was here before. Your girl could have known 'em, I suppose."

The cardigan where he had found the memo slip was a summer-weight one. She might not have worn it since last June. Mendoza apologized and looked to see if there was a manageress on the premises.

There was. She listened to his questions and said briefly, "The Beckwiths. They left because they were getting a divorce, and she's well rid of him. Last six months he was out of a job, and her supporting them

[180]

sewing—she did a lot of expert alteration work for The Broadway and private clients."

¿Qué mono? said Mendoza to himself. Another little ride on the merry-go-round. The phone number of the obliging seamstress, probably lengthening a hem, altering a new summer dress for Marion.

Her car still hadn't been located. He went back to the office and, as he came in, suddenly wondered if the lab had got anything from her clothes. There hadn't been any report. He called S.I.D. and got Marx. "Well, there wasn't anything to report," he said. "Nothing on the clothes but what you'd expect, flecks of her face powder, couple of her own hairs. And by the way, those prints from the Jackman house aren't in our records, we passed them on to the Feds." That, of course, was the little catch about fingerprints: if they weren't in anybody's records they were no use at all. "Just a minute, Duke's got something for you."

Mendoza started to say he thought Duke was on night shift, but the phone hummed at him. Then Duke came on and said happily, "Oh, we've got something pretty for you, Lieutenant. Did you know there's a whole new process for lifting prints from a dead body? It's not quite foolproof yet—Scarne and I've been practicing every chance we get for a couple of months, and it's damned interesting. It's a matter of the pores contracting at death, and you've got to use special equipment—these Kromekote cards—"

"Yes? So what have you got?"

"Some lovely clear prints off that rape victim on Friday night. One from her upper left arm, three from her left thigh. I've been doing some overtime, processing all we got. The rest of 'em aren't clear enough to make much of, but these are beautiful."

"Congratulations. If they show up in records—"

"I'm just going down to look." Duke sounded pleased with himself.

Mendoza swiveled around and stared at the gray sky out the window. It suddenly further occurred to him that he'd never looked up that parson, Whitlow, and his Good Samaritans. But, as per Miss Retzinger, he didn't suppose Marion Stromberg had spent any time that Thursday night chatting with a well-meaning minister. That was one thing they had all told him, all the people who had known her: she wasn't at all interested in religion; if she wasn't an atheist she was at least an agnostic. And if there was one thing he felt certain of, it was that Marion Stromberg hadn't lingered in the foyer of the Brown Derby to make a phone call to the Reverend Whitlow.

Linda Carr was still unconscious. Palliser and Landers, having spent the morning looking for rapists out of records, got to the Denny's on La Brea just after the two o'clock shift came on, to talk to the girls she had worked with.

The three girls who had just come in, Joan Tenney, Sandra Moore, and Ruth Hobbs, were excited and upset over what had happened to Linda. They were nice, ordinary girls, and they told Palliser and Landers this and that. The former boy friend wouldn't have done anything like that, they said. His name was Marvin King, he worked for a Ford agency up the block, and there hadn't been anything serious between them.

"But we've been thinking about something else," said Ruth, her eyes big and serious and admiring on Palliser, who was a good-looking man. "There are always guys coming in, try to make up to you—mostly it doesn't mean much, they're just kidding. Once in awhile you get one gives you a hard time, but Mr. Sorenson won't put up with anything real annoying. It's not as if we got the drunks coming in, not having a liquor license. But there was a fellow really got across Linda—she could put a guy down without any trouble usually, you know, just pass it off, but that one really bugged her. I'd have been a little scared of him myself."

"Who was he?"

"Who knows?" said Joan. "We've been talking about it. He used to come in around one or one-thirty, three or four times a week. He's a great big guy, with dark hair and funny eyes—kind of intense-looking. He acted like he really went for Linda, kept asking her for a date. He gave her a hard time, and she finally said if he bothered her again she'd get Mr. Sorenson to kick him out. Only he hadn't done anything really, you know, and you can't just throw customers out—I suppose Mr. Sorenson'd just have talked to him."

"He just came in off the street as a customer?" asked Palliser.

Sandra said, "I'm pretty sure I saw him once in one of those big Arrowhead trucks. A lot of places around here buy the Arrowhead water. One of their delivery trucks—it was parked down the street and I saw him get into it."

They didn't know anything more, and of course there was no reason to follow that up. But it was interesting.

They went back to the office to collect another handful of names from records, and came in just in time to take a call from Sergeant Bill Costello.

"Well, you told us," he said bitterly. "We've been round and round on it, Palliser. Even went through all Robinsons' employment records, turned the security guards inside out, and it's all a great big blank. In and

[183]

out they went, just like at Bullock's, and how they got the inside dope doesn't matter—there are just no loose ends to take hold of. And incidentally, harking back to your ghost, nobody with the M.W. initials, up to six months ago anyway."

"We run up against these things," said Palliser. "File it and forget it. Nothing else to do."

"Well, it was an idea," said Galeano philosophically.

"In theory, quite a good idea," said Grace. Galeano was driving; Grace sat back and lighted a cigarette, and his lean regular-featured chocolate-brown face wore slight amusement. "When you come down to it, Nick, most people are ordinary, reasonably honest and sane people—maybe because we see so many of the other kind, we expect to find them where they aren't."

Galeano just hunched his shoulders.

They had found the Armstrong house empty and were debating whether to wait or come back, when the woman drove up in a Chevy sedan and went into the house. They waited three minutes and rang the bell, introduced themselves, and she asked them in.

"What can I do for the police?" she asked, smiling. "Sit down, won't you?" She was a big woman with a warm smile.

"It's about Leta Reynolds," said Grace in his soft voice.

The smile vanished. "Oh, dear, that's a dreadful thing. Such a nice girl, Herbert said, and a good retoucher too. A pretty girl too, I'd seen her several times at the store. But I couldn't tell you anything about what happened." She was puzzled at their coming; she looked from Grace to Galeano. "Did you want to see Herbert?

[184]

He stayed on at the church to discuss something with the Reverend Farley."

"We were wondering," said Grace disarmingly, "if you minded your husband working with such a pretty young woman, Mrs. Armstrong."

"If I—" She stared at him. It dawned on her slowly what was in their minds and, at first, indignation hardened her expression and then she began to laugh. "You don't mean you're thinking that I—"

"When Mrs. Reynolds was first working for your husband," said Galeano, "she thought she might have a little trouble with him, she'd said. Being a little too friendly."

"Now that is too much!" she said. "You two listen to me and use some sense. Naturally Herbert appreciates a pretty girl as much as any man. But he's a good Christian. For the Lord's sake, we've got four grown children and Herbert's a deacon in our church! Just when was this girl killed?—last Monday morning—well, I was out shopping with my daughter Maureen from about ten till three in the afternoon, and if you think I've ever touched a gun in my life—"

Now Galeano said, "We missed lunch, Jase."

"So we did. Let's stop somewhere."

Hackett and Higgins were in one interrogation room talking to a possible rapist, and Grace and Galeano in another talking to a possible heister, at three o'clock. It was still sprinkling. Mendoza was smoking and shuffling the cards, and Lake had just come in to say, "It slipped my mind—Jackman called to say his sister had a slight heart attack, she's in the hospital."

"Damn," said Mendoza. He wanted to talk to the woman.

"Oh, she's going to be all right in a day or two."

"I got to talk to somebody here!" said a loud desperate voice. "Isn't nobody here? The sergeant downstairs said Robbery-Homicide—"

Lake and Mendoza went out together. Standing beside the switchboard was a tall youngish Negro. Normally he'd have been rather handsome; he had sharp Semitic features, he was medium black, he had broad shoulders; but he looked to be in a state of shock. "It's about a murder!" he said. "I got to tell you!"

"Calm down," said Mendoza. "Come in here." He got him to sit down in Hackett's desk chair. "Now what's it all about? I'm Lieutenant Mendoza. And you?"

"L-L-L— She shot Leta!" he said. "Oh, my God, and I didn't believe it! But I had to come—I had to come and tell you—" He gave a great sigh suddenly, and sagged in the chair limply. "I suppose I should've got ten traffic tickets—gettin' down here. I left Ventura—I don't know what time. I had to come and tell you."

Mendoza snapped to attention. He said, "Jimmy, fetch us some coffee, will you? And rout out everybody. I have a little idea we're about to hear an interesting story."

The coffee seemed to revive Len Reynolds somewhat. He calmed down a little, but he was still excited and upset. He looked at them, grouped around Hackett's desk there, and it was easy to see why the pretty and personable Leta had fallen for him; he was good-looking and his brown eyes were gentle and honest. "Oh, my Lord," he said. He finished the coffee and asked if he could have another cup; Galeano went down the hall to the coffee machine.

"Take your time," said Mendoza, offering him a cigarette.

[186]

Reynolds took a long deep breath, held it and let it out. "Thanks," he said to Galeano, and sipped coffee, took a drag on the cigarette. "I've got to—tell you how it was. I don't know if you know I've been up in Ventura. I went to night school after Leta and m—I broke up, she always said I ought to, and I got my diploma, and I passed the post office test. I got a good job up there as a carrier. And I've got an apartment. I've been there a couple of years. Well, about four-five months ago this girl moved into the apartment next to me. Betty Simms her name is. We'd said hello and nice day and like that, but she's no looker and it never crossed my mind to ask her for a date, look twice at her. You got to believe that! I never did. I think she's got a job waiting on table somewhere. But she's an awful pushy girl and she's been trying to make up to me every which way, all the while she's been there. God knows I never did n—anything to make her think— I've been real rude to her a lot of times lately, I didn't like doing that because I don't like to be mean, but—" he drank more coffee— "she's been a real pest. Bringing me cakes and asking me to her place for dinner— I was going to move just to get away from her, only thing to do. My God—but I didn't think she was a real nut. Only she's got to be—she's got to be."

He finished the coffee and cigarette, and got out cigarettes of his own. His hands were shaking. "I was— I—I don't work Sundays, acourse. I was sitting in the living room—looking at TV—about noon it was, when she came over. She never seemed to notice when I wasn't polite, she said she'd baked a cake for me—she was all smiles, just pushed right in. I said I didn't want it, I was busy, and she tried—she tried to put her arms around me—and she said, after what she done for me I ought to be nicer to her—she said—oh, my God—she said

[187]

she knew it was hard for me to pay that money to Leta all the time, so she'd come down here and killed her so I wouldn't have to pay her any more—"

"*¡Santa Maria!*" said Mendoza.

"I laughed at her! I thought she was crazy. I said how could she do that, and she got mad and said she had so. She got in my apartment and found Leta's address and— She went and got a gun and showed it to me." Reynolds' expression was part anger and part bewilderment. "A little bitty gun, it looked like a kid's play gun. But when she kept saying it—my God. I shoved her out and I bolted the door, and then I called Leta's folks—and they told me—told me about—" He put his head in his hands.

"My God," said Hackett.

"There was something wild about it all along," said Galeano. "A real nut you can say—"

Mendoza got up. "Jimmy, get me a line to the Ventura P.D."

Len Reynolds was suddenly crying. Unashamed, he brought out a handkerchief and mopped his eyes. "Leta *dead*," he said. "That crazy pushy girl. Not as if I'd ever—thought of her like that. Leta. I—I feel as if I'd killed her myself, you know? I never had anything against Leta—she was the nicest, sweetest girl I ever knew—I wasn't good enough for her, was all. And now—and now—" He blew his nose, got himself under a little control. "I'll never go back to that place again. That girl—"

Mendoza was talking to somebody at the Ventura police station.

About four o'clock Sanders called and talked to Palliser. He thought there was a chance that Linda Carr was about to regain consciousness. If she did, it might not be for long. Landers came in while they were on the phone, and he and Palliser left the suspect rapist waiting in an interrogation room and rushed over to the hospital.

She was moving restlessly in the high bed, and a nurse was standing by to see she didn't disturb the I.V. needle. She was moaning a little.

"Her pulse is better," said Sanders. He bent over the bed. "Linda! Linda, can you hear me?"

She stopped moaning and lay still for a few moments. Then her eyes opened—blank eyes, wide and blue. Palliser pushed Sanders aside and took his place. "Linda," he said quietly, "I'm a police officer. Can you tell us who hurt you?"

Slowly the eyes tried to focus on him. She said in a thick drowsy voice, "Didn't—kill self—after all."

"Linda. Who hurt you?"

She let out a little sigh. "Mike," she said. "Mike." She turned her face on the pillow and fell asleep; but her breath was coming easily, regularly.

The Hoffman funeral was at ten o'clock on Monday morning. Out of a sense of duty, Mendoza went to it. The only other people there were the men from the Hollenbeck station, some of their wives. And Cathy Robsen, sitting in a back row. The three caskets were closed, and it was a brief formal ceremony, with no graveside service.

Mendoza got back to the office at eleven-thirty, and Lake said, "They waited for you to open the ball."

In his office Hackett and Higgins were talking with a stocky blond man in a rumpled-looking gray suit. He got up as Mendoza came in and offered a hand. "You'll be the boss. I'm Roy Dodd, I talked to you yesterday.

[189]

We picked her up just where you told us, and I drove her down this morning. This is the damndest thing I ever ran across. The damndest. I didn't question her. Your baby."

Betty Simms was standing looking out the window. She was a big girl, broad-shouldered and broad-hipped and heavy-bosomed. She was wearing a bright-red wool dress and black high-heeled shoes. "Oh, we checked her car as you asked. It's a white Nova about eight years old."

"*De veras*," said Mendoza, watching her. She turned around. She was black, with a round plain face, broad lips, round little eyes under a bulging forehead.

"We also," said Dodd, "found the gun." He took it out of his pocket and laid it on Mendoza's desk: a tiny thing barely four inches long.

"Who're you?" she asked Mendoza.

He told her. "Sit down, Miss Simms. We've got some questions for you."

"All because he had to go and tell you," she said. "I never thought he'd do that. It was stupid, real stupid. I told him, he oughta be grateful to me, get him out of all that trouble—so he wouldn't have to pay her no more." She ran her tongue over her lips. "Nobody should tell the fuzz nothing, I thought anybody knows that. Then we could get married, see? Every girl wants to get married."

"Did you think Len wanted to marry you?"

"Well, I heard him bitch 'n' bitch to Mr. Chapman, he's the landlord, 'bout all the money he had to pay his wife. Len's a real nice fellow—at least I thought he was—and he's got a good steady job. Be nice to have regular money, if we got married and had some kids. That's what I always wanted, a nice fellow and some kids. But there was all that money he had to pay her. I thought, you know, if she was dead he wouldn't have to, and we could get married."

"Did he ever ask you to marry him?" asked Mendoza.

She simpered a little. "Oh, not in so many words, but a girl can always tell."

"How did you know where to find Mrs. Reynolds?"

"*I* was goin' to be Mrs. Reynolds. That was easy. I went in Len's apartment once and looked in the little book where he keeps people's addresses. Do you know he's got a picture of her in his apartment? I suppose it's to remind him how terrible it was bein' married to her."

"Like to tell us just how you did it?"

"I don't care," she said. "I had that little gun, I got it to protect myself when I was livin' in San Francisco, in the city. A girl's got to be careful, 'specially when she's pretty. I just phoned Mr. Shapiro, he's the boss where I work, I was sick and couldn't come in, and I drove down here and found the house. Twenty-seventh Street, and the number. I thought up the idea about the Avon lady on the way down. I used to know a girl sold Avon things. She didn't want to let me in, but I sort of went in anyway. And she said about not havin' time look at anything but I went all the way in and then I shot her with the gun."

"You know, Betty," said Mendoza—he was perched on the corner of his desk, gently swinging one ankle—"those payments Len was making weren't alimony. They were child support, for the little girl."

She turned up astonished eyes. "They was? You sure?" She looked disgusted. "And I *saw* the kid! She was right there! I coulda shot her too, just as easy, if I'd 'a' known that!"

Dodd said something under his breath.

"It really wouldn't have made any difference," said Mendoza. "Len wasn't going to marry you, you know."

[191]

She looked sullen. "He might have. There've been lots 'n' lots of fellows wanted to marry me. There was another fellow I nearly married awhile back—but he wasn't as good-looking as Len." She reflected. "I wonder if I could find him again."

"You're not going to have the chance, Betty."

"Why not? Oh. Oh, I suppose you're going to put me in jail awhile for shooting her."

"That's just what. Have you ever been in jail before?"

All of a sudden she seemed to lose interest. "I don't know," she said vaguely. "I don't remember."

"My God," said Higgins.

"Sergeant Hackett's going to take you over to the jail now. But we'll be seeing you again."

"O.K.," she said. She went out with Hackett quietly.

"My good God in heaven," said Dodd. Mendoza sat down at his desk.

"She's subnormal, of course. Arrested development? They've got so many new names for everything these days. Evidently she's been able to function, earn a living —but there may be progressive deterioration. Let the head doctors fight it out."

The phone rang and he picked it up. "Yes, Jimmy?"

"You've got a call from the director of the Humane Society. He wants to invite you to be the featured guest at their annual banquet. You're getting a lot of mileage out of that cat, Lieutenant."

"*¡Válgame Dios!*" said Mendoza.

Landers called the hospital about four o'clock. Sanders sounded worried. "I don't like this protracted unconsciousness," he said. "She went off into a natural sleep and then lapsed back again. I've got a hunch it's an involuntary retreat from reality, to avoid remembering the experience she's been through."

"But how long might that go on?"

"It might go on long enough," said Sanders, "to block it off from the conscious mind entirely. She might wake up with complete amnesia about what happened, simply because it's too terrible to remember."

"But you don't know that?"

"We'll have to wait and see."

Ken Kearney called about four o'clock on Monday afternoon. "Well, we're here," he told Alison. "I had the hell of a time getting hold of a U-Haul truck to bring 'em down. The sheep ranch was to hell and gone north of Los Alamos, and I had to go all the way to Lompoc to rent a U-Haul. Thought I'd never get 'em down here, but I did. They're up on the hill now, and Kate's feeling sentimental about our first spread when we had a few." He chuckled. Kate Kearney had been starting to move their possessions into the new place for the last week. "Like to come up and take a look?"

Everybody was excited about the sheep, and it had stopped raining. Alison brought El Señor in, the other cats being in already, and bundled the twins in parkas; Mairí bundled the baby in a warm sleeper and a blanket. There wasn't room for Cedric too in the Facel-Vega, and he was left staring after them lonesomely behind the driveway gate.

Up in the hills above Burbank, they left the last streets behind and wended up the blacktop road, with the twins asking excited questions. Would the sheep be girls or boys? Did they have names? Would they play like Cedric? Would they come in the house?

"No, no, lambies, sheep stay out on the hills where they belong."

"What are wethers, Mairí?" asked Alison.

"Well, *achara*, ah, mmh," said Mairí with an eye on the twins, "they'll be gentlemen sheep that can't have lambs."

"Oh," said Alison amusedly. "Very sensible of Ken. We wouldn't want lambs running all around every spring."

"We could then," said Mairí. "Twa or three nice lambs would butcher verra well, and home-bred lamb is far and away tastier than what you get at the market."

"Eat your own lambs? After seeing them running around? I couldn't."

"*Mamacita*, are we gonna eat the sheepses?" asked Terry uneasily.

"No, no, darling. The sheep are just for fun."

At that moment the gate came into view, their own iron gate of the entrance to *La Casa de la Gente Feliz*, and just beyond them in the new blacktop drive was Ken Kearney's car attached to a U-Haul trailer. He was standing beside it, tall and loose-limbed, and his little plump robin of a wife was standing beside him. Up on the hillside—the house was beyond the crest of the hill—were five white creatures loosely bunched together.

He came and opened the gate, shut it after the car. "Oh, they're pretty!" said Alison, surprised. The sheep she'd remembered vaguely were the thin, grayish, dingy sheep in Mexico, hopelessly foraging on thin pasture. These creatures were white and plump and woolly, and at her voice a couple of them *baaa*ed at her and started down the hill toward the humans. They had black faces and ears, and they looked absurdly as if they were wearing black silk stockings and high-heeled black shoes.

[194]

Their dainty slender legs looked too frail to support their bodies.

"They don't butt things, do they?" she asked.

"No, no. This must be the two were bottle-raised, the mother couldn't feed all four. They're tame as dogs." They came up *baaa*ing, and Alison felt the smooth black heads, the curled matted wool.

"Oh, they're darling. Look, Terry, Johnny—feel how soft!"

"Och, they do put me in mind of my own Highlands!" said Mairí sentimentally. "The dear wee black faces! Our Scottish sheep are nae sa' big, o' course. These are grand beasts, Mr. Kearney."

"What are their names?" he was repeating to Terry's insistent query. "Well, now, I don't know as they've got any names, Terry."

"But they got to have names. Everything's got names."

"They're graceful sort o' beasts in spite of their shapes," said Mairí. "To see a sheep houplin' ower a hill is a fine graceful sight. Och, it does put me in mind—"

"They're the Five Graces," said Alison with a laugh. "That's what we'll call them, Terry." The other three sheep were grazing contentedly a little way up the hill; she patted the silky smooth head so close against her knee. "They must have had very good care to be so tame." There was a sharp tearing sound and she staggered at a sudden pull.

"I should've warned you," said Kearney. "Now get away, you!"

The sheep so confidentially responding to Alison's patting had eaten a large piece out of her tweed skirt. She looked at it in dismay and then laughed. "I suppose it was attracted to the wool."

[195]

"That's a shame," said Kate Kearney, "a good skirt like that. It's not only wool. It's queer the things they will eat."

Kearney was explaining about the wool to the twins. "These were just born in February—they'll be due for a first shearing in April. Their nice wool coats are cut off, you see, and they'll be all clean and cool for the summer."

Terry said, "No. They gonna keep their fur coats." She was very decisive about it.

The A.P.B. had still not turned up Marion Stromberg's car in a full week.

The warrant came through on Betty Simms; but in all probability the psychiatric examination would take some time, and in the end she'd be committed to Camarillo.

The prints Duke and Scarne had so painstakingly lifted from the body of Consuela Rivera weren't in L.A.'s records. They had been sent to the F.B.I.

The autopsy report on the Jackmans had come in late Monday. All it told them was that the knife used had a blade about nine inches long, tapering from an inch to one-eighth of an inch. He had been stabbed forty-eight times, she fifty-three. There was more detail, but it didn't mean a great deal.

The P.R. man with the idea for a TV commercial had called back several times. When Mendoza went out to lunch on Tuesday with Hackett and Higgins, he was waiting to waylay Mendoza on the top step of the front entrance. He was a fat little man with an eager face and boundless energy. He pressed his card on Mendoza insistently. His name was Norman J. Yadkin, and he was with the Slocum-Traskins Advertising Agency.

"Look," he said, "look, Lieutenant, we did that great production for Rubinstein's new cologne—we did the Hercules luggage commercials, you must've seen those—Fantastic! Imagination, that's our specialty—we're one of the biggest outfits doing commercials in the business, because we're good, see? We've got the imagination to do *different* commercials, see?"

"I told you I'm not interested."

"But this has got to be the greatest ever, Lieutenant! You got to see it! Listen, it's the Crunchy Catty account —they got both canned and dry cat food—and the idea is this, see?" He was pattering along beside Mendoza, talking fast, while Hackett and Higgins, nobly choking down mirth, strode ahead. "Now we all know how fussy cats are about what they eat, right? So O.K., we get in with the human interest right away, the sympathy of all these people love cats, by running that great shot of you saving the poor little cat from the fire—that's a beaut of a shot, Lieutenant—and then we put the spiel—It Takes a Smart Detective to Discover What Cats Like Best—and we show a shot of you, with a lot of cats eating Crunchy Catty like they're starving, see— Please, Lieutenant, you can see what a great idea—"

"If either of you say a word—" said Mendoza, violently locking the door of the Monte Carlo.

"Well, it is quite an idea," said Hackett. "You could expand it, Luis. How I Became a Veteran Detective Through Tracking Down My Cat's Opinions. Silver Boy won't look at that Crunchy Catty stuff."

"If Alison has ever bought any," said Mendoza, "she won't be buying any more. ¡Dios!"

They came back from lunch; Palliser and Landers had been questioning a possible heister and had let him go—he'd had an alibi of sorts. It wasn't raining, but it was cold and gray. They lingered in the office; there was legwork to be done, but it would probably be unprofitable.

Sergeant Lake came in with a manila envelope. Mendoza slit it open idly and slid out the contents: the autopsy reports on Dick Sanford and Consuela Rivera. Sanford had sustained a skull fracture. Same as Marion Stromberg, he thought. The filing case: that had been obvious at the scene. He passed the report to Hackett; he was perched on one corner of Hackett's desk in the big communal office. He looked at the other report.

And he said, "¿Y qué significa eso? I'll be damned."

Hackett took his glasses off and looked up. "Something?"

"Something," said Mendoza. "The Rivera girl wasn't raped. Not even an attempt."

They were all surprised. "Well, that's a funny one," said Palliser. "By all the evidence, after the killer had disposed of Sanford—he probably never realized he'd killed him—he had plenty of time to deal with the girl."

"Suppose," said Hackett, "it was about the time the other cleaning people came looking for her, and scared him off?"

"Sloppy deduction, Arturo. They'd be coming in the back way and would have seen him. Look at the estimated times of death. Both Sanford and the girl six-thirty to eight."

They thought about it. "All right," said Higgins, "he'd just got back to the girl when something else startled him—one of the cleaning people in the alley, whatever."

"And he'd already killed her by then?" She'd been manually strangled. "Now, you've seen enough rape cases, George. She was strangled—when does that happen in a rape? Not every woman who gets raped is killed, but what they do tell us, the most dangerous mo-

[198]

ment, when the rapist's at the peak of excitement and violence, is—"

"When he's just done the rape," said Hackett. "That's so. Where does that take us?"

Mendoza's eyes were glittering. He lighted a new cigarette carefully. He said, "The way this looked, so obvious, the would-be rapist didn't know Sanford was there. That was—mmh—extraneous. The girl was the intended target." He emitted smoke. "Suppose it was the other way around, boys? Suppose Sanford was the intended target—and somebody didn't know the girl was there?"

"By God!" said Higgins.

The phone rang and Mendoza picked it up. "Yes, Jimmy. . . ." He looked at Palliser. "The hospital. Linda Carr's conscious."

Palliser and Landers went out in a hurry. "Jimmy," said Mendoza, "put me through to S.I.D. . . . Scarne? About those prints Duke lifted off that body last Friday night. . . ."

Linda Carr was still swathed in bandages, but she had a couple of pillows propping her head up higher, and her eyes showed awareness. "You can't talk to her long," said the nurse firmly. "Three minutes."

"All right," said Palliser. He bent over the hospital bed. She was alone in this two-bed room.

The blue eyes blinked. "Remember you—police officer."

"That's right. Listen, Linda. Can you tell us who hurt you?"

"He said—call him—Mike. Mike."

Palliser tried to think of the most vital questions to

[199]

ask her. "Where did he take you, do you know?"

Immense surprise widened her eyes. She croaked, "Where I—jumped out—window. Finally couldn't—stand —didn't mind if I killed myself—he left me untied in bathroom—I broke the window—and jumped out."

"What?" said Palliser.

"Woman there—never helped. Foreign. The man at the restaurant, he was there—before the bus—"

NINE

THEY HADN'T SEEN the original Traffic report; it had been phoned up to the office. They went back there in a hurry, and Traffic located it for them. The reporting patrolman was Moss, and he wouldn't be on until the shift changed at four o'clock, so they called him at home, hoping he was there.

He was. "What the hell?" he said, surprised. "It was Eleventh—the block just north of Alvarado, the right-hand side about the middle of the block."

It was a block of old apartment buildings, a few with shops on the ground floor. Palliser was driving; Landers spotted what they were looking for and said so, and Palliser pulled over into a red zone at the curb. In the grimy-faced tan brick building midway down the block, one of the second-story windows was broken, a rough piece of cardboard covering it from inside.

By the layout on the first floor, it should be apartment 7-B to the left upstairs. There wasn't any nameplate on the door; at Palliser's third imperative knock it opened halfway, and he shoved it all the way. The girl, standing there holding a baby, began to back away across the room; she looked terrified. There was a toddler about two on the floor. It was a shabby, dingy room.

"No Engleesh," she said. She was quite a pretty girl, dark, with a creamy, warm complexion.

They went through the place while she watched in fearful silence, and it was the place where Linda Carr had been held. There were the coils of wire on a closet floor, some of it still bloodstained, and they found her handbag on a shelf in the bathroom, all her I.D. in it, the billfold empty. Neither of them had any Spanish; Landers swore, found a public phone up the street, and summoned Mendoza.

The girl clutched the baby to her and huddled on the frayed old couch, watching their every move. She didn't seem much relieved when Mendoza arrived and started to question her. She looked at the badge and said, "I cannot read. It is police? You have arrested him."

"Not yet. Your name?"

"Alicia Contreras."

"And who is he?"

"My husband. Michael Contreras. Now I do not know how we will live, the babies and I. I have no English, I cannot work and take care of the babies. I am ignorant, I do not read or write. Please, it was because of this I did nothing, I could do nothing." She gestured apathetically.

"Your husband was holding a woman prisoner here."

She burst into slow tears and a spate of explanation. All her family was dead except her papa, a plague it had been, and she and her papa had come here from Sonora, because there would be work and good pay for him; it was four years ago and she was but fifteen. But they had no papers, and then her papa was killed in an accident in the street and she had nothing, she did not know what to do. But he had said he would marry her so she might stay here. "Who?" asked Mendoza. Michael Contreras, he lived near where they had lived then, and he was a born American. He was young and good-looking, and she did not know what else to do. And now there were the babies. Diego and Maria. She must think first always of the babies.

"You will tell me about the woman he kept prisoner here," said Mendoza sharply.

"Yes. She is not the first. But the others are all girls without papers, they do not dare go to the police and tell about it. He never kept another girl so long here. He made her have the sex with him while I watch, I do not want to but he makes me. He says he will cut my heart out, I untie her or give her food when he is not here. So I do not. I am much afraid of him," she said simply.

"Where is he? Does he work?"

She picked up a bundle from the couch beside her and gave it to him. It was a white jumpsuit; she had been mending a seam neatly. Across the left breast was embroidered in scarlet the name *Arrowhead*. "It is there," she said. Mendoza looked at Palliser and said briefly, "Go pick him up," and Palliser and Landers went out.

He looked through the apartment, which was reasonably clean; the children were clean and plump, solemn-eyed little things. "I did not dare disobey him," she said. "What will I do now? How shall we live?"

"Wasn't he alarmed when the girl escaped? Did he think this girl would keep silent like the rest?"

"No, but he said she must have been killed, she is killed when she jumped out, and he was tired of her anyway."

"For the love of God," said Mendoza.

"I was very sorry for her, but I am afraid of him, and afraid he would hurt my babies," she said timidly.

In the end he took her over to the jail. A couple of

the matrons spoke Spanish, though they were going to have a fight getting those babies away from her to deliver to Juvenile Hall. He wondered if the D.A. would want to hold her as an accessory. And where would she end? If the A.D.C. office heard about her, they'd turn her into a professional welfare recipient *pronto*. But she was very young, and at least she'd shown some guts and cunning in protecting her babies. Maybe not altogether a lost cause.

He called the lab out to process the place; judges liked evidence spelled out in black and white.

They didn't pick up Michael Contreras until he trundled the big Arrowhead truck into the company lot at the end of the working day. When he saw the badges he said, "Did that little bitch go and snitch?"

"If you mean your wife, no," said Palliser, watching him. Contreras was at least six-three, powerfully built; he looked like an ugly customer. "But you can guess what we want you for." They expected trouble, but he came quietly enough once the cuffs were on. At the jail, however, he refused to talk at all; he just sat and glowered at them, and they finally left him alone.

"I hope to God they put him away for a stretch," said Landers, "but would you bet on it?" He didn't have any record with them. It would be at least a charge of assault with intent, but a first offense, legally speaking. It remained to be seen what the D.A. would decide to do about the girl.

The day men had done some overtime on that, and Piggott and Schenke heard about it when they came on night watch; Palliser was still there finishing a report. "Brother," said Schenke, "what we do see on this job. People."

[204]

"Satan going roundabout seeking to convert souls," said Piggott, and he meant it seriously.

"He's finding a lot of takers," said Schenke.

The middle of the week was usually quiet, but occasionally they got surprised. It turned out to be a busy night. There was a knifing in a bar, and a hit-run, and they'd just got back from that when the desk called up a heist. That was at a liquor store on Beverly, and they both went out on it.

The patrolman was Bill Moss, and he was chatting with one of the two men in the place. Another one was just standing. And on the floor, propped up against a glass case of imported wines, was the flashy blonde female heister.

She didn't look quite as flashy as they'd heard her described a few times. The blonde hair was a long wig, and she had resettled it crooked so that some of her own dark hair showed at one side, and she looked sullen and shaken. She had on a red pantsuit, and the whole front of it was darkly and wetly stained from shoulder to hips. She was breathing hard.

"Evening," said Moss gravely. "You see we've got a present for you. Mr. Doyle, Mr. Murray, who own this place."

Murray started laughing. "If you could've seen Gene's face! Funniest damn thing I ever saw, and me thinking we were going to lose a day's take—"

Doyle was the one just standing. He was a great big sandy fellow, and plain on him were the marks of the ex-pro fighter still in training; the bulging biceps, the narrow waist, the litheness of quick movement as he turned. He had a heavy bulldog face with genial blue eyes, but just now he was looking faintly horrified.

"More cops," he said. "My God."

Murray was still giggling. "She came in here and put

the gun on me. We were just closing, I was counting out the take from the register. And she didn't know Gene was in the back room."

"My God," said Doyle. "I came out not knowing anything's going on, and she's got Dean up against the counter, her back to me—and I think to myself, that is a guy all dressed up like a female, because anybody knows that females don't go around pulling heists on liquor stores or any place else. And I'm in a dandy position, so I just catch the gun arm from behind and haul the guy around and bring one up from the ground—straight to the jaw, pow. And it's a female after all! Smack into that display of domestic wines. It's a female after all!"

In front of the rear counter where the register was, there was a mess of broken bottles and spilled wine all over the floor.

"If you could've seen your face!" gasped Murray. "When you connected—"

"My God, I never hit a woman in my life," said Doyle.

She spoke for the first time. "Nearly busted my jaw," she said resentfully.

"Well, my God, I'm sorry, lady—not that you had any business trying to heist us—why the hell are you going around pulling heist jobs? A dame ought not to be doing that."

"Damn it, I wouldn't be," she said querulously, "if I had a husband to do it for me, but he's in the joint for the last job he pulled."

Schenke and Piggott began to laugh then, and she held her jaw and groaned.

On Wednesday morning, with Hackett off, Mendoza

wasn't in the office five minutes, and the other men just drifting in talking desultorily, when Scarne came in. "How did you know where to look?" he asked seriously. "The crystal ball, I presume."

Mendoza grinned at him slowly. "So," he said. He went to the door. "George—Jase. Evidently that little idea off the top of my mind made a hit with the lab." Higgins and Grace came in looking interested. "It was a match?"

"The only trouble with these Kromekote cards," said Scarne, "is that you need the hell of a lot higher magnification—they take longer to process. Reason we only get back to you now. Duke spent all night at it, but I think we've got enough for you. There were three prints. We made nine points on one, eight on another, and eleven on the third."

"Not enough for court," said Mendoza. They had to show fourteen matching points on a fingerprint before the court would accept it as evidence. "But enough, I think."

"Oh, there's no question but it's his prints. There's a distinctive tented arch—two were the right forefinger, the other the left middle finger."

"*Muy bien,*" said Mendoza. He hunched a shoulder at Higgins and Grace. "Go get him. You'll probably find him at one place or the other."

Half an hour later, when they brought Newton in, Mendoza was sitting swiveled around to the window. The rain and gray skies had gone away, and it was very clear and cold. The back mountains glistened with new snow. "Sit down, Mr. Newton," said Higgins. Mendoza swiveled back to face the room.

"Sure," said Newton. "What's this about? Any way I can help you—"

"What," asked Mendoza, "was the argument about,

between you and Sanford on Friday night?"

"There wasn't any, I told you, we were partners eleven years, we got along fine—"

"Until last Friday night," said Mendoza. "Then you had a fight with him."

"I never saw Dick all last week. I told you, I got in a poker game Friday night, I can tell you the fellows I was with—"

"Possibly, later on. But at half-past six—or seven—or sometime, you were in the Wilshire store, and you had a fight with Sanford. We found your fingerprints there, you see."

Newton hadn't sat down. He was very natty in beige and brown sports clothes. He gave Mendoza an incredulous, contemptuous smile. "What's with you stupid cops anyway? I was part owner of the place, I was in and out, every reason my prints'd be there all around. You're the one wanted 'em to compare, weed them out from any others. So what if you found my prints?"

"You see, they were in a rather special place, Mr. Newton," said Mendoza gently. "They were on the girl's naked body."

Newton stood very still. "You can't—make fingerprints on a—"

"Oh, yes, you can. The difficulty up until recently has been to lift specimens clear enough to be read. But there's a new technique for that now. And three prints from the body—the girl's left arm and left thigh—are a perfect match for yours, Mr. Newton. And that proves that you were there, that you arranged that very obvious rape scene."

Very deliberately Newton smacked the flat of one hand down on the desk, in one display of temper, and uttered one heartfelt obscenity. Then he sat down. "All *right*," he said dismally. "So I lost the gamble. I thought it was worth taking."

"We'd like to hear about it."

"You'll hear about it," said Newton, "because it was a Goddamned accident. I was mad at Dick but I never meant to kill him, for God's sake. I'd suspected he was getting into the accounts, and I'd been doing some looking, and he had. He usually stayed late on Friday nights, and I dropped in to have it out with him. He tried to bluster it out, claimed there was some mistake—when I could show him the figures!—and I got mad and lammed him one. We were in the office, and he went down against that file case—I swear I heard his skull crack. And I was just going over to see—see if he was O.K.— when there was that damned girl, right outside the door! How the hell did I know the cleaning people came on Friday night? Mine come on Saturdays. She was scared, she'd seen the whole thing, and I could see she was about to let out a scream, so I just took hold of her by the throat to stop it, that's all. I kept telling her I'd pay her to keep her mouth shut, but all of a sudden I realized she'd gone limp, I—she was dead! I never meant—"

"It's a very easy way to kill somebody," said Mendoza.

"Now I know," said Newton bitterly. "Jesus, there I was with both of them, and one thing I did know— there'd be a crew of cleaning people around. I stood there just sweating, and all of a sudden I looked at her and thought what a good-looking chick she was—and the whole idea came to me right then. If the cops thought some nut was after her and Dick just got in the way, you wouldn't go looking for a reason on Dick. I thought it was worth a try. I got her clothes off, and made it look—" He shrugged and fell silent.

"But she wasn't raped," said Mendoza. "Which made

us think twice. You shouldn't underestimate us, you know." He laughed. "Especially our scientific lab boys."

Higgins stood up. "Come on, Mr. Newton. We'll get you booked in before lunch." Newton got up, looking surly, and preceded him out without another word.

"At least," said Mendoza to Grace, "we can stop hunting up the rapists to question. Shortsighted fellow, Mr. Newton. An accident—so it may have been, with Sanford. But I hope the D.A.'ll decide to land him on a Murder One for the girl."

"I'll take a bet," said Grace promptly. "He said that was an accident too."

"Go away and hunt heisters."

"There's one we don't need to. You haven't looked at the night report. And Bob left a note."

Mendoza grinned over the blonde. But with this latest little puzzle out of the way, his mind inevitably slid back to others. Why the hell the Stromberg car hadn't been picked up— Well, the only answer was that it was hidden somewhere. Why? Then he sat up. It could also have been driven across a state line by the day after the murder. They hadn't identified her for three days. That would be one very good reason that a six-county A.P.B. hadn't turned it up. And what the hell had happened to the woman? That colorless, conventional woman living the sterile quiet existence, not many interests, not much personality—on a rainy night, making a phone call from the Brown Derby, vanishing—getting stashed in Lafayette Park, dead, two hours later. Barely two hours later. After she'd had two more drinks. Where?

And just then Scarne called and told him the kickback from the Feds was in, on the prints from the Jackman house. They didn't have them. Nobody had them. They'd gone to NCIC too.

"¡Diez millónes de demonios desde el infierno!" said

Mendoza. The hell of that was, it didn't say that somebody somewhere didn't have them. The National Crime Information Center had been a good idea, and computers were very useful for shortcuts and storing information; but even NCIC didn't have enough computers to keep everything stored forever. As soon as a misdemeanor or felony was cleared up, anywhere in the nation, the information on it sent to NCIC by the local force was wiped out of the record.

The irrational one, the violent kook who had killed the Jackmans might be known somewhere as violent, as dangerous. He might even have killed before. And one thing Mendoza knew from long experience of dealing with crime: one like that would have given the warning rattle.

He got up and went out to the big office. Glasser and Wanda were talking, Glasser sitting on the corner of her desk; Grace was typing a report, and Galeano apparently daydreaming out the window. His black eye had faded.

"Goofing off," said Mendoza. "Where are John and Tom?"

Galeano jumped and looked around. "Down at the D.A.'s office talking about Contreras. They're in a little tizzy about the girl down there. Of course it's six of one, half dozen of the other. You can call her an accomplice because she could have walked out and come to us, but looking at it from her viewpoint—"

Mendoza wasn't interested in that right now. He said, "We're back where we started on the Jackmans. And I've had another idea. This joker didn't start out a criminal career stabbing an elderly couple over a hundred times. He's been in little trouble, and more trouble and possibly big trouble, before. It's going to be the hell of a job, but we're going to look through all the Traffic calls in that general neighborhood for the last three months."

"Oh, ow, please," said Glasser. "Say it isn't so."

"I know, I know. But I still say it's got to be that immediate neighborhood—he's somewhere around there. And if we come across the persistent prowler, the Peeping Tom—clothesline thefts—dog poisonings—it might point in some direction."

"You can think up more damned things to do," said Galeano.

"I'll put in a call to Traffic. Let them do the photocopying for us," said Mendoza abruptly.

When Higgins got back from booking Newton in and applying for the warrant, they were sitting around waiting for those records. They would wait awhile. Talk about tedious jobs—that, Landers was going to say, would take a month of Sundays. The Traffic records weren't kept long, like the current information at NCIC. They'd have filled Parker Center to the roof long ago. But they were filed for three months before destruction. Those were the records they'd be looking through, of the ongoing daily calls round the clock that had come across the central desk in that time. The citizens called in on a thousand and one things, little and big things, serious complaints and silly ones. When a squad car was sent out to investigate a prowler the driver never knew if he'd be meeting a drunk with a gun, a nervous burglar, or a bunch of cats knocking off garbage-can lids.

Mendoza said, looking at the relevant pages in the County Guide, "Say an arbitrary area—between North Broadway and Alvarado, between Sixth and Beverly. Anything inside that, and you know the kind of thing we're looking for."

They weren't so sure of that. But Mendoza usually knew what he was doing: if a higher curve than usual showed, of a prowler right around that area, it might carry some significance. And just occasionally the complaining citizen had some idea who was bothering him. If they could turn up one small lead. . . .

But the very idea of the job was mind-boggling. When the stack of Xerox copies came up from downstairs, they felt tired just looking at it.

Hackett spent his day off helping Angel sort out accumulated possessions; there was no sense paying the movers to transfer things that would be thrown away or given away. It was a nice day, and at least they were finished with the hot weather for a while. Mark was in school most of the day and Sheila was very good on the whole, but it was an exhausting job, and when Angel went out to start dinner he subsided thankfully into a chair with a Scotch-and-water.

"Calories," said Angel.

"Calories be damned, I need this," said Hackett. He felt more tired than he'd ever been at the end of a working day. He wondered what had been going on. He'd find out tomorrow.

On Thursday afternoon at one o'clock there occurred the sort of meaningful coincidence that happens oftener than fiction-writers would ever admit.

A very ordinary-looking middle-aged woman trudged into a bank in Beverly Hills and quite by chance stood in line at the teller's window presided over by Mrs. Thelma Wright. When, five minutes later, she laid a check on the counter Mrs. Wright looked at it with great, if immediately concealed, interest. The check had originally been made out and signed by Lorene

Taylor, who happened to be a close personal friend of Mrs. Wright, and it was a check she knew all about. It had been made out to Bullock's Department Store on November fifth; Mrs. Wright even knew what it had been for—a new camera for Mrs. Taylor's husband's birthday. The check was in the amount of seventy-seven-twenty. It had Bullock's official stamp on the back.

They had had a little discussion about it after the robbery at Bullock's. Mrs. Wright had said she didn't think the bandits would bother with checks, but Mrs. Taylor had decided to stop payment on it just to be sure.

Mrs. Wright looked at the woman presenting it; she had never seen her before. She was about forty, dowdy in a brown hat and brown coat; she had a homely nondescript face; she wore unbecoming glasses, and had a slight cast in one eye.

She said, "I've got plenty of identification." She was laying it out on the counter: driver's license, Social Security card, Master Charge card.

The check was endorsed, below the rubber stamp on the back, in what appeared to be a man's writing, "John E. Williamson for Bullock's." Under that it was endorsed by Grace Eberhart.

Mrs. Wright thought swiftly. The adrenaline coursed briskly through her veins, and her mind raced. She said as if just noticing it, "Oh, this is endorsed twice. I'll have to get the head teller to O.K. it before I cash it for you. I'll be right back." Gripping the evidence firmly, she walked over to the New Accounts desk and bent over to speak to Mrs. Hess there. In a breathless whisper she told her to get Denny at once to come and collar the woman.

So she hadn't seemed to go near Denny, who, mountainous in his blue uniform, was right across the bank.

The woman wasn't alarmed, was waiting for her; but Mrs. Wright had just begun to count out the cash when Denny's hamlike hand fastened on the woman's arm.

They took her into the manager's office and called the police, and the woman—who really seemed to be Mrs. Grace Eberhart—protested sullenly. "I didn't get the money," she said. "I thought it was worth a try, all you could say was no. I know it wasn't right, but I haven't really stolen anything, you don't have to bring the police in—"

The Beverly Hills police, of course, called Robbery-Homicide downtown. Hackett and Mendoza, with Palliser trailing along, got there at one-fifty. They found Mrs. Eberhart in tears, and had to hear Mrs. Wright's tale which she had already told twice.

"All right," said Mendoza, "where did you get the check, Mrs. Eberhart?"

"It was thrown away," she said. She wiped her eyes and her voice was plaintive. "I just thought I'd try if the bank would cash it. It's hard to get by these days, and my husband's been sick and can't work. I couldn't see just how to work it at first, on account of it being made out to a store, but I thought prob'ly it' d be signed first by somebody high up, one of the store's managers, like it was made over to me for some cleaning job or something. I got my husband to put down a man's name so it'd be different writing."

They looked at her incredulously. "Mrs. Eberhart," said Hackett, "didn't you know about the robbery at Bullock's?"

"What robbery? No, I never."

"Where did you get the check?" asked Mendoza.

"It was thrown away—it was in a wastebasket. I just thought somebody'd made a mistake. I even thought, people like that might not even miss it, know the money was gone. What do you mean about a robbery?"

It seemed that Mrs. Eberhart didn't watch television because it bothered her eyes, seldom read a newspaper because she wasn't interested in murders or politicians' doings. Her husband read the sports page but she never recalled his watching news on television. He wasn't interested either. "Except when there's a plane crash or something like that."

"Where—" asked Mendoza, and she rounded on him a little fiercely.

"I'm telling you whatever you ask, ain't I? You got me all flustered, think I'd committed a murder, all these cops around! It was in a wastebasket in one of the apartments I clean. People can get maid service with the apartments if they want, and people with the kind of money to live there, they mostly do. I'm *telling* you—acourse I remember which one. It was number twelve on the second floor. The Miramar Gardens, on Loma Vista."

The LAPD men breathed a collective sigh. "And isn't that nice," said Mendoza. "Just by a fluke."

"Fluke be damned," said Palliser. "I don't care how we caught up, just that we did."

"Don't be premature, John."

But as they came down the heavily carpeted hall of that very plush new apartment building, the Beverly Hills men backing them up, they heard faint voices and laughter past the door of number twelve; it was unlatched. Mendoza regarded the name-slot beside the door pleasedly. MR. AND MRS. NEIL WILMOT. He pointed it out silently to Palliser, who grinned and nodded. The ghost had turned up.

The two inside were taken completely by surprise. They were sitting lovingly close on the couch with a pair of martinis when the police simply walked in, and they hadn't even got up before they were informed they were under arrest. The Beverly Hills men kept an eye on them while the rest of them went through the apartment. There were a lot of expensive new clothes, jewelry, and eighty thousand dollars in cash in a suitcase in the closet.

"And thanks so much for the backup," said Mendoza to the Beverly Hills men.

They talked to them together in Mendoza's office, with Wanda taking brisk shorthand. Marcia Wilmot was a rather sharp-featured handsome woman who didn't look her age by five years. Neil Wilmot—apparently his real name—was also good-looking, tall and dark with a one-sided lazy smile.

Marcia did some understandable fuming about Grace Eberhart. "Just on account of a stupid greedy maid! It was foolproof—there was no way the cops could ever get a line—and then just one stupid little slip, and that damned maid!" She had missed just the one check when they dumped all the rest into the apartment incinerator, down the chute in the hall. They'd been cautious there too: afraid the seals on the bags wouldn't burn, they'd cut the bags up and buried them on the beach down at Santa Monica.

"Well, we had a damn good run," said Neil. "Worth it, baby?"

She laughed, looking defiantly at the cops. "I thought it was just terrible at first, when Neil went up for embezzlement at that auto agency, just after we were married. My husband a crook! And then I got to thinking, what the hell, you only live once, and what's the sense in slaving away at some dreary job just so you can say you're honest? What's the point? You might as well take what you can get and enjoy it."

"You certainly did," murmured Palliser.

"When Neil got out, I'd had this idea. Foolproof," she said wistfully. "It was super beautiful. Listen, I've worked in department stores all my life, I know how they operate. They mostly do things pretty much the same way. All you have to know is which elevator they use for the collection, where the Accounting office is, how they take it to the bank. And there's not that much difference in the set-up, most department stores. I got a job in that one in Philly, just long enough to get the dope, but I didn't have to, the one in Pittsburgh—I just took the wrong elevator once, landed up in the business office, apologized all over the place, and I had the set-up plain as a map."

"She's a smart girl," said Neil cheerfully.

"So damn smart I have to miss that one check," she said mournfully.

"So," said Mendoza, "now the ride on the merry-go-round is over, tell us who the other three men are."

They looked at each other and laughed. "End of story," said Neil. "Just say they're good pals of mine. They're lucky and we aren't. I'm a believer in the Golden Rule, Lieutenant. You don't get any names from us."

And they didn't. The Wilmots stood firm; it was one of the few instances of honor among thieves Mendoza ever remembered. When Hackett took Wilmot by the arm and Mendoza held the door for Marcia, to take them over to jail, they looked at each other again and Neil said, "Worth it, baby?"

"It was lots and lots of fun, darling."

He bent and kissed her lightly. "We'll be out in three or four years, sweetheart."

"I'll be seeing you."

"And you can't win 'em all."

"But you can't keep a good pair down either." They laughed and went out together.

Palliser started to call Bill Costello.

Higgins had spent part of his day off with a carpenter, figuring what that darkroom was going to cost. However they tried to cut corners, it wasn't going to be cheap; but he'd promised Steve. Higgins sighed and thought they'd just have to add a bit to the bank loan. If you were doing a thing, might as well do it right.

He said that to Mary, who was wasting a lot of paper trying to figure out the cost of paneling. "We don't have to do everything at once, George."

"Steve's going to have his darkroom," said Higgins. Margaret Emily came staggering toward him and he swung her up in his arms. She laughed, patting his face; she had her mother's gray eyes. And a good thing, thought Higgins, that she hadn't taken after him.

The dogged and tedious search through all the Traffic calls was not paying off. Even in the first stacks they had already gone through, no recognizable pattern showed; it was the same routine jumble all of them remembered from their days riding squads, the family disturbances, prowlers, complaints about neighbors, about noisy parties, about barking dogs: the drunks, the trespassers, the petty thefts. There were just the occasional felonies that got passed upstairs: burglaries chiefly.

So far, nothing was showing on this little piece of research.

And as it happened, Mendoza's two senior sergeants

were fortunate enough to be present that very next morning to see something new happen to Luis Mendoza. For Hackett and Higgins, inured to the necessary amount of paperwork the job entailed, had struck at the stacks of paper from Traffic. "There's nothing in it," said Hackett. "Or if there is it wouldn't tell us anything definite." They were sitting in Mendoza's office talking about the Jackmans when Lake came in and said there was a fellow here who said he knew something about Mrs. Stromberg.

"¡Vamos!" said Mendoza. "Don't tell me we're going to start to move on that! Shove him in, Jimmy!"

The man who came in, carefully shutting the door behind him, was a nice-looking gray-haired fellow; he looked about sixty. His dark-gray suit was as beautifully tailored as Mendoza's. He had blue eyes under strong tufts of eyebrows, and a humorous mouth.

"Morning," he said. "You the officers looking into this?" He had a newspaper in one hand; he showed it turned to the *Times* story and picture of Marion Stromberg.

"We are." Mendoza introduced them all. "Sit down, Mr.—"

"Benson. Chris Benson." He sat down and studied them one by one.

"You think you can give us some information about Mrs. Stromberg? Did you happen to see her that Friday night?"

"No," said Benson. "I hadn't seen her in more than a year and a half. I must say you all look like sensible men. I thought it over some time before I came in. I didn't know but what I'd get laughed at, and nobody likes that much. But the more I thought, I thought it was something you ought to know. I own a tailoring shop up on Ivar in Hollywood. I'm a widower—my wife died of cancer four years ago. Now I'm going to tell you about this plain, no point beating around the bushes. I suppose we're all men of the world like they say, and realize that just because somebody's got to be fifty, sixty years old, they don't necessarily lose interest in that old devil sex." He got out a packet of little thin brown cigars, sniffed one and lit it. "My wife had been sick for a couple of years before she died. Now, gentlemen, I've got too much sense to go out and pick up with a cheap hooker—and I'd feel a little strange with a young girl. All the women I know, mostly, were Nellie's friends—social acquaintances." He drew on the cigar.

"I'm going back about three years. I overheard a couple of my clients talking, one of them in for a fitting. They were joking about it. How these adult bookstores have bulletin boards, where people—make contacts. I expect you've heard of them.

"I thought it over awhile. I don't approve of all this pornography around—seems like people equate sex just for its own sake with freedom and happiness, which isn't sense. Nellie and I had a good thing between us, and I hadn't forgotten that. But there's loneliness too. I felt like a damn fool walking in that place. All the young people around, but some not so young too. You see, I was thinking—maybe there were other people who just wanted to—make contact. Lonely people."

Mendoza said, "*No creo en semejante cosa.* I don't believe—"

Benson ignored him. "I spotted this one card up there right away. It just struck me as honest. All it said was, *May*, and a phone number, and, *widow, 55, straight*. I memorized the number. Didn't get up the nerve to call for a couple of days, but I finally did. She sounded honest, too. Suggested we meet for a cup of coffee some place. It was a restaurant way down on Fairfax, I'd guess a place she'd never go usually. We talked—sort of sized each other up. We had about the same backgrounds. She was being plenty cautious, she said right away no last names. That was all right with me. It was later on, when I took her back to her car—it was dark and maybe that was easier for her—she came out plain. She said her husband had died a couple of years before, and she'd been used to a lot of action with him, she was feeling kind of desperate. She didn't know any men except her friends' husbands—kind of like me. She didn't want to get married again. She said she was nervous going in there, putting up a card—all the queers and kinky kind—but she was, well, interested in getting together with somebody for mutual satisfaction, you might put it."

Hackett and Higgins were listening, fascinated. If Benson had been a younger man he'd have come out with the frank explicit terms; but he'd grown up in an age of reticence, and walked cautiously around the subject with euphemisms.

"She wasn't a fool, she was a lady, and she was protecting herself pretty sensibly too. How do the British put it?—no names, no pack drill. She wouldn't have taken up with any riff-raff—but neither would I," said Benson dryly. "Cut a long story short, we thought we suited each other all right."

"You mean—" Hackett was enthralled.

"I've got a house on Courtney Street. Pretty well shielded by shrubbery, and all our old neighbors who knew me have moved away anyway. She used to come there, after dark. We had something going for a while," said Benson. He looked at his cigar, which was nearly smoked through, and hesitated, and for the first time he looked embarrassed.

"Good God," said Higgins. "That—that conventional

—what was it you said, Luis, cardboard figure, color-less—visiting the sick and doing good works—"

"Go on," said Hackett to Benson.

Benson put out the cigar in the ashtray on Mendoza's desk. He looked down at the floor, and he was looking a little flushed. He said, "Well, to put it plain, she was crazy for it, she couldn't get enough. I—quite frankly, she was a little too much for me to handle."

Hackett laughed. "They do say, some older women— there was Ninon de Lenclos, George. And Sarah Bern-hardt. But what a story. That prim matron, sipping tea after shopping with her lady friends—"

"Well," said Benson, "it occurred to me that her husband must have been quite a fellow. She was— Well, after awhile I got the idea that she was seeing another man. I don't know if that was so, or how she—made con-tact. Probably the same way we had met."

Hackett chortled. "You have handed us an epic, Mr. Benson."

"I don't know about that," said Benson soberly. "It was a year and half ago I went down to San Diego on a visit to my married daughter, and when I came back I— just didn't call her again. May. That was all I ever knew her by—May. But," and he tapped the newspaper, "that's her all right. Well, gentlemen, that's about it. I'll just say that one of Nellie's old friends and I are planning to get married, and that's that. But May—" he looked at the picture thoughtfully— "I've got to tell you, I don't think she'd have taken to doing without it for a year and a half. She was—quite a lady for action, gentlemen."

"Of all the damned queer stories," said Higgins, "this is—"

"What occurred to me," said Benson, "is that— Well, I was very sorry to learn that something like this had happened to her, you know. But I did wonder—and I expect after all I've been saying, you're wondering about it too—if she had been still, er, making contacts, well, it could be she'd got a little less cautious in the kind of men she picked up with."

Hackett said, "Yes, of course that's the implication. What do you think, Luis?"

But Mendoza, for the first time that anyone remembered, was stricken speechless with astonishment.

TEN

About five minutes after Benson went out, there was a call to an attempted heist at a supermarket, with some wild shooting going on; they all went out on that, and it occupied some time, with the market manager and one of the heisters shot dead and the second heister wounded.

When they got back, Lake had a little news for them. The blonde lady-heister had refused to talk, but had now been identified through her prints; she had a little pedigree for forgery from four years back. Her name was Emily Bellucci, and her husband Tony was doing time for armed robbery, in Susanville. And the D.A.'s office had decided not to charge Alicia Contreras, was turning her case over to social services.

By then, of course, Mendoza had recovered his usual equilibrium. "Don't," he said to Hackett, "make it such a salacious little dirty joke, Art. Human beings and human nature. And I disagree with you that Marion Stromberg had got down to picking up anything male, and inadvertently ended up with a violent hood of some sort. *De seguro que no.* She was exactly what Benson tells us, cautious and covering up—she wasn't about to lay herself open to blackmail or any other kind of danger. Whatever man she was—mmh—meeting at the moment, she'd have sized him up very carefully, just as she did Benson."

"So how come she'd taken up with one who ended up killing her?" countered Hackett. "At least we know now what that phone call was—my God, she wanted action all right, a night like that in that downpour of rain—"

"We don't know how she was killed," said Mendoza. "But I'll lay a bet, if and when we do come across that one, Art, he'll be just such another one as Benson—a widower, a bachelor, around her own age, somebody like herself without many social contacts—and fairly fastidious."

Hackett gave a crack of laughter and said that wasn't exactly the word he'd have used. "And why should a man like that steal her car? When the A.P.B. hasn't turned it up in eleven days—"

"You can fill that in for yourself," said Mendoza. "He didn't. Somebody else did."

"Why drag your heels on it, Luis? Anybody can see what must have happened to the damned-fool woman."

"If you do, it's more than I can," said Mendoza stubbornly. "If there's one thing I can claim some knowledge of it is—"

"Women," said Hackett. "I think you've lost your sure touch, boy."

"I was going to say, human nature," said Mendoza. But of course the entire office was titillated by Benson and his interesting little story about Marion Stromberg.

Schenke, sitting alone on night watch with Piggott off, got called out at ten-thirty to a rather queer thing.

It was a quiet block on Reno Street, but a good many neighbors had been attracted out by the screams and the barking, and could supply answers for him: Mrs. Nora Reid had lived in the old four-unit apartment for years. She must be getting on for eighty, they told Schenke. She always took her dog out for a last walk around the block about ten o'clock; and tonight about that time a good many people heard screams and snarling and came out to find the poor old lady sprawled unconscious on the sidewalk, her handbag missing, and the dog, as one woman put it, "slavering at the mouth." Schenke wouldn't have quite said that. The dog was excited and had blood on its muzzle. It was a brown-and-white mongrel about the size of a large fox terrier.

The old woman hadn't a mark on her; it looked as if she'd been knocked down on the sidewalk. But there was a good deal of blood around, and it made a regular trail leading down the block to the corner. Using a flashlight, Schenke followed it up to the corner, where it tapered off: some temporary bandage slapped on?

Everybody said the dog was a good watchdog, would have taken after anybody who attacked the old lady. As it evidently had. Schenke found her handbag in the street just past the corner; the billfold in it contained four dollars and some change. Somebody called her daughter up in Hollywood to come and get the dog; she had lived alone.

Well, it was to be hoped she would go on living; she had a concussion and was still unconscious when the ambulance had come. Schenke got Duke out from the lab to get samples of the blood, and Duke said, squatting over a splotch on the curb, "You know, this looks like arterial blood to me, Bob. The way it was pumping out in spurts. I'll bet that dog caught somebody in a vital spot—femoral artery for choice."

"Yes," said Schenke. It could conceivably turn into a homicide. He went back to the office and alerted all the emergency wards and clinics around to report anybody in with severe dog bites. Nothing else came in, and he had time to write the report on it.

Palliser got in early on Saturday morning; even Farrell wasn't there. He hadn't sat down when there was a call from the desk downstairs: the emergency ward at the General. "Yes?" said Palliser. It was a doctor talking about a patient with dog bites. The patient was still there, they'd been asked to inform this number, the doctor understood it was a police matter. "Thanks very much, we'll get back to you, Doctor," said Palliser. And then Farrell came in and behind him Mendoza.

The night report explained the dog bites. Palliser went over to the hospital with Glasser. The old lady would probably be all right, but of course she could have been killed; she was little and thin. "I don't know what the Homicide office is doing in this," said the doctor who had called. "He's only a child. We ought to track down that dog, he said it attacked him without any provocation at all—I've called Animal Regulation."

The child was twelve-year-old Billy Bowes, who lived in the block down from Mrs. Reid; his mother had brought him in last night, and was glad to see the police taking an interest. Her boy might have been killed—just going up to the pizza parlor on Third to bring back a snack for everybody, and it must have been that great big dog of Tomlinson's, the thing was always getting over the fence, and it had attacked Billy for no reason at all, it ought to be shot, he'd been bleeding like a stuck pig.

They went into the ward to see Billy, who'd had some blood pumped into him and was sitting up, still feeling sorry for himself. He was a big fat lump of a boy who undoubtedly outweighed the old lady by twenty pounds.

Palliser said, "It wasn't the Tomlinsons' dog that bit you, was it, Billy?"

"I dunno," he said. "I guess so. The only dog around there."

"What about Mrs. Reid's dog?"

He plucked at the sheet. "That little ole thing."

"He went after you pretty hot when you snatched her bag, didn't he?" said Glasser. "Gave you some trouble you hadn't expected."

Billy was surprised. "How'd you know that?"

"Because we're detectives," said Palliser patiently. "Was that the first time you'd done anything like that?"

The boy jerked his head once. "I—I saw her comin' along the sidewalk—everybody says she's got lots of money. I never thought that little no-count mutt would take after me like that."

It was a piddling little thing to waste time on, but technically speaking it was assault. There'd be all the paperwork, and Billy would come up before a juvenile court judge and be put on probation. But maybe he'd been scared enough that he'd think twice in the future before acting on impulse.

There were a couple of new heists to work, left over from Thursday night. Wanda, Grace and Galeano were still working through the Traffic records. Mendoza was fidgeting around the office, after having re-read all the reports on Marion Stromberg and the Jackmans, when around noon Glasser slapped down the report he'd been reading and said, "This is a Goddamned waste of perfectly good time, Lieutenant. Nothing's going to show."

"*Claro que no*," said Mendoza absently. "Probably not, Henry. I was woolgathering again. And damn it, I never talked to Jackman's sister, she might—"

Higgins looked up from his typewriter. "It's a bastard, Luis, but there's just no handle on that one. If there were anything to point a direction—but there isn't."

"No," said Mendoza. And after a moment, "And of course it'd be no damned use at all to look at that bulletin board. Hell."

Glasser, Galeano and Wanda went out to lunch. Higgins finished his report, covered the typewriter, and had just said, "Come on, Luis, let's go and have lunch," when Sergeant Farrell got a new call. A body, in an apartment on Hoover. "Oh, hell," said Higgins.

They went to take a quick look. It was a pleasant, unpretentious furnished apartment in a six-unit place, and the owner lived on the premises. It was the owner who had found the body, coming to put a new washer in the faucet in the kitchen.

"He only moved in last month," said the owner, whose name was Thorkild. "His name's James Amberson. I don't know much about him. He seemed to be a very nice fellow, a quiet tenant. I do know he was a retired Navy man—career Navy, he was in twenty-five years." Prodded to remember anything else, he said, "Well, he introduced me to his sister once, she came to see him. I think her name's Suttner."

The body was that of a Negro male about fifty, and it looked as if he'd been beaten to death. There was a heavy-duty wrench on the floor near the body, covered with blood. It had, at a guess, happened last night.

Higgins called for a lab truck and they looked through the place desultorily. There was an address book by the telephone, and an address and phone number for Suttner in it: View Park. Mendoza was still looking abstracted; Higgins took him out to Federico's and they had lunch, late. Now there'd be all the paperwork on this thing, but if Higgins read the signs right at least

Mendoza was admitting that his little idea about the Traffic records was a dud.

They went out to View Park after lunch. The Suttner house was a sprawling brick place with an immaculate shaven lawn, and old trees shading it. The Suttners were both home, and after the first shock and grief had spent itself they poured out emotion and information in quantity. Mrs. Lucy Suttner was a buxom brown woman, still rather pretty at forty plus; he was darker and quieter, a dental technician at a laboratory downtown.

"If he only hadn't taken up with that woman!" she burst out. "I know that's what's behind this—you know it's got to be, Clyde! Didn't I try to tell him—he was a plain fool to get married for the first time at nearly fifty! Just retired from the Navy, he made chief petty officer, a good pension, and he has to meet that woman! Oh, she puts on a good front, and of course she flattered him and buttered him up no end, just looking for an easy meal ticket—any woman could see through her kind, but men—"

"Well, I'm bound to say even I saw through her," said Suttner wryly. "Myra Carpenter, he met her at a party somewhere, and she really got him corraled—of course she's quite a looker."

"Well, he found out!" said Mrs. Suttner. "He wasn't married to her a month before he found out! She's got a son by her first marriage, and he's a wild one—we heard he's got a police record and I'll swear he's a dope addict —always at her for money, and the money she took off Jim! And bringing his no-good friends around—"

"But we understood," said Higgins, "he'd just moved into that apartment."

"Last month. He'd had enough, and he came to his senses and saw what a fool he'd been. He'd left her, he was going to divorce her. And I know she's behind this somehow! Her and that terrible boy of hers. Oh, why did Jim have to meet her? He could have had such a good life, the pension, he was only fifty. . . ."

They told Mendoza and Higgins where she was living; they supposed she was still there, an apartment on Hampton Court in Hollywood.

"This," said Higgins as they got back into the Ferrari, "looks pretty damn obvious, doesn't it? He was going to divorce her, so they had the bright idea of killing him while she was still eligible for his Navy life insurance. It makes you tired, Luis."

"Yes," said Mendoza, but he still sounded abstracted. Instead of heading for Hollywood he started back downtown. "You can write a first report on it, George," and then he was silent all the way back to the office.

There, he told Farrell to get Jackman for him; and he so far remembered his manners that before asking the question he wanted to, he enquired after the well-being of the family. "Well, the funeral was yesterday," said Jackman. "We got the notice that we could have the bodies. They're buried up at Forest Lawn. At least it was a nice day."

"Yes," said Mendoza. "Is your sister better?"

"Oh, yes, she's O.K. I got a cleaning service to—deal with the house," said Jackman. "We'll put it up for sale, of course. No reason to keep a place down there."

"I never talked to her. I'd like her address."

"Oh, surely."

It was Mrs. Helen Burley, an address in Burbank. Somebody had said her husband was manager of a chain market. He found the place, tucked away at the end of a dead-end street; it was a good-sized Spanish house behind a good deal of shrubbery.

She was tall like her brother, but had once been

pretty and was still nice-looking; she had kept a good figure and there was little gray in her brown hair. She asked him in, and asked, "Have you—found out anything?"

He didn't tell her there was nowhere to look. "I wanted to ask you, Mrs. Burley—you see, you saw your parents later than any of the rest of the family, didn't you?"

"That's right. It was two weeks ago today. Oh, dear. We were all busy getting ready to go over to the wedding, you know. Oh, they'd have loved to go—their youngest great-granddaughter—but of course the trip would have been too much for them. They were looking forward to hearing all about it." She blinked. "I'd just run down to take Mother a pan of leftover gelatin salad, we'd be gone a week, no sense wasting it."

"Do you remember what they talked about? Did they mention any little worry, any disturbance, anything at all unusual? However casual?" This was, of course, a waste of time; there'd have been nothing; they'd had no warning.

"There wasn't anything wrong, no," she said in mild surprise. "That's a sort of backwater, that street, pretty quiet. But crime these days—" She cast her mind back. "We just talked about ordinary things, the wedding mostly, and the awful prices—whether they might get a new TV set, the old one was about on its last legs. And Mother was saying how the neighborhood had changed, so many of the people they knew moved away or died—we'd got talking about old times when Bill and I were growing up down there. Oh, she told me the house next door had finally got rented and the people just moved in—they seemed nice enough, they'd come asking to use the phone, theirs not in yet."

[233]

"Yes," said Mendoza. Nothing, of course.

"She said she thought their son might be retarded, he looked a little odd. Poor souls. I can't think of a worse cross—thank God mine were all just fine," said Mrs. Burley placidly.

"You think there's anything in this?" said Hackett.

"Mrs. Burley didn't realize that the Burroughs aren't young people, or she might have done some thinking and worrying about it," said Mendoza. He braked the Ferrari and they got out. The old Jackman house looked already deserted, though you couldn't tell from outside that it was empty. The house beside it was just another pleasant old California bungalow, one of the porch steps cracked, its paint a little dingy. They went up to the porch and Mendoza shoved the bell.

When Mrs. Burroughs opened the door he said to her, "We'd like to see your son, Mrs. Burroughs. May we come in? You never mentioned that you have a son—of course there wasn't any reason to, was there?"

She backed away and put one hand across her mouth. In the house for the first time, they saw it held the usual shabby nondescript furniture of a rented place. Harry Burroughs was there, relaxed in old clothes and slippers, reading a newspaper. He got up and came over.

"*Did he do it?*" she whispered. "Was it him, was it Tommy? When I heard, I was afraid—I was afraid, because you never know what he'll take into his head to do. But he's never done anything—anything as bad as that. I looked the best I could—he doesn't like anybody touching his things—I told you, Harry, I looked, but I couldn't see anything with blood on it—and—he's never done anything as bad as *that*." She was trembling all over.

"They told us he'd be better at home," said Burroughs tightly. "My God, my God, if I thought he'd done that—" He was a tired man, defeated by life. He took off his glasses and rubbed his eyes. "He's got medicine he's supposed to take, some kind of tranquillizers. He's what they call schizophrenic. The doctors told us that ten years ago when he was eleven, when he started to act—queer. He was up at Camarillo two years after that, and then they said he'd be better in a home atmosphere, as long as he takes the medicine. He'd be home awhile, and then he'd throw a tantrum and—do things—"

"He wouldn't know what he was doing," she said. "Like when he killed that kitten—he didn't know. But when they sent him home again this time, we thought— the neighbors in Montebello knew about him, we thought maybe if he could start fresh somewhere where nobody knew—not that he ever goes out much except to the library—"

"He's always reading," said Burroughs. "He's always quiet, doesn't like to go out of the house. That's why it never crossed our minds it was possible—God, it isn't possible! He's a smart boy—the doctors said the ones like him usually are. Only their brains don't work just the way other people's do—and they get what that one doctor called fixations. Like the way Tommy all of a sudden got so religious, the last time he was in Camarillo. You never know what he'll go off on—"

"Religious," said Mendoza. "What sort of religion?"

"Oh, he's always spouting about Satan and hellfire and Armageddon. They always told us, just don't cross him, just let him do what he wants and see he takes the medicine. It keeps Amelia pretty tied down. But—you— coming asking— You don't think—"

"Where is he?" asked Mendoza.

"In his room." Her voice was barely audible. "It's

where he is all the time. Reading and thinking." She pointed the way down the hall mutely.

It was the back bedroom of the two, about twelve feet square. There was a single bed, an armchair, a chest of drawers. As they stopped in the doorway, the young man sitting in the armchair by the window looked up sharply. "Tommy," said his mother in a weak voice behind them.

He was quite a good-looking young man, dark and tall and well built; but there was a wildness about him that was nearly a tangible aura. His eyes moved in nearly constant restlessness. In one lithe movement he was on his feet. "Who are they?" he asked her loudly. "Tell them to go away!" He had been reading a Bible.

"Now, Tommy," said Burroughs, "don't be like that. You ought to—"

"You're not supposed to tell me what to do! Nobody's supposed to tell me what to do, order me around —Dr. Locke said so! Tell them to go away!"

Mendoza said, "We just want to look at the knife, Tommy."

"No."

"Just for a minute."

"No. You want to take it away." He gave them a sudden secret smile, and his eyes were terrifying. "I might need it again."

"Oh, Christ," said Mrs. Burroughs. She turned and reeled down the hall drunkenly.

The ambulance attendants handled him expertly, but he fought like a cornered beast all the way, until they got him tied down on the stretcher. Burroughs would have seen that before; he just sat waiting for it to be over. He sat on the couch and he said sickly to them, "But the doctors ought to know—all you can do is believe what the doctors tell you. Dr. Locke said he'd be all right, no trouble, if he just took the medicine, and we always saw that he did. If—if he could do—*that*—why did the doctors—keep letting him out?" He put his head in his hands.

It was, of course, a good question. They called up the lab; by the time Marx and Horder got there the Burroughses had retreated into their bedroom and shut the door.

At the very back of the walk-in closet in the back bedroom, rolled in a paper bag, they found the bloody shoes and the bloody knife. In the garage they found the can of black spray paint.

"And let us hope that this time," said Mendoza savagely, "he gets sent to Atascadero." That was the asylum for the criminally insane. "They don't get let out of there quite so easy."

This was one time he'd like to pull rank and delegate somebody else to break the news to the Jackmans. Only he wasn't built that way.

On Sunday morning they all went up to the new place. Alison and Mairí were busily plotting where furniture should go—some of the new furniture had already been delivered—and the twins were wild to introduce him to the sheep. They were uninterested in the house entirely, and led him firmly out and down the hill again. The sheep had vanished utterly from where they had been on the hill five minutes ago.

"They runned away!" said Terry.

"They're around somewhere, *niños*." They located the five sheep just over the crest of the hill, busily munching on the flourishing weeds. At least they seemed to be doing the job expected of them.

"Five Graces, Mama said." Johnny was pleased with the sound of that and repeated it thoughtfully several times.

At their voices, two of the sheep headed for them and thrust smooth black heads for patting. They were oddly attractive creatures, thought Mendoza, remembering Alison's experience and keeping well out of the way. They looked very pastoral and peaceful there on the empty hillside, and the only negative thought that crossed his mind was that they had unexpectedly loud bass voices.

If he could have foreseen the trouble those sheep were to cause. . . . But the crystal ball was not operating, and he merely regarded them with vague benevolence.

There were three new heists on Saturday night. This week there would be arraignments scheduled for Contreras, the heist woman, and Newton. One of the assistant D.A.'s, unaffectionately known to the LAPD as Nervous Nellie, monopolized Mendoza for an hour on Monday morning, discussing the relative merits of charges on Newton ranging from involuntary manslaughter to murder two.

That morning the central desk got a routine call for a squad car, and Zimmerman landed at a middle-class frame house on Diana Street and asked the young woman at the door what the complaint was.

"Well, I don't really think there's anything in it," she said hesitantly. "But Stewart's never been one for telling lies, and I just wondered. It's my little boy Stewart, he's five."

"Yes, ma'am," said Zimmerman patiently.

"Well, he and his sister spent yesterday with their grandparents—my mother and father—and when we brought them home Stewart was saying he'd seen a man put a lady in a closet in the house next door and she was dead. He says he went into that yard to get his ball back, and saw it through the glass door. Mom and Dad just laughed and said he was good at making up stories." She was silent, thinking. She was a pretty girl in the mid-twenties. "So did Bob—my husband. But he keeps talking about it. I wondered. The house next to Mom and Dad's is up for sale. It does have a sliding door at the side." She was apologetic. "I know it sounds silly, but I wonder if somebody ought to go and look?"

Zimmerman thought too. He got the address, but he wasn't going to yell for the front-office boys when it might be just a kid's story; they'd cuss him out from here to there. He drove past the house, got the name of the realty company from the sign, and went there. One of the salesmen drove back with him and let him into the house. They looked, and in the closet of the master bedroom was the body of a woman in a nightgown, nothing else. There wasn't any I.D. anywhere. She'd been shot in the head.

So then he called the front-office boys.

Resignedly, Grace and Galeano went out on it. It was the house next to the corner, and first they asked the neighbor in the corner house to see if she knew the woman; she looked, gave a shriek, and said, "My God, it's Cindy Hamlin! Stewart did see something after all! My God, they just moved away two months ago, her husband got transferred to Bakersfield—how did she get here?"

It was a nice house on Edelle Place; a block away,

this would have belonged to the sheriff's department. The husband, Randolph Hamlin, was manager of a chain shoe store, the neighbor told them. Presumably he should be at the store, up in Bakersfield; unaccountably he wasn't. They had turned the lab loose there.

Also on Monday morning, Hackett finally found Myra Amberson. Her son, Doug Carpenter, had a pedigree of narco selling and assault, so they had his prints; and his prints were plastered all over the wrench that had battered James Amberson to death. Hackett got tired of dealing with the stupid, stupid people. He brought her in to question her; she was a nice-looking black woman, smartly dressed, with coy manners and a brittle laugh.

"I don't know where Doug is, honestly," she said. "He's twenty-three, he lives his own life." She shook her head archly; she had on dangly earrings and they rattled. "That's just awful, if he did kill James like that, Sergeant. He must have been high on something, to do that. James would have come back to me—he was going to."

Hackett put out an A.P.B. for Doug Carpenter and came back to the office to find Mendoza fulminating on the phone.

"Are you telling me that your cretinous uniform branch never checked—? . . . *¡Santa Maria!* How do they remember where to bring the squads back at end of shift? Nearly two weeks that A.P.B.'s been out, and nobody—nobody at all—thought to look. . . . All I know is, if I was watch commander at Hollywood, your God-damned stupid patrol units would shape up or get off the force! Yes, you may tell that to Captain Andrews, from me, with bells on! Your damned excuses for patrolmen have set us back two weeks on a homicide case!" He slammed the phone down, noticed Hackett, and said shortly, "Hollywood's just spotted Marion Strom-berg's car. Would you have a guess? Probably right there all along. In the visitors' parking lot at the Holly-wood Presbyterian Hospital."

"What?" said Hackett. "Why wasn't it noticed be-fore?"

"Because it never occurred to any of the idiotic Traf-fic men working out of that precinct to look in a hospital parking lot, of course. The only reason it got noticed just now was that a woman went into unexpected labor at home alone, and called for a squad. The gallant bone-headed officer duly rushed the lady to the hospital and on his way out did a double-take and checked the plate number. They're towing it in."

"Well, we come all sorts like other people," said Hackett.

"Not on this force," said Mendoza. "We're supposed to be smarter." He was slightly mollified a couple of hours later when Marx called up to tell him they'd picked up a couple of good latents from the inside of the passenger's door, and would check them with records. There had been a bright-red handbag on the front seat, with all her identification and forty-three dollars in it.

Grace and Galeano wanted to talk to Randolph Hamlin about his wife's body and they couldn't find him; so on Monday afternoon they put out an A.P.B. for his car. The lab hadn't finished processing the house —the body wasn't going to get autopsied for at least a day or so—when the car was spotted parked up on the Sunset strip, with Hamlin sound asleep inside it. The patrolman brought him in.

He had the hell of a hangover, and he said to Grace

[241]

and Galeano, "Bitch, bitch, bitch. She couldn't stand Bakersfield. She didn't like the house. Bitch, bitch. Twenty times a day, she said it over and over, I wish I was back in the old house. So—" he yawned hugely— "I put her there. That's where she wanted to be."

At four o'clock that afternoon, a doctor at the emergency ward of the General called in to say that he had a man there with some knife wounds. Higgins was in the middle of a follow-up report on Amberson, but went out to see what it looked like.

It wasn't anything for Robbery-Homicide. The man had unwillingly given his name as Charles Chidsey. He was a smallish man about thirty, and he was mad at the doctor for calling in police. "Only I was bleeding so much I didn't know if I could get home without passing out, and my wife won't be home until six." He was a teacher, he wouldn't tell them where. "Damn it, I have to finish out my year's contract, and then I'm getting out. Maybe out of teaching altogether—teaching! Dealing with hop-heads and hoods! Oh, I couldn't be assigned to the nice high school up in Flintridge where I applied—at least the kids there come from homes that have toilets and don't use the halls—oh, no, I'm white, so I have to come down here to balance the racial quota! God, I never had any prejudice before but I'm sure as hell growing some! And no, I'm not going to tell you who the Goddamned louts were who pulled the knives on me—do you think I'm crazy? All a judge would do is put them on probation, and next time they'd kill me!"

It wasn't a case for Robbery-Homicide. Yet.

Marx called at five o'clock on Monday to say that the prints from the Stromberg car weren't in records, had been sent to the Feds.

[242]

For once the F.B.I. was commendably prompt. At ten o'clock on Tuesday morning the kickback came in. The prints belonged to Andrew Clifford; he had spent thirty-five years in the Air Force, retired as sergeant two years ago.

"*¡Paso!*" said Mendoza, and brought out the phone book. "And kindly don't tell me there are dozens of Cliffords with whatever initials." He had picked up the Hollywood book, and ran down the C's to all the many Cliffords. "Romaine, Rosewood, Orange Grove, Delongpre, Outpost—Catalina. *Ya lo creo.* That's our boy. Go and see if you can pick him up."

"The crystal ball told you?" asked Higgins.

"If you'd just do a little elementary thinking, *amigos.* It was a cold night and he had to get home—he wouldn't leave the Buick far from where he was going, and Catalina's two blocks from that hospital."

Higgins and Hackett looked at each other and went out.

They brought Andrew Clifford back with them forty minutes later, and introduced him to Mendoza. Clifford was in the mid or late fifties, an upright stocky man with thinning brown hair and a stubborn jaw; he was casually dressed in sports clothes. He looked at Mendoza appraisingly and Mendoza studied him with equal interest.

"Exactly the type I predicted, isn't he?" he said to his senior sergeants. "Outwardly a very respectable citizen. Good manners, good background, clean and neat. She wouldn't have settled for less."

Clifford's grim mouth relaxed a trifle. "You think you know all about it?"

"No, Mr. Clifford, I don't know anything about it. You're going to tell me."

Clifford had sat down in the chair beside the desk. He looked down at his hands. "I thought I'd cleaned my prints off every place I'd touched in the car. I'm damned sorry you caught up, Lieutenant—but in one way it'll be a relief to have it off my conscience. I like to think I've always been an honest man. You seem to know about May."

"Marion Stromberg."

"Was that her name? I never knew it."

"We knew there'd be a man. Where did you—mmh—pick each other up?"

Clifford said slowly, "I'm a bachelor. I got out of service, I settled here because I like the climate, but I didn't know anybody here then. I haven't had a permanent home for years, of course. Now—well—not being exactly as naive as I was when I joined up at eighteen, I know where to find a woman if I want one. But I happened to wander into one of those porn stores on the boulevard, right after I landed here—I don't go for that stuff, but they had some Oriental carvings in the window I wanted to look at—I spent some time over there after the war, I like their art. Well, being there, I looked around, and spotted that bulletin board. I got a mild kick out of it, and just on impulse I stuck up my phone number. That was all. So what? The fags or the kinks call, no sweat, hang up. A chick maybe I look at."

"She called you," said Mendoza.

"That's right. She didn't sound young, but hell, neither am I. The years catch up. They slide by, and all of a sudden. . . . Well, I met her for a drink. We looked each other over. And—"

"You thought she'd do?" said Mendoza.

Clifford smiled slightly. "No, sir. I felt damned sorry for her. You see, she'd never had anything else. Than just the sex." He was silent; he got out a pack of cigarettes, lighted one, and said to it, "There was a girl in

London in nineteen fifty-three, a special thing and we'd be together forever—only she got herself killed by a damn stupid drunk driver. I felt sorry for the woman. And don't tell me I just obliged her. I liked her too."

"All right, we'll take that as understood and go on to specifics. That Friday. November the sixth," said Mendoza. "She called you about eight o'clock."

Clifford raised his eyebrows. "You've been doing some detective work. That's right. We'd always used my place—I told you I never knew her full name, where she lived. She said she was coming over, and hung up before I could tell her not to. You see, my sister and brother-in-law were staying with me, they'd flown out from Chicago three days before, they'd be there for a week or so. They just left last Saturday. And they had my car. I hadn't felt like going sightseeing with them that day. I expected them back any time, nine, ten o'clock.

"Well, she came, and she was annoyed when I told her that, that she couldn't stay. I said, come on, we'll go out and have a drink anyway, and we went to a place down on Beverly. It was raining like hell."

"She had two daiquiris," said Mendoza.

"That's right. She was restless and she was annoyed with me. Hell, I hadn't wanted to come out at all, and I was annoyed with her. I was driving. When we got back in the car I went down Beverly looking for some dark side street and I ended up on Lafayette. I said O.K. if she was so hot, I took hold of her maybe a little rough—and she was insulted, she wasn't going to do it in the car like a slut, and there we were in all the God-damned rain and I'd rather the hell be home where it's warm, waiting for Allie and Chuck to come in—I swear I didn't know I was going to do it, I just backhanded her one and revved the motor at the same time, and she was thrown against the dash—" He passed a hand over his mouth.

"Oh, yes, I see," said Mendoza.

"She fell off the seat. I—she was limp. I put the brake on, I— Well I never meant anything like that," said Clifford. "And just then there was a police car passed six feet away from the Buick, and I was sitting there shaking, half off the seat where I'd been feeling for her pulse—and I was thinking of Allie and Chuck coming back and wondering where the hell I was, out in the rain—and cops asking how I happened to be with her when I didn't even know her name, and everybody she knew saying I was a liar, she'd never be up to anything like that.

"I don't excuse myself. It was maybe a damn cowardly thing to do. But she was out of it, she wouldn't feel anything. I just got her out of the car quick and drove off. It was ten minutes to ten. I was damned sorry about the rain—hell of a place to leave her—"

"But it stopped."

"Yes, by the time I got back to Hollywood it had stopped. I thought if I left the car in the hospital parking lot it'd be found sooner or later."

"Sooner or later—how right you were," said Mendoza darkly.

"I walked home. Allie and Chuck had just got in, wondered where I was. I said I'd just gone up to the drugstore for cigarettes." Clifford sat back and reached for another cigarette.

"That's very much the kind of story I expected to hear," said Mendoza.

"Which means you don't believe it."

"Luis—" said Hackett.

[246]

"Now, Art, you should trust my instinct for human nature. It's not an edifying story but it's an understandable one, Mr. Clifford. It's the kind of thing I had a strong hunch was what really happened."

"God, I'm sorry, I'm sorry," said Clifford heavily. "That poor damned woman. It was all she understood. The surface. You know?" And after a silence he asked, "So where do we go from here?"

"I think, to a simple charge of involuntary manslaughter, and probably probation," said Mendoza. "You can't even say she invited trouble. She was so cautious —up to a point. But the accidents will happen."

They still hadn't picked up Doug Carpenter, but they would sometime. It would be a moot point whether the D.A.'s office decided to charge Myra Amberson along with him.

There were three heists still making legwork, and there would probably be others coming along. But for the moment Mendoza's mind was at rest; the really annoying little puzzles were cleared up—until the next one happened.

And tomorrow was also a day.

He went home, to El Señor demanding his share of rye, and Bast, Nefertite and Sheba circling under the dining-room table demanding samples because it was fish, and Cedric coming in proudly in the middle of dinner with a very dead bird.

"Och, the creature—such a household this is—" Mairí pursued him armed with a broom and dustpan.

Alison had been having discussions with the movers, and everything, she said, was settled. "December tenth. Anything we haven't sorted out by then will just have

[247]

to come along, and we'll sort it at the other end. That's a very useful word of Mairí's, sorting things, it can mean such a variety of—"

The phone rang, and Mendoza went down the hall to answer it. Dr. Robert Douthit the vet was on the other end. He said, "Just a little favor, Mendoza. A friend of mine writes the veterinary column for the biggest national cat magazine—you know the one. The chief editor wants to do a one-page feature on your rescuing that cat from the fire—that was quite a thing —and he couldn't get through to you on long distance the other day. Knowing this friend of mine had contacts here, he asked— Now look, Mendoza, I know you don't go for the publicity, but it's a specialty magazine—not too many people would see it. They can buy a copy of the *Times* photo—all they want is a shot of you and the cat in its new home. A sort of before and after piece, you see. We've got it all set up with the new owner, she's been very cooperative. It's entirely at your convenience, whenever you're free in the next day or so. Look, it won't take half an hour of your time—"

"Oh, hell and damnation," said Mendoza, "this is blackmail."

"Not at all." Dr. Douthit chuckled. He had looked after the Mendoza animals for years, and unwillingly Mendoza capitulated.

Knowing cats, he wasn't surprised at the outcome. He showed up at the house on Portia Street on Wednesday morning; Douthit was there with a local photographer who set up his outfit and got everything arranged; he posed Mendoza against Mrs. Meeker's living-room drapes, focused and set his lens, and said, "All right, now let's get the cat."

Mrs. Meeker succeeded finally in coaxing Merlin down from the refrigerator top (also a favorite brooding place for El Señor, Mendoza reflected). "Come, pussin, nice pussin, we want to take your picture with the nice man who saved your life—"

He should have known what would happen. Merlin was placed in his arms tenderly, and at the exact moment the photographer snapped the shutter, he spat in Mendoza's face, drove his hind legs into Mendoza's chest, and departed rapidly from the scene.